Sworn to Remember

by

Maria Imbalzano

Sworn Sisters Series, Book 2

Sworn to Remember

Cover Art by *Diana Carlile*

The Wild Rose Press, Inc.
PO Box 708
Adams Basin, NY 14410-0708
Visit us at www.thewildrosepress.com

Publishing History
First Champagne Rose Edition, 2019
Print ISBN 978-1-5092-2580-4
Digital ISBN 978-1-5092-2581-1

Sworn Sisters Series, Book 2
Published in the United States of America

The volleyball guy got off his stool and crouched on the floor. "Let me help."

His voice was deep and smooth. A thrill ran up her arm as he handed her some errant coins. She found his eyes. Beautiful blue eyes. Caribbean Sea eyes. Familiar eyes.

"Hi, Sam." His brow furrowed as he said her name, although his tone indicated no question.

She froze in place as she stared at him. "M…Michael McCain?" His name fell between them.

He nodded.

Her pounding heart thrummed in her ears. Michael. It couldn't be. And yet…those eyes…

He smiled. "I didn't realize it was you the other day. But I see now."

They were still crouched on the floor, and Michael reached out to take her hand and raise her up with him. Her head swam, and she grabbed the counter to steady herself. After all these years. He looked completely different. Gone was the long, shaggy hair. The lanky physique. Instead, he was built like a man who frequented the gym, and his sun-streaked hair was combed into place. Her teenage crush stood before her looking amazingly gorgeous, and that old familiar current flashed through her.

Praise for Maria Imbalzano

"It didn't take but a few pages to become wrapped in a story woven with fine threads, and twists, that captivated me to the final page....I wait with anticipation for *Sworn to Remember* in the Sworn Sisters Series, Book 2."

~*Esquire*

~*~

"Just when your heart may drop, it's picked back up and squeezed with love and put back in and cradled and pumped back to life!"

~*Trully*

~*~

"Nicki and Dex have amazing chemistry and their heat is scorching both in and out of the bedroom...If you enjoy a novel with a strong heroine, an eclectic group of caring friends, and a hero that just won't give up, then check out this book."

~*LJT*

~*~

"A love story so beautiful and sensual that it will keep you in a trance till the last line. Couldn't put it down and excited about book 2."

~*Lillian N.*

Dedication

To my real sister, Joanne,
who is strong and sensitive and sweetly nostalgic

Chapter One

Adultery, extreme cruelty, desertion.

Samantha Winslow could hear the hatred and betrayal jump off the pages of the Divorce Complaint as she hastened down the hall toward her office, coffee in one hand, papers hot off the printer in the other. She reviewed the causes of action she had drafted a half hour earlier and muttered, "Ben Calloway, you are a slimy bastard."

Her secretary, Carol, sprinted two feet behind, attempting to catch up. "What do you want to do with the Townley Marital Settlement Agreement?"

Tossing her hair over her shoulder, Sam continued to march down the hall on the thirty-third floor of her firm's New York City high-rise. "Call Mr. Townley and find out if he can come in at two. I need to review it with him, but I have some changes to make first."

"Will do," replied Carol, in her usual good mood.

"And call Judge Hurley's secretary to find out if the Russo motion can be heard at eleven on Friday. I have to be in Judge Persky's courtroom at nine." She glanced behind to assure Carol followed in her wake.

"Already confirmed."

Sam slowed her pace. "Did you call Mr. Hill to come in and sign his Complaint? He's going on vacation next week. I want that Complaint filed before he leaves."

"I called him yesterday and left a message."

"Well, call him again," she demanded, then thought better of her tone. "Please." Stress had a way of making her take her frustrations out on the wrong people. Stopping in front of her office, she turned to Carol with a sheepish grin. "It's only ten o'clock and I'm already behind."

Carol accepted her indirect apology with grace. "I know. Mrs. Calloway's waiting for you in Conference Room Two. And Mr. Calloway and his attorney are out in the reception area." She dropped her voice conspiratorially. "Mr. Calloway's pacing and snarling into his cell phone. He doesn't appear to be in a good mood."

"And he hasn't even seen a copy of this Complaint yet." Sam grinned as she held up the document in her manicured hand. "He's the one who wanted a four-way conference this morning. I'm sure he was hoping to get his wife to cave in early and settle before she learned of his little affair. Now that she knows, that's not going to happen." She buttoned her navy pin-striped suit jacket and slid her hand over the matching skirt to remove any possible wrinkles. "When she told me what she found out yesterday, the venom practically dripped from her voice. Her plan may be to castrate him this morning."

"Sam!"

"Sorry." She smiled ruefully at Carol's blush. Her secretary's prim and proper attitude amused Sam since this wasn't the first time Carol heard similar comments from the divorce attorneys at the firm. They all felt they earned the right to be a little crass, given their dealings on a daily basis.

"Good luck." Carol handed Sam the revised

Agreement in the Townley matter for her review, then turned to leave. "I'll be at my desk if you need anything."

"Thanks." She'd need more than luck to get through this day.

She tossed the Agreement on her desk atop the other piles, if they could be called that. Just under the paper mountain was a stack of at least ten phone messages she had yet to return. But first, the Calloway meeting. She grabbed her yellow pad and three sections from the file, all the while thinking about the Calloways—and couples like them.

Why was it the errant husband always hooked up with the younger woman who worked with him? What about the sanctity of marriage? What happened to the promise to love and honor till death do you part? Melissa Calloway was a beautiful woman—smart, charming, elegant. She had given up her promising career as a designer at Calvin Klein when she married ten years earlier. Her new role demanded her availability at a moment's notice along with managing her husband's personal life. And she did so with dedication and loyalty. She ran his household, raised the children, catered his parties, and sat on charitable boards, all with an ease and grace that made him look like the perfect husband, father, and businessman. Too bad he hadn't returned the favor.

Sam headed toward the door but didn't make it out before Carol stopped her in her tracks. "Did you see the front page of *The Post* today?"

"Of course not. Who has time?"

"This you'll want to see. One of the paralegals had it." She held out the paper to Sam.

Ben Calloway stood front and center, wearing a tuxedo, his arm around a young beauty dressed in a designer frock. The Metropolitan Museum of Art served as the backdrop. The banner read, "Real Estate Magnate Calloway Escorts New Assistant from Red Cross Event." Smaller letters under the photograph queried, "Has Melissa Calloway been replaced?"

"Oh, no!" Anxiety swept through her body. "Do you think Melissa has seen this?"

"Probably not. She's sitting too calmly in the conference room." Carol looked over Sam's shoulder at the ticking bomb.

"I better cancel this conference before it even gets started. It's bad enough she only recently learned of the affair. War's going to break out when she sees the evidence plastered on the front page of *The Post*."

The next hour felt more like days after Sam shared the photo with Melissa, who ranted, raved, cried, and threatened. If only people could control their emotions, her job wouldn't be so difficult. Sam finally managed to calm her for the time being and suggested she make an appointment with her therapist, since the public humiliation would stay with her long after she left the office. Some things in life weren't fair, and Melissa Calloway certainly didn't deserve her husband's flagrant disloyalty and the mortification his careless actions brought with it.

Cases like this made Sam appreciate her marriage more than ever. Her husband, Tom, gave her the freedom to pursue her career without demanding that she cater to his needs. They were independent, yet connected. He understood the long hours and myopic focus that would soon reward her with a partnership.

She glanced at the only photo she had on her computer desk, hidden behind the monitor. She and Tom gazed into each other's eyes on their wedding day, exuding love and happiness. Sam smiled at the memory, then pushed it out of her mind. Too many more important matters vied for her attention.

The day passed in a flash, with client meetings, phone calls, and dictation intersecting each other willy-nilly. It was a few minutes past six, according to her watch. By now all the secretaries were gone, and the buzz and hum of computers, telephones, and voices had subsided. This was the time in the office Sam liked most. No distractions.

At least that's the way it was supposed to be. So why was her phone ringing? She glanced at the caller ID to identify the culprit. Tom's phone number flashed across the tiny screen.

"Hi, Tommy," she teased, using the childhood name his mother still called him. "What's up?" She continued signing letters Carol had left on her desk.

"I thought we could meet for a drink at Winston's." Horns honked in the background. He must be cruising the sidewalk, enjoying the spring weather.

"Are we celebrating something?" Sam turned her focus from work to her husband.

"Can't I invite my wife out for a drink after work on a Tuesday night?" Annoyance over her question wended its way through the line.

"Sure." She shrugged for her own benefit. "What time?"

"How about seven?"

It would take her at least forty minutes to get there, so she would only have twenty minutes to get done what she needed for tomorrow morning's court appearance.

"Seven thirty would be better."

A sigh escaped. "Okay. I'll see you then."

She placed the receiver in the cradle and tapped her nails on its surface. It wasn't like Tom to be cranky. And he hadn't laughed like he usually did when she called him Tommy. Something must have gone wrong at work. He'd been preoccupied lately with the prospective purchase of some company in California somewhere. She'd make a point of asking him about it. Let him vent, get it off his mind. He deserved her attention, and the realization she didn't know much about what was going on with this new deal brought her up short. Tonight would be the perfect opportunity to focus on his career instead of hers. Maybe turn his mood around.

Sam was late, of course. She was always late if coming from the office. It irritated Tom, but no matter how hard she tried, she could never stop herself from dictating one more letter or responding to one more email. Walking through the door into the mahogany and stained-glass bar, she inched through people standing three deep. Chattering customers took up every stool and space available. Her eyes moved around the dimly lit room, taking in the happy scene as she sought her husband.

And there he was in the thick of things, eyes on the flat-screen TV, immersed in a sporting event. Even from this distance, his handsome features showcasing baby blues, blond hair, and angular cheekbones gave her heart a kick, as she noticed other women in the bar notice him. But she was the lucky one. He was hers.

Tom pulled on a longneck bottle of beer as she approached.

"I see you started without me." She moved to kiss him, but he turned his head, and she grazed his cheek.

"You're late." His smile was missing. He must have had one hell of a day. "What would you like?"

"A glass of Chardonnay and a quieter spot would be great."

"That could be arranged." He ordered her drink and requested a table in the back.

Once seated, Sam relaxed into the calming atmosphere, and the cool liquid slid down easily. "This is much better." She smiled at her husband across the booth. "I was planning to work on Denise and Ben's case tonight. They want to adopt their nephew, Bobby. But I'm glad you had this idea."

"I don't want to talk about your cases right now."

The sting of his words smarted. "I thought you'd be interested in this particular case. Denise and Ben are your friends too. We were both devastated when Ben's brother and his wife were killed in a car accident."

He didn't apologize or respond to her statement.

Biting her lip to keep from saying anything that would tip this conversation into an unnecessary argument, Sam injected a modicum of concern into her voice. "What's wrong? Is something going on at work that's bothering you?"

"No. Well…yes, I guess. In a way."

"What is it?"

"I've been meaning to tell you." He looked down, avoiding her eyes, as he shifted in his seat.

She leaned forward. "Tell me what?" A twinge of anxiety shot through her system.

"I'm leaving for California for business on Saturday."

The twinge subsided. He often travelled for business for a day or two. "This Saturday?"

"Yes."

Something was off. The silence seemed to make him squirm even more.

"When will you be back?"

"I'm not sure. I'm planning on staying until the end of August. Maybe September."

"What?" Her voice escalated with her shock. "It's April. You never go away for four months. What about our vacation?"

She fleetingly realized they had no vacation plans. She was usually too busy to book anything, so Tom planned their time off.

He ignored her question. "Our company is in talks with a similar company out in San Diego. We're going to spend the next few months meeting with the president and vice-president, the company's accountants, you know. Doing the due diligence and determining whether we should purchase it or not."

Tom played with his beer bottle as he spoke, not looking at her.

"Why are you springing this on me now? You must have known about it for months."

"I wasn't sure I'd be going. Joe and Sherry were originally supposed to go."

"That makes more sense." Joe was the president of the company and Sherry, the comptroller. "What happened to change the plan?"

Tom's jaw tightened as he set his beer bottle on the table. He looked up and boldly locked eyes with her. "I talked Joe into letting me take his place."

Stunned, she looked at him hard, trying to gauge his reasons while attempting to keep her cool. "Why? Do you have some burning desire to see the sights in San Diego?" Sarcasm punctuated her words, but she couldn't help herself.

"No. I decided I needed to go."

His choice of words pricked at her skin. "What's really going on here, Tom?"

"You're married to your job, Sam. You work twelve hours a day, including Saturdays, and when you are home, you're either reading a law publication or working on some file."

Anger bubbled up inside her, but she battled it back. It would only make matters worse.

"Of course I'm always working. I'm a lawyer. I work at a big firm. I want to make partner. You know the requirements." Her effort to calm down evaded her. "I thought you understood. You never said my hours bothered you before."

"Well, they do. They did. But you were too busy to notice." His voice was tight, as if speaking through clenched teeth.

"So when you finally do tell me, it's on your way to California?"

"I'll probably be back in September. I think some time apart might be good for us."

"How could time away be good for our relationship? And what do you mean you'll *probably* be back in September?"

She sounded like a shrew, but this conversation had turned wicked, and she couldn't understand where it had come from. *Was he that unhappy*? They both worked hard, although if truth be told, she did spend substantially more hours at the office. He seldom complained. Instead, he went off to an art-show opening or movie without her. And didn't they always go out together on Saturday nights? Sometimes the two of them and sometimes with his coworker, Sherry, and her fiancé, Russ. It was comfortable, easy.

He didn't answer her question, but she had more. "Is Sherry going for the whole summer too? Is Russ on board with this?"

"Sherry and Russ broke up." If their table hadn't been so dimly lit, Sam would have sworn Tom's face tinted red. "As a matter of fact, I've been seeing Sherry." The words came spilling out, unchecked, unasked for.

She must have heard him wrong. "What do you mean you've been seeing Sherry?" His silence stretched on for too many guilty moments, piercing her heart. "You're having an affair?"

He barely nodded.

A false laugh escaped. "You're kidding. Right?"

"No. I'm serious." His eyes focused on hers, saying much more than his words.

The room spun, and she reached for the table to steady herself. "Does Joe know about this?" Surely the president of the company wouldn't allow it.

"Yes."

Sam's blood pulsed through her veins to the beat of the throb in her head. She squinted her eyes as she looked at him, trying to find a shred of doubt on his face. Anything to undo his words.

"When did it start?" As if that mattered.

"A few months ago."

"So when the three of us went to the movies last month, you were already having an affair with her? You took us out together?" Her words came out brash and loud as shock set in.

Tom's face burned even redder. He lowered his lids.

"You bastard. Sherry is my friend too. How could you sneak around with her behind my back—or should I say, right in front of me—and pretend everything's fine between us?"

Bile rose in her throat, and she fought to keep control, grabbing the cloth napkin and squeezing it into a ball. How could he do this to her? Cheat on her. And worse yet, with one of their friends. It was unconscionable. Despicable. Uncharacteristic.

She tilted her head as if to see him in a different light. "When did you become such a snake?" Her voice's volume rose with each word.

"Don't name call, Sam. It doesn't become you." He glanced around as heads turned their way. "And could you please lower your voice?"

"You expect me to be charming when my husband tells me he's moving to California for four months, maybe more, to hook up with the younger woman in his office? How cliché, by the way." Hysteria rose to the surface. "You're not supposed to be looking for love on the job. You're supposed to be married to me." Her throat clogged with panic as she fought to continue. "You're supposed to be in love with me."

His face paled, but a steely silence met her words.

"Why did you make me meet you here?"

"I thought it would be easier to have this discussion in a public place."

"Easier for whom? Did you think I might stab you if you told me this in the privacy of our home?"

"No, of course not. I knew it wouldn't go well, and I didn't want to…to…"

"You didn't want to what?"

"Shhhh…calm down." He glanced over his shoulder, bringing her attention to the audience she'd unwittingly garnered before responding. "I didn't want to be alone with you." The pity on his face made his words even more injurious.

She stared at him with her mouth open, her face burning with indignation and anger. Tears stung the backs of her eyes, and she blinked to keep them from falling. She wanted to scream, lash out with hurtful words, words that would slice through his heart and cause him at least one-tenth the pain he was inflicting on her. But the right words were nowhere to be found. How could she deal with this inconceivable betrayal in a sentence, or even a paragraph? She threw the balled-up napkin at him, hardly a sufficient weapon.

He caught it and placed in on the table. "I know I'm a coward, but I was afraid you would cry and beg me to stay. I didn't want you to try to dissuade me. I packed my clothes today and moved into a hotel. I'll be leaving Saturday. There didn't seem to be any point in arguing about this."

Retorts swirled and collided in her mind. Some angry, some panicked, some pleading, some irrational. But she was in a public place and refused to be humiliated while trying to make sense of his bombshell. She'd be damned if she were going to start sputtering non sequiturs and begging for more time to deal with it all. Yet his words echoed through her being, tearing through every shred of her loosely held composure, grating on her nerves like fingernails on a chalkboard. Tom didn't want her to try to dissuade him. He didn't even want to be alone with her!

She slid out of the booth, never taking her gaze from his. Poise and steadiness seemed of utmost importance as she stood slowly, testing her legs for support before she turned and walked through the bar toward the door.

The sounds of lively chatter among coworkers and friends seemed muffled as if she moved under water. A blur of color and form wavered in slow motion with no crisp delineation from one person to another. Mottled. Like an impressionist painting.

Out on the sidewalk, Samantha pointed her body in the direction of their apartment, and she placed one foot in front of the other, willing herself to get there without collapsing.

Breathe in. Breathe out.
Step left. Step right.
Look straight ahead. Don't think. Just move…
Keep moving…

Chapter Two

It was the Friday before Memorial Day, and the beach was not yet home to the thousands of vacationers who streamed to the Jersey shore for sand, sun, and fun. But there were some.

Sam jumped back from the surf, as a frigid wave crashed over her feet. How had she ended up here? Although the Jersey shore was not a bad place to spend her exile. Bruce Taylor, one of her work colleagues, had been kind enough to let her borrow his bungalow in Crescent Beach. But a change of scenery hadn't changed the movie running through her brain. She bit her lip to keep the tears from spilling out. She and Tom once shared a vacation house with friends in the Hamptons when they first started dating. They'd spent the summer laughing and kissing on the beach, experiencing the dawn of new love.

She turned at the sound of laughter. A rowdy bunch of guys foreshadowed the holiday mood as they pummeled a volleyball over the net, testosterone causing them to slam the ball from one side to the other. Gusty laughs and colorful language echoed over the beach before getting lost in the roar of the ocean. A group of young women in short-shorts and midriff-baring tops preened nearby, cheering on their boyfriends or acquaintances or strangers, the relationships a mystery.

Sam stepped up her pace, hoping to pass the sand court without notice. She wasn't in the mood to contend with catcalls or other offensive noises if the spirit struck the exuberant bunch. Just then, the volleyball whizzed past her head and plopped in the ocean at her feet, spraying icy water up her legs and onto her rolled-up jeans.

"Damn." She hopped back from the offending object.

"Hey, lady. Could you get the ball?"

Lady? She almost screamed as she plucked the ball out of the ocean and threw it hard, pounding the man standing before her, right in the chest. A huge red welt swelled on his skin where the ball made contact.

"I'm sorry." She covered her mouth with her hand.

"What's your problem?" The stranger rubbed his chest, a thin film of sweat giving his tan a glistening sheen. He scooped the ball up and turned in one liquid motion.

"I said I was sorry," she replied to his back, as he sprinted off, revealing well-muscled legs.

A hot flush crept up Samantha's face as she shoved errant strands of hair under her baseball cap. What was wrong with her? He'd only asked her to get his ball. But the use of the term *lady* pushed the wrong button, making her feel old and crotchety. And here she'd been worried about catcalls!

Thirty-three isn't old, right? Besides, he looked the same age. But he had a vitality about him that made him appear younger. Maybe it was the Hawaiian-patterned swim trunks that hung low around slim hips. Or the thick, layered, chestnut hair, finger-combed off his forehead, accenting the chiseled lines of his face. Or maybe it was his easy smile directed at a statuesque woman in the entourage, before he tossed the felonious ball to one of his teammates.

The guy looked familiar. Probably one of those faces that reminded her of a movie star. *Why are you staring at him?* She chastised herself, then smirked. As if looking at a man while wallowing in the agony inflicted by another was somehow sacrilegious. She willed her body to move along before he caught her. But not before she witnessed one of the young women caress his chest as if to erase the mark Sam had left with his ball. *Oh, brother.*

Leaning over, she rolled up the hem of her jeans even farther, as the waves crashed hard around her feet, spewing mist and sand up her legs. As a child, she had loved to play tag, running up to the surf and skipping back, trying not to let the white foam touch her feet. A fun game for a simple life.

She walked on, the grains of sand sifting between her toes, cool but soft. Her hand grasped at the strands of hair obscuring her view and tucked them back under her cap. It didn't stop the wisps from whipping into her mouth with every step, but it gave her something to focus on.

I've become a cold, bitter woman. Only thirty-three and I've lost my lust for life. How could I have let this happen? And what am I going to do about it?

She sat on the sand and hugged her knees, attempting to keep the cool wind from penetrating her body. The sun had set and dusk turned to dark. Waves continued their incessant rolling and crashing as the tide backed away from her.

No more games with the surf. No more

distractions.

The time had come to deal with the issues. Tom. Herself. The future.

Alone.

****

Sitting at the kitchen table of Bruce's beach house, Sam stared at the words she'd typed on her laptop. Her finger hovered over the mouse, hesitating, as indecision played havoc with her plan. She reminded herself that her email message was addressed to her best friends since high school—The Sworn Sisters they called themselves—even though she hadn't gotten around to sharing her trauma with them. She hadn't been able to. Opening the wound to let the blood flow required guts. Lancing the scab to prevent infection seemed the necessary thing to do, but she hadn't steeled herself for the shrieking pain which would accompany that action. But she was close.

They loved each other like sisters, supporting each other through thick and thin. True, they didn't get together as frequently as they would like, living in different cities, although not too far from their New Jersey hometown of Lawrenceville. In fact, Alyssa still lived there while Denise lived a few miles north in Princeton. Only Sam and Nicki ventured to the big cities, with Nicki in Philadelphia and Sam in New York.

While they all lived within driving distance, their careers or family responsibilities won out over frequent get togethers. When they did come together, they picked up where they'd left off, as if they'd seen each other last week.

Sam turned her attention back to her email and

took a moment to reread her silly poem, hoping it would convince her friends to come.

Remember the days when we were full of doubt,
Yet Friday nights were definitely girls' night out.
We spent hours primping to look just right,
Then partied till midnight, knitting our group ever so
*   tight.*
It's fifteen years later, and I'm still full of doubt,
Looking forward to each of you hearing me out.
So give me a call or drop me a line,
Advise me which weekend you can fit into your time.
My address is in Crescent Beach, isn't it a pity,
The residence of the moment is not New York City?
Bring your swimsuits, your shorts, your flipflops, your
*   memories,*
Leave behind your jobs, your chores, your headaches,
*   your families.*
You have no choice but to come and reminisce,
Your friend Sam needs your company and some bliss.
I hope you can arrange to free up your plate,
Just email or call me to work out a date.
                    Love, Sam

Was she ready to share her painful story?

She clicked the *Send* button, and her note flew off into cyberspace.

Now for a distraction. It would do no good to stalk her inbox since her friends had commitments and weren't tied to their computers, or at least their personal emails. Casting her eyes on the pink, flowered shoe box sitting on the end table, she plopped on the couch and sighed. A very small container for high school memories, but it was all she'd saved. And for some reason she'd brought it with her to Crescent Beach.

Was she turning nostalgic, or was there a deeper meaning for reaching toward the past?

Lifting the lid, she picked up a few photographs. She and Alyssa on their first day of senior year smiled back at her, their hair long and straight, their eyes bright with enthusiasm. Of course, Alyssa's uniform skirt was a little shorter and her makeup a little bolder. So like Alyssa, always trying to be noticed. Having four sisters would do that to a teen. The next photo was Denise and Sam as Santa's helpers holding brightly wrapped presents in front of a Christmas tree at the local nursing home. Denise, dressed as an elf in three-quarter length pants and pointy shoes, had her hands on her hips and a funny grin on her mouth. Sam wore a cute little red dress and hat trimmed in fake fur. Where in the world had they gotten those outfits?

The next picture was high school graduation. The three of them, plus Nicki, linking arms, dressed in white caps and gowns instead of their dreaded Catholic school uniforms, all looking off in the distance, as if seeing their futures while clinging to the past. They weren't smiling. But then again, a black cloud had hung over the occasion, threatening to ruin their celebration. It had taken cumulative willpower and the mantra to think positively to get them through that night without breaking down, but they had done it.

Sam placed the photos on the couch beside her and lifted a red satin book from the box. Her fingers traced the word *Diary* etched in gold, and she smiled to herself.

She fanned the pages, then turned to the first entry.

At least an hour passed before she reached the end. Closing her eyes, she leaned her head back against the sofa as the facts surrounding the last high school party at Alyssa's came crashing back as if it were yesterday.

Sam picked up the graduation picture. Nicki's eyes were bright with unshed tears, her lips drawn down. Those last few weeks leading up to graduation had been so painful. For all of them. Even though it was Nicki who'd been pregnant, they all shared her emotions. And although they tried to support her and keep her spirits up, more tears fell during those days then during each of their lifetimes.

Not only had Nicki's misfortune surfaced, but so had Michael McCain's. Sam had had a major crush on him despite his ambivalence toward her. He disappeared the night of Alyssa's party. No one expected him to leave town twenty-two days before graduation. He was the star pitcher for the baseball team. Accepted to Fordham in the fall. Which led the police to initially believe he'd encountered some trouble that night. The fight between him and Carl had given way to speculation and investigation. The tension between him and his father—another avenue to explore. But nothing ever came of it. Because there had been no evidence of foul play, and he'd already reached the age of majority, it became less of a violent crime case and more of a missing person case. Eventually the matter was dropped.

Although not before graduation. Instead, their commencement ceremony, which should have been a joyous occasion, took on a sense of depression and confusion. The answers were missing; security gone. It seemed as if the student body as a whole ached to put as much distance as possible between their once beloved school and their optimistic future.

At least that's the way Sam had felt.

The bittersweet memories of those final days of high school skipped and twirled through her mind, sometimes fuzzy, sometimes sharp as a knife, threatening to bring back to life those adolescent growing pains. Sam pushed them away. Who needed them when she had her current pain to deal with?

Tom. She whispered his name, and her breath caught in her throat as her eyes stung with fresh tears.

Maybe her diary could help now, as it had when she'd been a teen; her secret friend who held her thoughts without fear of judgment, retaliation, unwanted advice, or loose lips.

She wished she could pick up a pen, turn the page, and begin to write.

But she couldn't.

Chapter Three

The sun's brilliance pierced Sam's eyes as she left the house at seven thirty the next morning to walk into town. She breathed in the salty sea air as she pushed her sunglasses into place. In some ways, she felt infinitely better than she had in weeks.

Sam approached Melanie's Coffee Shop on Crescent Avenue, a cute, cozy café with white eyelet curtains tied back to permit a glimpse into its inviting interior. A throwback to earlier days, the décor included black and white checked linoleum, gray Formica tables, and red leatherette seats. It was a place for locals that perhaps, in time, would feel comfortable.

But not yet. So she avoided the counter and sat at a two-person table by the window. Having ordered a cup of coffee, she opened her newspaper and began reading, only to find herself distracted. She glanced at her watch for at least the third time since she arrived. A hard habit to break. She couldn't quite grasp the concept of having nowhere to go or nothing to do. Feeling conspicuous, she inhaled the earthy aroma of her coffee, hoping its perfect roasted blend would envelop her in familiarity. She sipped it and focused on a news story about the redevelopment of Asbury Park, but her mind wandered, and she fidgeted in her chair, trying to get comfortable. But it wasn't the chair.

Edgy and unsettled, she folded the newspaper, paid

her check, and walked out onto the sidewalk, barely fifteen minutes after she'd arrived.

Ridiculous. She came to a standstill. Ten weeks stretched before her. Only ten weeks to pull herself together. It would be harder than any case she'd ever tried. But she was a fighter. She could beat this. Turning around, she walked straight back into the coffee shop, taking the only open stool at the counter between two men, one dressed in tattered jeans, a sleeveless T-shirt, and a hardhat sitting on the counter before him, the other in dress pants, shirt, and tie.

"Decided one cup wasn't enough?" The jolly waitress poured Sam another.

Sam shrugged. "Thanks." She could feel the construction worker assessing her.

"I've never seen you in here before." It sounded more like an accusation than a statement. "Here for the summer?"

"Part of it." He'd get bored if she kept her answers short.

"Nice. How is it the wives get to spend their days on the beach with the kids while the husbands go off to work? Doesn't seem fair." He shook his head but had a patronizing smile on his lips.

"What makes you think I'll be spending my days on the beach with the kids?" Sam's ire surfaced. This unexpected irritation was becoming a bad habit.

"That's what all the ladies your age do around here."

"What a ridiculous generalization." She stirred her coffee a little too hard, and it splashed onto the counter, puddling around her cup.

"Hey, Mike, aren't I right?" The construction

worker peered around her.

The businessman barely looked up from his paper. "Sure. Whatever you say, Steve."

"Don't you think this lady has it made? She gets to play with the kids while her husband slaves away at his job?"

The man glanced at Sam a moment too long, then returned to his paper.

Damn! Sam bit her lip and squeezed her eyes closed as a flood of embarrassment rushed through her, his familiar face imprinted on her brain. Just her luck to sit next to the guy she'd assaulted with his volleyball the other day. Maybe he wouldn't remember her.

She exhaled slowly.

"She doesn't have any kids with her now..." He paused, the hint of a grin on his mouth. "And she didn't have any kids when she was walking on the beach the other night, either."

Oh, he recognized her. She shifted in her seat, waiting for more, but fortunately he was silent.

"The kids are probably with the nanny." Steve continued to push the conversation. And all her buttons too.

"You know it's rude to speak around me," she snapped. "I am sitting right here. And the fact is, I don't have any kids. And I don't have a husband." The words tumbled out before she caught herself. A slip of the tongue. "But I do have a job, so you can be assured that no one, other than me, is paying for this luxury vacation." Her biting sarcasm guaranteed she would make no friends this morning.

"With that attitude, no wonder you don't have a husband," Steve snorted.

Seconds from exploding, Sam fought to keep silent, afraid of what would come pouring forth. She had to get out of here.

Rifling through her purse, she threw some money on the counter, then spun on her stool toward the exit. As she stood, her newspaper slipped out of her hand, then her wallet, and all the change jangled to the linoleum floor. *Could this get any worse?* Her face burned as she stooped to capture the out-of-control coins. Coming back into Melanie's had been a very bad idea.

The volleyball guy got off his stool and crouched on the floor. "Let me help."

His voice was deep and smooth. A thrill ran up her arm as he handed her some errant coins. She found his eyes. Beautiful blue eyes. Caribbean Sea eyes. Familiar eyes.

"Hi, Sam." His brow furrowed as he said her name, although his tone indicated no question.

She froze in place as she stared at him. "M...Michael McCain?" His name fell between them.

He nodded.

Her pounding heart thrummed in her ears. Michael. It couldn't be. And yet...those eyes...

He smiled. "I didn't realize it was you the other day. But I see now."

They were still crouched on the floor, and Michael reached out to take her hand and raise her up with him. Her head swam, and she grabbed the counter to steady herself. After all these years. He looked completely different. Gone was the long, shaggy hair. The lanky physique. Instead, he was built like a man who frequented the gym, and his sun-streaked hair was combed into place. Her teenage crush stood before her looking amazingly gorgeous, and that old familiar current flashed through her.

"Are you okay?" He broke into her trance and handed her some coins.

"No. Yes," she quickly amended, dragging her eyes from his, as she put the handful of change into her wallet. Dozens of questions collided, vying for the chance to get out. But now was not the time.

She tried for a smile and hoped to sound natural. "I can't believe you're here."

"Did you miss me?" His killer grin sent her insides fluttering. But only for a moment.

He was playing with her. His indifference to the angst he'd put his classmates through fifteen years ago called up a surprising frustration. Perhaps unjustified, since he'd been the one hurting enough to leave. But real just the same.

"We thought you were dead!"

His grin disappeared, and he lowered his eyes. "I'm sorry. I had to leave town fast."

She searched for a calm she didn't feel. Could seeing him in person dredge up long buried emotions from the past? He certainly didn't deserve her ire, but she needed an explanation. "Is that all you have to say?"

"For now." He paused, then touched her arm. A gesture of comfort?

"Why didn't you call one of us? Let us know you were all right." She couldn't seem to let it go.

"Sam, you caught me off guard here. I didn't expect to run into you. It's been years since I left—since we knew each other. Maybe we can talk about it some other time. But not now." His eyes pleaded with her to understand.

She nodded. Perhaps this coffee shop, with its eclectic mix of locals and vacationers, wasn't the best place to dissect the past. Besides, everyone had secrets. If he didn't want to talk about it now, she'd have to abide by his wishes. "Sure."

Noticing some wayward coins, he squatted to pick them up. Sam stood there watching the muscles in his shoulders bunch beneath his shirt. The familiar hum and buzz of adolescent attraction seeped through her blood, and she dug her nails into her palms to kill it. Her schoolgirl crush couldn't recur this easily, could it?

"Do you need a hand?" She extended hers to help him up, calling upon her courtroom skill of staying in control no matter what the pressure.

He took her hand as he rose, and that telltale jolt of electricity sizzled up her arm. She almost started laughing at the absurdity of it all.

"See you, Michael," said Steve as he slid off his stool. "Maybe I'll see you too, vacation lady." His chuckle highlighted the pleasure he derived from causing such a stir.

Sam gave him her best stern look. There was no point in entering into another war of words with this chauvinist.

"Steve's just teasing," explained Michael.

"He's rude and presumptuous." How could anyone not take offense to his assumptions?

"Well then, it seems you two have something in common."

"Excuse me?" She arched her eyebrow, unsure of whether he was teasing or serious.

"You were pretty rude the other day when I asked you for the volleyball." A lazy smile crossed his face.

"Rude? You called me lady."

"I guess if you're not"—he shrugged—"then it could be considered a slur."

Heat burned her cheeks, and she opened her mouth to speak and then closed it. Is that what he thought? Her high school crush? Appropriate words abandoned her. This was all just too much.

At the risk of acting more the fool, she made a snap decision. She turned on her heel and marched out the door.

****

Sam arrived back at the house an hour later. The first thirty minutes she'd spent walking off her anger, directed mostly at herself for reacting in such an inappropriate way. By the second thirty, she'd realized her inability to get along with strangers, or old acquaintances, could doom her stay in Crescent Beach. Carrying around too much baggage made for a grouchy Sam. Steve had only been teasing her. She shouldn't have gotten so indignant about it.

Perhaps she could forgive Steve, but she had a harder time with Michael. Running into him after all this time without obtaining a decent explanation for his disappearance grated on her nerves. Although she'd stopped thinking about him sometime during college, the old memories had come hurtling back with a vengeance. She'd expected more from him then "I had to leave town."

Perhaps, if she tried, she could understand his reluctance to explain away a painful past, especially to someone he hadn't counted on running into. But his impoliteness in reminding her of their little altercation the other evening had her burning with embarrassment. Worse was his comment about her being a lady—or not.

And to think that an hour ago, she'd succumbed to her teenage infatuation by mooning over his gorgeous eyes and strong shoulders.

Obviously, it was best to leave the past in the past.

And hopefully, she wouldn't run into Michael McCain again.

****

A car horn beeped in the driveway, and Sam's spirit soared. It was nearly seven on Friday evening, and the day had passed like weeks.

Nicki was here! Thank God, because she could not spend one more minute alone with her thoughts.

She hustled outside to greet her friend, and behind her were Denise and Alyssa. All of her Sworn Sisters.

"Oh, my God." Tears escaped, but they were happy tears for a change. She hugged them each in turn. "What are you all doing here?"

Denise responded, "We got your email invitation but didn't realize it was an emergency until Nicki called us the other night. She told us you and Tom had separated. If we can't drop everything for our Sworn Sister in need, then we're not the friends we thought we were." She gave Sam a lopsided smile. "How are you holding up?"

Despite the melancholy that had taken over her body and soul, Sam's mood did an about-face as she took in her best friends. "Much better, now that you're here. Welcome to Crescent Beach."

Everyone talked at once, as Sam led them into the

house, straining from the effort of lugging Nicki's "overnight" bag.

Nicki, oblivious to Sam's struggle, followed with nothing but her oversized purse. "Where'd you find this little cottage?"

"One of my friends at the law firm. He and his family don't use it until August, so he offered it to me when he learned about my forced leave of absence." She glanced toward the kitchen. "You must be starving. I don't have much to offer. I thought only Nicki was coming."

"You're in luck," said Denise. "I made stuffed mushrooms, bruschetta, and a Mexican dip. I know they don't exactly go together, but I wanted to make sure everyone had their favorites. I'll be right back." She strode out the door and headed toward her car.

Wonderful Denise. They were lucky to have her as part of their group. Knowing their tastes, she catered to each of them, no matter how busy her life was with her husband and kids.

"I brought wine and beer." Alyssa followed Denise out to the driveway.

"I could use that." Nicki settled onto the couch without inserting herself into the fray; the opposite of her usual take-charge demeanor.

It didn't take long to set out their meal. Appetizers were enough for them, as long as it included an adult sensible beverage. Sam pulled out some cheese and crackers, gathered glasses and napkins, and watched her friends as if on the outside looking in.

The hum of the others catching up swirled around Sam, and while she wanted to know what was going on in their lives, focus abandoned her. She had to remind herself her Sworn Sisters had given up their Friday night to be with her. She needed to join in.

"Nicki, how's the music business doing?" asked Alyssa as she took a swig of beer from the bottle.

"Great. But a little too busy. I'm at work six days a week, and on Sunday I can't drag myself from bed."

"How'd you get away this weekend?" Sam's guilt kicked up a notch. Hopefully, Nicki wouldn't have to work late every night next week to make up for this little visit.

"I told my boss I was going out of town." Nicki flipped her long blonde hair over her shoulder, a familiar trait. "I'm sure he assumed I was flying to Vegas or somewhere equally decadent, but no need for him to know the details."

Sam eased back on the sofa, attempting to relax. "Thanks. To all of you. I'm sure it wasn't easy to get away on such short notice." She raised her wine glass in a silent toast to her friends.

Alyssa verbalized their sentiment. "To the Sworn Sisters. May we always be there for each other."

They drank, and Sam allowed the comfort of their friendship to pour through her with the wine.

"Not to bring this party down, but we are here for a reason." Nicki zeroed in on Sam. "We know you and Tom are separated, but we don't know any of the details. If we're going to slice and skewer him, we need specifics."

Sam inhaled a fortifying breath, then put her wine glass down, knowing the sooner she got through this, the faster they could deal with it and move on to other, much more pleasant topics. With a heavy heart, she told them about the night Tom called her at work and asked her to meet him for a drink. Although she had shared what had happened with a few colleagues at work, she had only given abridged versions, not delving too far into her life or its consequences with anyone.

Now, telling it to her very best girlfriends, she realized her story wasn't much longer than the few sentences she had strung together on other occasions. Questions came flying at her from all directions, but most of her responses were the same. "I don't know. We never discussed that. I don't know. It never occurred to me." She sounded like a complete idiot—naïve, clueless, uninvolved in Tom's life, and worst of all, oblivious to his needs.

Sam kept this realization under cover and hoped her Sworn Sisters didn't see her as she was starting to see herself. Being the good friends they were, they gave all the appropriate responses, shredding Tom and coddling her. She needed that; craved it. Hearing out loud that Tom was a slug, an ass, a jerk, a cold-hearted weasel, and not deserving of her love reinforced the silent screams resonating in her head as she hurled similar accusations at him through telepathy.

"This conversation is exhausting." The strain and angst from pulling apart the inner workings of her marriage settled deep in her bones. Being her loyal friends, they didn't lay blame on Sam and instead found fault in everything Tom did. In the end, they pronounced him a skank. What would she do without them?

"I'm sorry, Sam." Denise patted her leg before stacking some empty plates on the coffee table. "We're here to support you, not make you miserable. Let's change the subject. I'm going to put the mushrooms in the oven. Can I get anyone anything?"

"I'll take another beer." Alyssa drained her bottle.

"I'll get the wine." Nicki stood to retrieve the bottle from the kitchen.

And just like that the conversation veered from Tom to reminiscing about their high school days, boyfriends past, and crazy trips they'd taken.

"This is a much more civilized way to enjoy the Jersey shore than the way we did it in high school." Nicki glanced around the living room before taking a baby bite out of a nacho.

Sam pushed her friend's lack of appetite aside and snickered. "Four of us in a raunchy hotel room with a double bed was the only way we could afford a beach getaway back then."

"At least you ended up with a space on the bed," complained Alyssa. "I always got the floor with the gross carpet."

"You're the one who brought a sleeping bag," Nicki pointed out. "Our very own Girl Scout. Always prepared."

"That's because I had four sisters who made me sleep on the floor when we went on vacation. Why my parents had us all stay in the same room with two double beds is beyond me. It wasn't fair." Alyssa huffed that memorable and oft-repeated refrain.

Sam sympathized with her friend. The middle child between two older and two younger sisters, she was the odd one out.

"Oh, Alyssa. You can't still be carrying around that 'poor me' attitude." Nicki, who was usually a little more sensitive to Alyssa's plight, was clearly having none of it tonight.

Sam zeroed in on Nicki's face. Normally it held an easy smile, especially if accompanied by a teasing barb. Not tonight. Her tactless comment and closed expression chilled the air. Something was going on with Nicki. Something not so good. Perhaps it had to do with Dex, her man of the moment.

Denise must have sensed the tidal wave about to crash and jumped in with a comical memory from a karaoke bar where the four of them gave their best rendition of "Respect" complete with dance moves. That returned the laughter, which continued well past midnight, through story after story of their minor embarrassments, silly pranks, and major friendship.

It wasn't until eight the next morning, with the sun glaring through a broken slat in the blinds, that Sam awoke. As happened every morning since she last saw Tom, a deep sadness settled around her soul, which she needed to banish. She looked over at Alyssa who had a pillow over her head, dead to the world. Picturing the mess they'd left on the coffee table the night before, Sam pulled herself up and crept downstairs, intending to quietly clean up, but Denise had beaten her to it.

"What are you doing up so early?" Sam followed Denise into the kitchen with the last of the empty beer and wine bottles.

"It's not early. I have kids, remember?"

Sam's eyes watered, and she turned to hide her emotions while taking her time to prepare coffee. "I can't tell you what it means to me that you came. You have your hands full with your two toddlers, as well as Bobby."

Denise smiled. "Are you kidding? When Nicki called and told me what happened, I couldn't get here fast enough." She sipped her coffee. "I hope it helped. I know we can't take the pain away, but whatever you need—if it's to talk or hang out or get away from it all—call any one of us. Or all of us. We're here for you, just as you'd be for us." Denise eased her arm around Sam's shoulder and hugged her. "We're the Sworn Sisters."

Sam laughed through her tears. "And my best friends."

"Laughter is good for the soul. We have to do this more often."

"Do what more often?" Alyssa's eyes were barely open as she padded into the small kitchen, pushing away strands of long brown hair that had escaped her ponytail and fallen across her face.

"Get together and laugh," said Denise, draining the remains of her coffee cup.

"I'm in. Where are your mugs?" Alyssa began opening and closing cabinets until she came to the right one. "I have to be at work by noon. What time is it?"

Denise looked at the clock on the kitchen wall. "Almost nine. I'm sorry, Sam, but I have to go soon too. I can't leave Ben with all three kids all day."

"No problem. I'm so happy you were able to get away last night." The buoyancy Sam experienced from having her close friends at hand sank a few levels, but she rallied back. "After we got past the first hour dealing with my issues, I had a blast. At times I was laughing so hard, I was crying. I can't remember the last time that happened."

"Me neither." Denise put her coffee mug in the sink, accompanied by a tired sigh.

With two children under four and now responsible

for her deceased in-laws' son, Bobby, Sam doubted that Denise's exhaustion was merely from one late night.

"Don't think you have the rest of the weekend to yourself, Sam. I'm staying." Nicki breezed into the room, looking like a soap opera star in a white silk nightgown with her long blonde hair brushed straight. She headed for the coffee maker.

Sam's spirits lifted with Nicki's declaration, and the women picked up where they'd left off the night before, talking non-stop about anything and everything.

After a while, Alyssa confessed to an anomaly as she pointed to Nicki's attire. "I bought one of those for our honeymoon... I won't be needing it anymore."

Although Alyssa and David had broken up six months ago, Sam saw the pain surface in Alyssa's eyes. Another minefield. "It won't be long until you find someone else." Sam spun her positive words around Alyssa despite her own trauma.

"I don't know if I'll ever trust a man again. I knew David for eight years. I thought we were soul mates." She winced. "I hate that expression. I don't know why I even said it, but you know what I mean. I never thought he'd cheat on me. Why ask me to marry him if he didn't plan on being faithful?"

Sam knew the answer. Because Alyssa longed to get married. Badgered him into an engagement. Her four sisters were married. She was the last one. She desired what they had. And David and Alyssa had been together forever. Cheating was his way of getting out of marriage. But now was not the time to have that discussion.

Nicki chimed in. "You're lucky you found out and broke things off. It wasn't meant to be."

Was it that simple? A wrong choice made somewhere along the way that came back to bite her in the butt years later? Sam didn't agree. Couples needed to work through their differences, not pick up and move on, leaving one partner devasted and wondering what had just happened.

Far too soon, Alyssa and Denise had to leave, putting an end to their deep, and sometimes insightful, discussions.

Sam hugged them as she walked them to their car, leaving Nicki inside in her nightwear. "Please come back to visit."

Alyssa quickly volunteered. "I've penciled in a few weekends after consulting my work schedule."

"Really?" Sam didn't know whether to be ecstatic or upset. "Do you think I need a babysitter?"

"Of course not. I think you could use a friend to get you through this. And I have the time." She rolled her eyes dramatically.

"Then I'll see you soon."

Sam waved as they left. Walking back toward the house, she couldn't help but thank fate for bringing them all together.

Chapter Four

"I'm so glad you're staying. I miss you." Sam hugged Nicki, needing the physical and emotional connection to bolster her sagging heart.

Nicki squeezed her back, then held her at arms' length. "You are not a mush woman. You are going to tell me all the reasons why you are better off without Tom. Understand? And you are going to believe them."

Sam exhaled, hoping to expel the negativity Nicki demanded she do. "Why don't we put on our bathing suits? We have all day to labor over my sad story at the beach."

"Do we have to go to the beach?" Nicki glanced out the window as if searching for a flash rain shower, but the sun shone with conviction. "I'm not in the mood, and I don't want to subject myself to getting more wrinkles around my eyes. I'm not keen on skin cancer either."

These complaints had never come from Nicki's mouth before. She loved the beach. What was going on with her? "There is sun screen. And you could wear a hat. I even have a beach umbrella you could sit under."

Nicki's brow furrowed.

"Never mind. If you don't want to go to the beach, we can sit on the porch. Or ride bikes around town. Or play tennis." Sam paused, attempting to gauge Nicki's interest in any one of her suggestions. "How about going out for lunch? The Reach is a few blocks up, across from the beach. Then you can at least see the ocean, without actually going near it."

Nicki perked up. "Now that sounds like a good idea. I'll go get ready."

Nicki came downstairs an hour later, dressed in a blue, silk, flowered sundress and strappy, heeled sandals. Gold bangles graced her wrists, and hoop earrings peeked through her long, blonde hair when she moved. A designer bag swung from her right shoulder.

"Where do you think you're going?" Sam withheld an eye-roll, taking in Nicki's over-the-top outfit.

"To lunch. I need to look good in case I meet the man of my dreams."

"This is the beach, Nicki! People don't dress like that. They wear shorts, or a bathing suit and cover-up. You look like a million bucks."

"Thanks. That was the goal." Nicki brushed her hair over her shoulder and placed her hand on her hip in a camera-ready pose.

"And what do you mean about meeting the man of your dreams? I thought you were dating Dex."

"We broke up." Nicki's voice rasped, and she averted her eyes, focusing on a modern painting on the wall. "I'll fill you in at the restaurant. Let's go."

"I'm so sorry, Nicki. What happened?"

Her jaw tightened. "We'll talk about it later."

Sam decided not to push if Nicki wasn't ready to discuss it.

Unfortunately, Nicki's avoidance of the subject pivoted her focus onto Sam. "You can't wear that."

Sam looked down at her beige shorts and white tank top. "Why not?"

Nicki prodded her up the stairs to her room, then rummaged through her closet without so much as a request to invade her personal space.

"What are you doing?" Sam sighed, realizing her grumbling stomach would be put off a bit longer.

"Looking for something a little more appealing." She brushed through the garments in no time. "There's not much here to work with."

Of course not. Because Sam left most of her city clothes in the city where they belonged. Crescent Beach was a casual retreat, a summer vacation destination. And her forced sabbatical location.

She watched Nicki with a blend of amusement and astonishment as Nicki redoubled her efforts. She finally pulled out a white slim skirt and a black and white halter top that Sam had purchased at a local boutique. Kind of elegant, kind of sexy.

"This is better. Meet me downstairs when you're ready." With that, Nicki whooshed out of the room, leaving Sam to follow her instruction.

Sam did as she was told, and Nicki nodded in approval when she came into the living room. *Thank goodness.*

"Is this a halfway decent place we're going to? Might I meet a gorgeous, gainfully employed stud?"

So Nicki was moving on quickly. But would she ever find who she was searching for? Her relationships never seemed to last longer than three months. "It's a popular spot, and yes, I believe there will be men there."

Nicki finally smiled. "Lead the way."

****

The Reach was packed—and noisy. Not exactly

what Sam had in mind but typical for a Saturday afternoon eatery at the shore. At least Nicki was satisfied, so they might as well settle in at the bar, as they waited the estimated forty-five minutes for a table.

Fortunately Sam could see the ocean from her perch since she wasn't going to be able to enjoy it in person. Not that she enjoyed much these days. Her head throbbed to the rhythm of the waves, and she wasn't sure an alcoholic beverage was the best choice before she got something in her stomach, but Nicki ordered two margaritas without discussion.

She sipped at hers, hoping the tequila would not only kill her headache, but distribute some much-needed spirit into her blood. Nicki filled the air with chatter about her music clients, which Sam found blissfully soothing since she could come in and out of the conversation without much thought. Until the second drink when Nicki turned back to the matter at hand.

"I thought Tom was one of the good guys. It's hard to believe he would do that to you."

Fresh pain washed through Sam, made even sharper when she thought of Tom with Sherry. Unbridled words poured out as she lamented over the loss of her marriage, the loss of her husband, and the loss of her self-esteem.

"Some days it feels like I'm living a nightmare, and some days the pain is so acute I can't get out of bed. I thought he loved me. I guess I took it for granted. Took him for granted. I assumed he was happy."

Although Nicki had heard most of this the night before, she didn't shut Sam down through her detailed recitation. Instead, she comforted and supported her.

"Time heals all." Sarcasm peppered Nicki's remark, which seemed out of place given her eagerness to meet someone new. "And it looks like you have the time."

A suffocating heaviness pressed on Sam's chest as she recalled her meeting with Phil Bennett, the managing partner of her firm. "It's hard to admit this out loud, but after Tom left, I could barely function at home, much less at the office. I went through the stages of grief—denial, bargaining, anger. Now I'm just depressed." She spun her glass, making the ice settle. "My personal problems were interfering with my professional life. Before this happened, I was on track to become partner in September. Now, I'm not so sure. I got the impression our managing partner thought I should have sucked it up and moved on." Her voice shook with incredulity. "And you know, I've felt the same way about some of my divorce clients who wallowed in their sorrow. Now I know what it's like."

Nicki gave her a sympathetic smile.

"Worse yet, clients were calling to complain I wasn't being responsive to their needs. That kind of bad press does not bode well for positive votes from the partners." Sam inwardly cringed. Even now, weeks removed from the angst-ridden meeting in which Phil had delineated her faults, she wanted to scream. *How dare he*! She had done her best under the circumstances.

Nicki nodded, placing her hand over Sam's, and an all-encompassing compassion, sprinkled with love, seeped into Sam's soul. And for the first time, it didn't elicit tears.

"Maybe the rest of the partners don't know."

Nicki's optimistic spin would have been Sam's preferred interpretation, but she knew otherwise. "In the scheme of things, a ten-week leave of absence is a drop in the bucket compared to the time you've spent in the office over the past seven years."

Even Nicki knew she was a workaholic. A twinge of remorse shot straight to her heart. If she hadn't spent all those hours in the office, maybe she would still have Tom.

"Why did your boss give you so much time?"

"He must have determined it was a bargain compared to the prospect of upping the firm's malpractice insurance if I stayed." Sam chuckled without mirth.

"I'm glad to see you've kept your sense of humor through all this."

"I'm all cried out. But don't worry, there's always tomorrow."

Despite the fact she looked at it as a punishment, Sam knew she was useless to her clients, who needed her to be strong. She vowed to herself she'd paste her bruised and battered ego together with crazy glue, if need be. She had to turn this around. The offered break would be her salvation. She would regroup, figure out what had happened to land herself in her clients' worst nightmares, and fight through the fog to come out with a clear and sunny view of her future.

She'd be back at least a month before the vote for partnership, and she'd have that month to bust her butt working, as well as lobbying the partners to make her one of them.

No use reliving the past. She couldn't change it. And she was so tired of thinking about it. Talking about it. It was time to change the subject.

"What happened with you and Dex? And don't tell me it's no big deal. I can see it's affecting you."

Nicki shrugged. "I didn't know him well. We met on a cruise, dated for eleven weeks, then broke up. No harm no foul."

So Nicki was going to skim the surface and blow off her relationship with Dex as another mistake. Apparently, their split happened over two months ago, although she hadn't said a word about it to Sam. Not that they got together very often, but phone calls and emails were not uncommon. Maybe that was all there was to it.

Instead of dwelling on the details of her breakup, Nicki did a one-eighty and relayed hysterical tales of diva behavior by the music artists she worked with—a valiant attempt to prove she no longer cared about Dex.

So Sam let it go. At least for now.

She glanced at the entranceway where traffic was heavy, but they slowly advanced on the seating list. Nicki had been right to dress up. Sam felt sophisticated and elegant and sensed more than a few appreciative looks from the men passing by. Much needed attention to boost her ailing self-confidence.

Nicki elbowed her. "There's a very handsome guy standing at the end of the bar looking at you."

Sam swiveled in her seat to follow Nicki's gaze. A tall, gorgeous man in khaki pants and navy-blue golf shirt stood beside a beautiful brunette in a pale-yellow outfit. They looked like they were straight out of the pages of *Vanity Fair*.

"Yes, he's good-looking from what I can see of him." Sam turned back to Nicki. "He's with a woman.

Probably his girlfriend…or wife."

Nicki considered this information for a moment. "Or first date. Or sister. But I guess you probably should stay away from him. What good would it do to find a man here in Crescent Beach when you're moving back to New York in two months? You certainly don't need any more complications in your life right now."

"That's for sure." Sam nodded her agreement.

Not that she had any intention of getting close enough to any man to feel more than annoyance at his audacity to live. Tom's betrayal had morphed her feelings toward him into a disdain for all his species.

After sitting at the bar for close to an hour, they were finally seated at a table by the window.

Although Sam had been starving earlier, the drinks and conversation, especially about Tom and Sherry, had her stomach in knots. "I'll have the spring mix salad," Sam told the waitress taking their orders.

"Oh, no, you don't," Nicki interrupted. "We're having thick, juicy burgers. You look like you've lost weight, and that's not good."

Sam was about to disagree. Besides, since when was losing weight a bad thing? But she didn't have the will to argue with Nicki. It would be easier to nibble at a burger.

After ordering, they talked about the latest fad diets, the must-see plays in New York, and the designer fashions of the moment before Sam circled back to Nicki's state of affairs. "It seems you're ready to jump back into the dating scene."

"Absolutely. But I don't want a relationship. Just a stable of guys to do things with on the weekend."

Her flippant words belied the sadness in her eyes,

telling another story. Did her split with Dex affect her more than she was willing to let on?

"You not having a boyfriend? I don't believe you. I can't remember a time when you've been without a partner—significant or otherwise. You attract men like bees on honey." The tall, slim body. The straight, blonde hair. The cornflower-blue eyes. Not to mention the brains, the dry sense of humor, and the exciting career.

"Not the right ones. I don't think there are any right ones." Nicki's eyes widened at the size of the burgers when delivered. After taking a bite, she segued back to their conversation. "I'm sticking with what works for me. I don't get too involved." She leaned over the table as if to share her secret. "Anything over three months and they're history."

"That's a short period of time. How can you ever get to know a guy well enough in three months?" Sam could honestly say she didn't know her husband after being married for three years.

"It only takes a night. The point is, I don't want to get to know them well. I learn a little bit about the guy while going to nice restaurants, plays, sporting events, wherever. But I make sure they know my philosophy. No strings. No commitment. Just sex. Just fun."

Sam held her burger halfway to her lips. "Fun. How does one go about meeting someone like that?" Her "all work, no play" life needed to be revamped. Although she highly doubted she would follow Nicki's advice.

"You work in a predominantly male world. You can easily meet eligible bachelors at your bar association functions or Chamber of Commerce events.

But make sure you don't form any attachment."

"What happens if you fall for one of them?" Not that she would.

"That won't happen if you stick with the plan. Your life can become uncomplicated by the ups and downs of a relationship. I love my career as a music exec. I get to travel. Meet talented artists. I come and go as I please, without compromising or bending to someone else's will. It's great to be uncommitted." Resolve was written all over her face.

Sam could no longer mask her suspicion. "Are you really happy, or are you trying to convince me, as well as yourself, that everything's perfect without having a meaningful relationship?"

"Just because you have a bachelor's degree in psychology doesn't mean you can analyze me." Nicki grimaced while she meticulously poured ketchup on her fries. "Do you truly believe I need a man to make me whole? Well, I don't. As a matter of fact, I'm much happier now than when Dex and I were together. And my guess is, once you get over the pain of losing Tom, you're going to find you can be happy on your own too." She smiled playfully.

"Maybe I'll try it your way. When I'm ready." If that time ever came. "It sounds good…but…"

"But what?"

"I always pictured having a family one day. Children." Were these words coming out of her mouth? Especially given her current state of mind. And should she be saying them to Nicki after what she'd been through? Or had Nicki totally repressed her pregnancy experience and moved on?

Nicki set her glass down with a thud. "Have you

lost your mind? Why in the world would you want kids? They mess up your career, ruin your body, and throw up in your hair."

It was as if the past had never occurred. Not that Nicki had wanted to keep the baby, or even contemplated it. She'd only been eighteen and had her life ahead of her. But now she was talking as if she'd never been pregnant and given up her child for adoption.

Sam circled back to herself, careful not to include Nicki as part of any shared fantasy. "I pictured having a loving husband, a beautiful four-bedroom house in the suburbs with a pool, and two little, adorable kids calling me Momma and telling me they love me."

"It sounds dreadful." Nicki cringed, as if sickened by the thought. "Stop making it appear so idyllic. You should know better than anybody. You're a divorce lawyer, for God's sake." She shook her head. "And wasn't Tom the perfect husband at one point? What if you had kids with him and lived in that great big house with the pool? Then *poof*!" She snapped her fingers. "He's gone. What do you do then? Sell the compound and drag those little rug rats into the city to live in a two-bedroom apartment because you can't afford the mansion anymore? You try to juggle your career with day care, and you're always late picking up the kids, while Tom flies in once a month from San Diego to do the daddy thing."

"Enough." Sam held up her hand in defeat. "I get it. Children make things harder. And you're right. I'm glad I don't have them with Tom. But someday…" Sam sighed.

Nicki's negative point of view hit a little too close

to home. Sam's situation would have been even more disastrous if she and Tom had children. Yet she didn't want to believe she might never have that dream. This conversation was depressing. Nicki's critical point of view was obviously the direct result of having been pregnant at eighteen. Sam couldn't have known what Nicki went through. Although Nicki would have everyone believe the whole trauma had no effect. Once she'd had the baby and given it up for adoption, she'd never spoken about it again. Boy or girl, healthy or not, no one knew but Nicki. But did her silence mean there was no psychological damage?

"I'm sorry if I raised a bad subject." Sam pushed her plate away, leaving most of her burger uneaten. "I'm not thinking clearly."

Nicki waved her hand, dismissing her apology. "Don't worry about it. You don't have to tiptoe around me."

Sam acknowledged her words but noticed the defensiveness in her voice. Maybe she did have to tiptoe.

Chapter Five

"Aren't you glad we came out tonight?" Nicki's high-wattage smile answered the question from her point of view.

Sam raised an eyebrow in response as she looked around the bar of The Bentley House. The jury was still out. She'd tried to ward off Nicki's insistence that they investigate the club tonight, but she'd given up the fight after twenty minutes. A futile attempt from the beginning.

"Oh, come on. Admit it. You're having fun." Nicki elbowed Sam to punctuate her point.

Although high maintenance, Nicki guaranteed a good time. And while Sam shifted through the emotional gears that came with losing her marriage, Nicki only allowed her a certain amount of sympathy before changing direction and insisting on another topic. Maybe she was right. Partying through her depression had a certain lure.

For the next two hours, Sam tried valiantly to put her cares behind her as she and Nicki alternately danced, drank, and talked to new acquaintances. Bodies writhed and swayed on the minuscule dance floor, with eyes sparkling and mouths laughing. The summer party had started, and Sam and Nicki found themselves right in the thick of things. Nicki was, of course, more animated and friendly and dragged Sam into inane conversations, making her participate whether she wished to or not.

Near midnight, Sam had enough. She pulled Nicki away from some dull accountant. "It's getting late," she shouted near her ear. "Are you ready to go?"

"What's the matter? Is Mr. CPA boring you?"

"A bit." Sam was hot and tired and no longer in the mood to put on a happy face—at least with strangers.

"Okay. Let's blow this joint." Nicki turned to her admirer. "See you around town. Cinderella here needs to get home before twelve."

Sam pulled Nicki through the sweltering masses, trying to avoid contact with other revelers' clammy skin, since hers was hot enough. When they finally slithered through the front door, the cool air breezed over her as if she were standing before an open refrigerator. Heavenly. Now she could complain in earnest to Nicki about the people they'd met while they headed toward Sam's car.

"Damn." Sam stopped in her tracks as she spotted a policeman slipping a ticket under her windshield. "Wait," she shouted, then sprinted the half block to intercede. Out of breath, she puffed, "What are you doing?"

"You're illegally parked, ma'am. Your meter ran out. I'm giving you a citation."

She hated the term *ma'am* more than *lady* but decided to let it go. She had a more pressing problem right now.

"It must be broken. I know I put enough money in that meter to stay parked here until one. And it's only"—she glanced at her watch—"eleven fifty-five."

"You must be mistaken, ma'am. These meters are

checked regularly."

If this baby-faced cop with the crew cut called her ma'am one more time, she was going to pop him. She yanked the ticket off the windshield and glanced at the penalty.

"Ninety-five dollars! You must be joking." Her shriek pierced the air, but she didn't care. "There is no way I'm going to pay ninety-five dollars to this municipality, which has broken meters." She handed the ticket toward the officer, as if he would take it back. "You might as well void this, because you've made a big mistake."

"Sorry, ma'am." His calm, reasonable voice was even more infuriating. "Once I write the ticket, it can't be voided. Not that I would if I could. You violated the law." Was that a smirk aching to get out?

"Listen, sir." Sam gritted her teeth in an attempt to minimize her angry tone, her fingers digging into her hips. She stood her ground, only inches away from this boy who couldn't be much past his teen years. "Burglars violate the law. Drug dealers violate the law. People who put enough money in the meter to cover their stay do not violate the law." She held the ticket in front of her and tore it in half.

Her attempt at intimidation was not working. His jaw tightened, and he opened his pad and began writing.

"What do you think you're doing?" This time her voice grated on her own nerves.

"I'm issuing you a second citation for disorderly conduct."

"What?" She was just about to grab his ticket book when Nicki jumped in and pulled her back.

"Whoa, Sam." She turned her around and whispered near her ear, "Calm down and be reasonable before he decides to throw you in the slammer for the night. You're not making any points arguing with him, and he's looking less and less happy with your attitude."

Sam looked over her shoulder and watched the cop tear a second ticket out of his pad. He handed it in her direction, but she refused to take it.

Nicki accepted the offending citation. "Sorry, officer. My friend's husband took off with another woman, and she's a little hostile. We'll just go now so you can continue doing your job."

She pushed Sam into the car and closed the door, then ran around to her side. "Let's get out of here," she demanded, slamming her door shut. "But don't speed."

Sam tried for silence on the ride home, but her wrath couldn't be contained. "It's impossible to believe the police in this town have nothing better to do than check parking meters. How pathetic. Shouldn't they be worried about the real criminals here?"

Nicki's laugh did nothing to lighten her mood. "My guess is there's not much crime in Crescent Beach. The town is made up of yuppies who rent for the summer. And the locals are probably law-abiding citizens given the size and value of these houses. The police must lie in wait for people like you who miscalculate the number of hours of fun they're going to have. I'm sure you made his day by being obstinate on top of it."

"I know I put enough money in that meter. You should have checked."

"Me? You're always so careful about obeying every law I never even thought to check."

Sam ignored her remark. "Ninety-five dollars! That's outrageous. And who knows what penalty the disorderly conduct charge carries. I'm going to fight it in court."

"Oh, they're going to love you." It was hard to ignore Nicki's sarcasm. "After they hear you were dancing and drinking at The Bentley House all night, do you think you could convince the judge there's something wrong with the meter and not your memory? And then, when he learns you ripped up the ticket..."

"How dare he charge me with disorderly conduct! All I did was show him what I thought about his little citation. He's lucky I didn't smack that smug, self-satisfied look right off his face."

"No. You're lucky. You would have definitely been spending some time in the local jail for that." Nicki opened her window and inhaled the fresh air. "What's gotten into you, Sam? I've never known you to have such a bad temper before. You've always been the voice of reason. The mediator who unruffles feathers, not the antagonist."

"Well, things have changed. And I'm not going to let people walk all over me anymore." Not Tom, not that baby-faced cop, and not the town prosecutor.

She'd fought with the big boys before and won. The Crescent Beach prosecutor was probably some sixty-year-old geezer putting in his time before he could collect a nice, hefty pension. She could picture his clipped gray hair rimming a bald dome, tweed jacket, faded dress pants, and scuffed loafers.

She would show this town how the game was played. She wasn't about to roll over and pay these outrageous fees. She would fight for justice. Here was her chance to get back in the legal arena and kick some butt.

And she had every intention of doing so.

****

"Earth to Sam." Nicki deposited her suitcase near the door on Sunday evening as Sam sat on the couch sipping iced tea.

Sunday nights were always disheartening, bringing an end to the weekend and thoughts of six days of work ahead. Since she wasn't working, Sam should have felt differently about it, but she couldn't shed the melancholy.

"Do you have to go?" Sam wore her best pout as she rose and went over to Nicki.

"You'll get through this, Sam." Nicki hugged her. "But you should deal with it now. There's no use dragging it out."

"What do you mean?"

"When Dex and I broke up, I kept thinking he'd change his mind. He was crazy about me and I was crazy about him. But he wants to marry and have children. I was good with the marriage part. Not so much with the children part. I didn't believe something like that could get in the way of us being together forever. I kept hoping he'd come to his senses eventually and see it like I saw it. That we could be happy—just the two of us. I couldn't move on. Because not only was part of me thinking he'd change his mind, I also hoped I'd change mine. I wasn't at all sure I had made the right decision. And I miss him so much."

Now, finally the truth was coming out. Forty-eight hours after her arrival. So their breakup really did affect Nicki despite her false bravado.

Nicki sighed. "But I haven't heard from him in two months. He hasn't come to the conclusion he can't live without me. And I haven't decided I'll have children so I can be with him. When it's over, it's over. Move on. Don't spend your nights crying over what could have been. Don't question his decision or believe he might change."

Sam nodded, a bit in a daze, and sank onto the sofa. Nicki was telling her to file for divorce!

"Don't look so shell-shocked, Sam. You know I'm right. Tom left you for another woman. Even if he does dump her, are you going to want him back after what he's done to you? You're strong, Sam. You can do it. You'll find your way." Nicki sat beside her, taking her hand.

A surge of warmth melted through her chill. "Thanks, Nicki. Thanks for listening to me, for letting me vent. And for the advice." She inhaled, hoping Nicki's words would sink in with her breath. "You know. Maybe I am getting stronger. It still hurts that I failed at marriage. I never thought I'd be in this position. But the pain is duller. And less frequent. I can breathe again."

"This is a good place to get away from it all. You're lucky you were able to take a leave of absence. When Dex and I broke up, we were in the middle of a merger with Yukon Music. I couldn't take off the weekend, much less ten weeks. But we all get through it, one way or another."

Sam knew Nicki was right. She had said the same thing to her clients over and over.

She sighed a cleansing sigh, then smiled. "It's been a good weekend, in an odd sort of way. Having my

Sworn Sisters here to support me means the world. Thanks for coming, Nicki."

"Anytime, Sam." She stood, rummaging through her purse for the car keys.

Sam bit her lip, a new habit to stem any stray tears. "Oh, I almost forgot." She perked up. "Did you get the invitation to our fifteenth high school reunion?"

"No. And please don't tell me we've been out of high school for fifteen years."

Sam picked at a thread on her shorts, debating whether to broach the subject she'd been meaning to raise all weekend. "Remember Michael McCain?"

Nicki's face paled, and she sank back onto the sofa. "Yes." Her voice croaked into a raspy whisper. "He disappeared the night of Alyssa's party. A few weeks before graduation."

"Well, I ran into him the other day. At the local coffee shop." Sam held her breath, anxiety gnawing at her insides over Nicki's possible response.

"What?" Nicki's eyes registered astonishment, then disbelief.

Sam's own reaction was similar when she'd recognized him. Actually, her heart had nearly leapt out of her chest. "I couldn't believe it either. It's shocking."

Nicki stared at a candle on the coffee table as if in a trance. After a few seconds, she raised her eyes to Sam's. They glistened with tears. "What was he doing in Crescent Beach?"

"I don't know. I never asked him that specifically. I did ask why him why he didn't contact anyone back then to let us know he was all right."

"What did he say?" Nicki stood and began pacing. "We thought something bad had happened. That he might be dead. Yet he shows up here fifteen years later? What has he been doing for the past decade and a half?" Her voice escalated with her questions.

While Sam had anticipated upset, she hadn't expected resentment. She better start talking fast. "It was a weird coincidence seeing him there. I was stunned…and embarrassed. A few days earlier, I had hit him with a volleyball. I was walking on the beach, and this ball plopped in the ocean right in front of me, spraying me with frigid, sandy water." She babbled on that this stranger had called her *lady*, when he asked for his ball. "I hate that term lady. It makes me feel old. I threw the ball hard, hitting him right in the chest. At the time, I didn't know it was Michael. He looked different, and I wasn't focusing on him. I was deep in thought about Tom. And Sherry." Hopefully, her explanation would appease Nicki somewhat. "Then I ran into him in the coffee shop."

She paused, giving Nicki time to say something, anything, but Nicki just stared at her with mouth agape.

"Since I didn't get any information before leaving the coffee shop, I Googled him the second I got back to the house. The latest mention was that he was a partner at a medium-sized New York City law firm."

Nicki's pallor matched the color of the painted white walls.

Could Michael's resurfacing make this much of an impact on her? They hadn't talked about him in fifteen years. "Are you feeling okay?"

"I…I can't believe he's in the area. That none of us ever heard from him." Nicki's voice cracked, and she stood abruptly and headed for the kitchen.

Sam hadn't expected this reaction. It seemed a bit

emotional after all these years. What was going on with her? Should she go to her or give her some space? As she vacillated, Nicki came back, her eyes noticeably red.

Sam rose and hugged her. "I'm sorry I dumped this on you right before you were leaving. I knew it would affect you; I just didn't gauge how much. You spent a lot of time with him senior year. I remember that summer being so worried about him, speculating about what might have happened. I guess he didn't want to be found."

"I have to go." Nicki's hasty end to their weekend stunned Sam.

She moved between the door and Nicki. "No, don't go yet. You're upset. Let's talk. I'm sorry. I didn't mean to shake you up." She shouldn't have blurted out her news. But how could she have expected this reaction? She'd obviously sent Nicki into a state of shock.

"I'm okay." Nicki gave the tiniest fake smile. "I have a long drive and a busy day at work tomorrow. I need some time to let this sink in. I'll be fine. The ride will do me good."

Sam hugged her again, but Nicki's body was stiff. "Call me when you get in so I know you've arrived safe."

"Will do."

With that, she was gone.

Chapter Six

On Thursday, Sam sat at the kitchen counter drinking coffee when the ringing phone distracted her from her thoughts.

"Hi, Sam. It's Carol, slaving away here in the office. Sorry to bother you again, but you said to call if I needed you. By the way, how was your weekend?"

"The weekend was four days ago." Sam scowled as she recalled the insanity that settled in Crescent Beach on weekends during the summer. "It was a little crazy here. Tons of people. Tons of booze. Tons of partying." As a matter of fact, everywhere Sam and Nicki went, there had been gangs of happy revelers—shouting, never talking—about where they had been, where they were going, and where they were going after that. "Of course, I took no part in any of it."

"Of course not." Her assistant's easy agreement confirmed Carol knew, more than anyone, that Sam worked twelve-hour days, six days a week, and rarely participated in fun activities.

She probably wouldn't believe her if Sam admitted she'd caved in to Nicki's insistence that they go to The Bentley House. What a change from her younger days when she and her friends had embraced the single life, partying till dawn. But now she lived on the other side of the road. No longer single, at least legally, slightly older, and a resident of sorts who wanted her adopted town back to normal.

"What's up?" No doubt a list of problems.

"Melissa Calloway wants to file a Complaint against her husband's assistant for alienation of affection."

Sam sighed. "She won't get anywhere with that."

"She wants to talk to you about it."

One of the other associates, her competition for partnership, had stepped in to represent Melissa Calloway in Sam's absence, but Melissa demanded Sam's opinion on everything from alimony to the division of dining room chairs.

A satisfied grin tugged at Sam's lips. She grabbed her yellow legal pad. "What's her phone number?"

Although she had taken a leave of absence, the frequency of phone calls from the office suggested she would be working more than anticipated on her sabbatical. Given her prior fear of having too much free time on her hands, a few hours of work each day proved to be the perfect balance she craved. And she felt a huge sense of satisfaction that her clients held such stock in her advice.

After discussing three other cases, Sam remembered her little brush with the law. "Is Scott Baker around? I want to talk to him about a municipal court case I have here." She added a little white lie. "I'm representing someone who got two tickets the other night. I have some questions."

"You can't stay away from practicing law, can you?" Carol chuckled. "He's in court this morning, but I'll have him call you when he returns." She segued onto another topic. "What do you do down there when we're not bothering you with work?"

"I jog on the boardwalk in the morning, shower, then walk to a cute, little coffee shop around nine for breakfast." She didn't share the fact that this later hour assured avoidance of Steve. And Michael, who was probably back in New York anyway.

"Have you met anyone to hang out with?"

Sam grimaced. Hardly. Her angry outbursts assured she would have a hard time in that department. Who would have guessed that the pain of a husband's betrayal would assert itself through rudeness to strangers? "I wouldn't call anyone here a friend. But I have been making a conscious effort to talk with the locals at the coffee shop." The later crowd proved a chatty bunch. "Then I deal with whatever issues you and the gang at work raise. At some point, I go to the beach and read. Glamorous life, huh?"

Carol sighed. "It sounds wonderful."

"It sounds better than it is. Don't forget the reason I'm here. I was about to have a breakdown, remember?"

"I'm sorry you're going through such a tough time. But I know you. You'll come out of this stronger than ever."

"Thanks for the vote of confidence."

Sam wasn't so sure. Even though hanging at the beach sounded relaxing, she often caught herself staring at the ocean, watching the waves roll in, then out. She thought about Tom. About his betrayal and the reasons for it. Had she really put her career before all else, including him? Was she that driven that she had become married to her job, as he accused, or was that his justification to absolve all guilt over his illicit affair?

In looking back at their life together, she realized that the perceived simplicity of it had, in reality, been a complicated maze of emotion, past history, and future goals. The baggage she carried with her into the marriage, although well hidden, fueled her every step, her every choice. Her father's infidelity and eventual defection, her mother's struggle to support them, while seemingly a way of life for far too many families, had clearly taken its toll. She could no longer ignore her past, as she thought she could. It had insinuated itself into her life, driving her to gain financial independence through her workaholic ways. Before moving on, she would have to deal with it.

During her soul-searching afternoons on the beach, Sam struggled to work through the pain and loss, each day dealing with different emotions. Scathing anger one day bridged into sorrow and hurt the next. And she found herself interchanging the ogre—one minute it was Tom, the next, her father. She guessed she needed a professional counselor, but she was determined to try it her own way first.

How was she able to be so strong for her clients and such an emotional wreck when it came to her own life?

Eight weeks would never be enough.

****

"All rise," boomed the sheriff's officer as he escorted Judge Litner to the bench.

The familiar words sent a jolt through Sam's body, and she felt the same anxiety-fueled adrenaline as when starting a trial. *How ridiculous*! This was municipal court. Two frivolous tickets had brought her here, not a hotly contested divorce case. Yet she couldn't control her pounding heart as she waited to plead her case. The thrill of the contest tantalized far more than the complexity of the matter.

Her olfactory senses were already heightened by the familiar scent of polished, old wood and righteous authority, as her eyes settled on the raised bench where justice would be meted out. The seal of the municipality hung proudly on the wall behind the judge, who peered over his reading glasses at the crowd of the accused, all squashed among dozens of others in pews behind the bar. The noise died down immediately—the quiet power of authority.

The prosecutor stood when the judge addressed him for the first case.

Sam did a double take, then her stomach plummeted.

Michael, dressed in a charcoal gray suit, white shirt, and blue silk tie, entered his appearance. Her jaw tightened, and a throb in her head began. What happened to the bald guy she'd imagined? And why was Michael, a big city lawyer, working here in Crescent Beach?

She had no answer to that question, but she had plenty of time to scold herself. She had gotten completely out of control with a policeman, and now she'd have to explain her actions in front of Michael. As if he didn't already think she was half crazy walking out on him at the coffee shop in a huff.

She slunk down in her seat and moved her head directly behind the woman's in front of her, praying he wouldn't see her. But she didn't have to worry. He barely looked out at the sea of culprits. He would obviously deal with them one at a time.

By ten o'clock, Sam realized Judge Litner was in a bitter mood, which got exponentially worse as he listened to excuse after excuse as to why this one or that one ran a stop sign or breezed through a red light or didn't pay the meter.

The two ninety-five-dollar tickets started to seem insubstantial compared to the tongue lashing she'd receive when it was finally her turn. No one was getting a break. Michael, in his role as prosecutor, wasn't offering anyone a lesser charge, and the judge wasn't finding anyone not guilty. Even worse, Judge Litner was adding court costs as insult to injury. If only she had just paid her fines and waived her right to this charade. But it was too late.

By noon, the courtroom crowd had thinned. In no hurry to face Michael McCain, Esquire, Sam squirmed restlessly on the wooden bench. Her back hurt, her butt hurt, and her pride was soon to be hurt.

"Samantha Winslow," called the court clerk in a loud voice.

Her body jerked to life as the judge and prosecutor looked over the gathered assembly, waiting for someone to rise. Sam stood slowly, eyes to the ground, as she stepped her way over feet and legs to get to the end of her pew. She wore one of the two suits she'd brought with her, a navy designer skirt and jacket that had fit in perfectly in New York City but looked oddly out of place in Crescent Beach. Her fellow offenders had hardly bothered to dress for this solemn occasion. Cut-off shorts and jeans populated the court room. Occasionally, a pair of khakis showed up.

Sam willed herself to look Michael in the eye. She refused to appear embarrassed, or worse yet, guilty, as she held her head high and approached the bench. She licked her lips in preparation to speak, but Michael spoke first. He gave no sign of camaraderie as he read the charges against her.

"Your Honor, Ms. Winslow is charged with failing to place sufficient money in the meter on Saturday, June sixth at eleven fifty-five p.m. Her car was parked at meter 323 on Ocean Avenue, not far from The Bentley House."

Sam's cheeks burned in fury. How dare he insinuate to the judge she was partying at a bar!

He continued. "Officer Barlow then issued a second summons for disorderly conduct when the defendant allegedly ripped her parking ticket in half."

The judge glared at her, and she swallowed, struggling to find her voice, willing it to be strong and even. "Your Honor, I parked my car at that meter at ten p.m. after having had dinner with a friend at a local restaurant. I personally placed enough money in the meter to cover us until at least one o'clock. We came back to the car a little before twelve. I know what time it was because I looked at my watch." She glanced at her wrist. "When we arrived at the car, a police officer had just written out a ticket, and I patiently explained to him the meter must be broken because I had paid more than enough." Sam cautioned herself to stand still and refrain from parading around the courtroom giving her speech, as she would have in family court. She had to keep remembering this was municipal court, and she was the defendant.

She continued. "He ignored my citizen's complaint—made no attempt to check the meter or write a note to have it repaired. Instead, he insisted I had violated the law, with a smug attitude, I might add. Your Honor, I am a law-abiding citizen; in fact, I'm an attor—"

"Is Officer Barlow in the courtroom to testify?" growled Judge Litner, sounding none too happy that he might have to hear from him.

Sam and Michael turned at the same time toward the masses behind them. Shuffling and whispers permeated the air, but Officer Barlow did not appear. Sam breathed a sigh of relief, holding her grin in check. *That will shut Mr. Prosecutor up.*

She turned back to the judge. "Your Honor, the prosecutor cannot prove his case without the officer's testimony." A swirl of elation rushed through her at her victory. "I respectfully request that all charges be dropped."

"Ms. Winslow, the meters are presumed to be in good working order unless we receive notification from the municipal maintenance department. Mr. McCain, have you received any such notification?" Litner peered down at Michael over the rim of his glasses.

This couldn't be. The judge wasn't supposed to be asking the questions. And certainly not of the prosecutor who wasn't even a sworn witness.

"Objection, Your Honor," she said in a clear, loud voice.

Litner turned his withering gaze on her. "Ms. Winslow, are you objecting to me?"

Of course she was. But she shouldn't admit it. "Your Honor, I object to the question being asked of an officer of the court who is not a sworn witness in this case."

"Objection overruled," he boomed. "Mr. McCain?"

"No, sir. We have not been notified of any broken meters."

Sam's temporary triumph screeched to a halt as the judge returned his stare to her as if she were a common criminal. Her heart jack-hammered, and her mouth dried up like powdered cement.

The judge glowered at Sam before speaking, using measured words to underscore his unhappiness. "I will dismiss the charge of disorderly conduct for lack of corroborative testimony." He looked pained. "However, Ms. Winslow, I would caution you to hold your temper if you find yourself in that situation again. I am not usually so lenient when it comes to disrespect of the law."

He then scowled at Michael. Apparently no one in his courtroom was safe. "Mr. McCain, in the future, make sure that the officers writing these tickets appear in court. I don't like to dismiss serious charges."

"Yes, Your Honor."

The judge continued. "With regard to the parking meter citation, I find the defendant guilty as charged. Ninety-five dollars plus fifty in court costs." He banged his gavel, and Sam jumped. "Pay the clerk on your way out."

"But Your Honor—" Sam stammered, shocked at the swiftness of justice when it came to her case. For hours she had heard case after case drone on.

"I ruled, young lady. You're dismissed." He stood, handing over files to his clerk. "There will be a short recess."

She looked to Michael, who angled his head in the direction of the door, his eyes following, an apparent signal to leave before she got hit with a contempt of court charge. Irritation heated her cheeks, and she bit her lip to keep from arguing further. Turning on her heel, she clicked her way over the warped, hardwood floor toward the court clerk. Her pulse pumped to the beat of her anger over this preposterous system of justice.

She should have written a letter prior to her court date. She should have called the municipality and asked them to check her meter. She was furious with the judge, furious with Michael, and furious with herself. She knew better. It was her livelihood to always be prepared. Why did she think she could just show up, plead her case, and they would believe her?

Sam tore the check out of her checkbook and practically threw it at the clerk, her teeth clenched tightly in an effort to keep any stray, nasty words from flying out. When she pushed at the heavy wooden door that led out to the hallway, it suddenly eased open as a man's hand gave it more weight from behind.

"Tough luck," he said, presumably to her.

She turned, and standing within inches of her was Michael, with a grin on his face and a twinkle in his eyes. Then the steam rushed through her head and forced the words out of her mouth.

"Luck has nothing to do with it. It appears that in this court room, the Rules of Court are irrelevant if the judge can ask the prosecutor whether a meter is broken on Ocean Avenue and the prosecutor can testify there are no reported broken meters."

The sarcasm dripped from her voice, but it didn't seem to faze him.

"First of all, this is municipal court, Sam, not the Superior Court of New Jersey. The rules are a little more relaxed here. Secondly, I do check with the maintenance department to see if there are any problems with the meters. We hear that excuse dozens of times a day, so I'm prepared." His blue eyes flashed, but she couldn't tell if he was insulted or amused. "For such a beautiful woman, you sure do have a bad attitude." He shook his head. "Tearing up a ticket in front of a policeman... I didn't remember you as being so crazy."

How dare he compliment her at the same time he insulted her!

"Why were you so stern when you counted off the charges against me to Judge Litner? Like I was some serial offender."

He had the audacity to laugh. "You walked up there like you were about to defend the civil rights of all mankind. I couldn't resist, Sam."

His gorgeous smile almost took the air out of her sails. Almost. But she wasn't ready to give it up and let him off the hook. Because there were other things bothering her, much more than his prosecutorial tone in the courtroom. Questions he hadn't wanted to answer the other day in the coffee shop. Questions he surely wouldn't want to answer standing in the hall of the Crescent Beach Municipal Building.

"Don't call me Sam as if you know me. You left us fifteen years ago without so much as a goodbye, leaving us to think the worst. Do you know how many months we worried about you? How we hounded the police, posted fliers, called everyone you knew?"

"And then you all went away to college and started your new lives," he said quietly. "Michael McCain forgotten. But that's fine, Sam. I mean Ms. Winslow.

Because I survived."

"Well, congratulations. You clearly didn't need your friends then."

His jaw tightened, and he took a step back. "You don't know what you're talking about."

"Then explain it to me." Exasperation punctuated her words. Why was it so difficult for him to tell her about the past?

"Not now." He looked around as if to point out the traffic in and around the halls. "Maybe some other time. I have to be back in the courtroom in fifteen."

He turned and walked down the hall.

Sam stood there in shock. She wanted to scream that she didn't have a bad attitude. She wasn't crazy. He could have admitted the meter might have been broken. Believed her. His arrogance matched his powerful stride. A far cry from the Michael McCain she'd known in high school. Yet he still possessed those aqua eyes. They had flashed as he counted off his defenses to her fighting words. But they were just as beautiful when calm.

She turned and headed out the front door, walking in the direction of her temporary home, all the while talking under her breath as if clarity would come from within.

After she covered two blocks with her fast-paced stride, beads of sweat dripped down her back. She hadn't removed her suit jacket, and the oppressive temperature of the day closed in around her, making her feel like she was wrapped in plastic. The early afternoon sun baked the cement sidewalks, which seared through the soles of her heels, putting her in a worse mood than when she'd first left the courthouse.

But her physical discomfort paled in comparison to her emotional distress. Was Michael right? Did she have a bad attitude? Her first three altercations with him could hardly prove otherwise. And it wasn't like her to disrespect authority. In retrospect, she couldn't believe she had ripped up her parking ticket in front of a police officer. She rolled her eyes and mentally thumped her head with her palm to knock some sense into it.

Although she had reason to be miserable, her purpose in fleeing the city had been to pull herself together. She needed to reach down deep inside and find the Sam she used to be. Before the collapse of her marriage. Maybe even before she became obsessed with becoming a partner. The person who loved the law, who yearned to learn new things, who enjoyed spending time with friends and meeting new people. Not the person who thumbed her nose at authority and started arguments with strangers. And old friends. She had become cynical, bitter, and non-trusting.

And she had a bad attitude.

Unacceptable.

By the time she reached her destination, Sam's anger had faded, replaced by the goal to search out her former self. She needed to change.

And she only had seven weeks to do it.

****

The next morning, Sam slid into a pair of white shorts and a pale-blue tank top, then pulled her hair back into a ponytail, all the while encouraging herself to make a change. She couldn't permit Tom's horrid betrayal to turn her into a hostile person, a witch. She was better than that. She had to rise above the sludge he had dropped her in before he'd left for San Diego.

Tom was a selfish, egotistical bastard who only craved current gratification. And he acted on it without any thought to its consequences. She was through castigating herself for not seeing the signs, not giving him what he needed, not being a good enough spouse.

Stepping into her flip flops, she bounded down the stairs and out the front door, feeling lighter and happier than she had in days.

She brought her laptop to Mort's Office Supply so she could print out a Marital Settlement Agreement she needed to review, then headed for Melanie's Coffee Shop. It was earlier than she usually arrived, and not an empty stool remained at the counter. She took a table near the window, ordered the usual, and poured through the forty-page document before her.

She was almost finished when the chair across from her scraped against the floor.

"Mind if I join you?" a male voice asked, not waiting for her to answer before he sat down.

Sam raised her eyebrows, but held her tongue. "Good morning, Michael." She strove to sound friendly, in deference to her decision to get rid of the attitude.

"I see you're in a better mood than you were yesterday." His smile lit up the room and sent her insides into a tailspin.

"It's very nice of you to leave it at yesterday." He could have thrown in the other two times for good measure. "I apologize for my rude behavior and horrible comments." She pursed her lips to keep from illuminating her sins.

"Fines and court costs can make a person out of

sorts." His warm tone took a one-eighty from the previous day. Perhaps he felt a tad guilty for being so haughty.

"And broken meters," she said, allowing her mouth to get in the way of her resolve to let it go.

"Actually, I had someone from the inspection office go and check out your meter. You were right. It was broken."

She tightened her grip on the cup. *Be nice. No outbursts, no matter how understandable.* "Why are you telling me this? Aren't you afraid I'll throw this cup at your head?"

"The thought did cross my mind." He chuckled. "It's too late to get your money back from the municipality. So it looks like I owe you a hundred forty-five bucks."

She un-gritted her teeth. "Do you always reimburse the people you wrongly accuse?" She tinged her skepticism with amusement.

"Of course not. And I wasn't actually planning on giving you cash. I thought I'd take you to dinner."

She looked into his clear blue eyes, but no evidence of a joke lurked within their depths. Her heart kicked at her ribs with their intensity. She wasn't ready for this, was she? She didn't need more complications in her life. Although he was only inviting an old acquaintance to share a meal.

"Why in the world would you want to go out to dinner with a crazy woman?"

He winced. "Sorry for the slur, but you were pissing me off."

"So the truth comes out." She smiled despite his stinging candor. "But don't worry. You don't have to make it up to me. It's nice of you to admit your mistake." She refused to go out to dinner with him just to appease some sense of guilt.

She met his eyes once more. Dangerous. It was best to leave before she got herself into trouble. Gathering her document, she placed a few dollar bills on the table. "Maybe I'll see you around town again. Although hopefully not in traffic court." She grinned, flirting just a little, then left.

And she couldn't stop grinning as she walked down the street. He had looked dumbstruck at her rejection. Like women didn't ever turn him down. It felt good. Powerful. Great for her ego. Yesterday he'd said she was beautiful, and today he invited her out to dinner. She wouldn't dwell on the fact that in the same breath he'd pointed out her bad attitude and his dinner request sprang from some misplaced duty to repay her.

Why ruin it?

Chapter Seven

Michael and his group of raucous friends played volleyball on the beach nearly every night at six. At least those who could get away from work on any given night. It was the perfect time of day with the sun hanging off to the west, guaranteeing three more hours of daylight, without the intense heat of the afternoon. A cool breeze blew off the ocean, and sea gulls hunted and pecked for clams in the broken shells along the water's edge. Surfers took over the waves, now that the lifeguards were off duty, and an occasional family remained, allowing their children to play in the sand as parents sat on their blankets and watched.

A lone figure walking along the surf caught Michael's attention, and he missed his chance to spike the ball over the net. "Hal, take my place." He threw the ball to his teammate and sprinted toward the ocean, sending sea gulls running in all directions.

"Samantha. Wait." His voice broke through the noise of the surf.

She turned. "Michael!"

"I was playing volleyball and saw you walking." As if that explanation covered up the fact he'd been looking for her, hoping she would show up.

She didn't say anything, so he continued. "I hope I'm not interrupting you."

"No. Of course not. I was…thinking."

Her eyes shone magnificently in the evening sunlight, violet, a color he had never seen on anyone else before. How had he not noticed them in high school? Rich, dark hair was pulled back into a sleek ponytail—granting him a glimpse of her long neck. Not a hint of makeup covered her pretty face bronzed by the sun, drawing his attention to full, kissable lips.

He dragged his eyes downward, taking in very long, very gorgeous legs—legs he wouldn't mind having wrapped around his hips. He smiled at the thought, then shook his head to dispel the image.

"Do you mind if I walk with you?"

"No—"

Definitely not an enthusiastic response. Her melancholy voice threw him off. She was usually so full of fire around him. "Is something wrong?"

She gazed out over the ocean as if deciding whether to answer his question or ignore him. At least a minute passed in silence. She looked young, vulnerable, much different than she had in court yesterday, dressed in a power suit, ready, willing, and more than able to assert her rights.

"No. As a matter of fact, I'm doing much better now, thank you."

"Were you sick?" He had seen her this morning at Melanie's, and she was fine.

She chuckled. An open friendly chuckle. "Not a physical illness. I'm in Crescent Beach on a mental health sabbatical. I needed a break from the city, from my job…from my life." She glanced over at him and gave an embarrassed smile. She looked like a cover girl, fresh, young, and pure, with a face that could compete with the highest-paid supermodel. The first three times he'd seen her here, a scowl was permanently marring that countenance. But this morning, she appeared to be a changed woman. Dr. Jekyll, Ms. Hyde.

"High-powered job?"

"I suppose. I'm a lawyer too. Big firm. Park Avenue. I do family law, divorce, custody, domestic violence."

This took him by surprise. Although that explained her aggressiveness in municipal court. In high school she'd been quiet, shy. But extremely smart. She'd been chosen as the valedictorian for high school graduation. In several respects, it made sense. She certainly had the disposition to be a trial lawyer now, tough, assertive, argumentative.

He watched her as she walked beside him, her eyes straight ahead, hands in pockets. Her smile gone. Introspective, maybe sad. He didn't want to pry. He hated when people interfered in his affairs, and yet her demeanor intrigued him. Was she wondering how much of her recent life to divulge? Or had she decided she'd said enough?

"I used to work in Manhattan too," he volunteered.

"Yes. I know."

"You do?" If she'd known, why hadn't she ever tried to get in touch with him? And why had she reacted like she'd seen a ghost when they ran into each other at the coffee shop?

"I recently found out." She paused as if deciding whether to admit how. "I Googled you after we ran into each other at the coffee shop a few weeks ago." She glanced at him. "Why did you leave the city?"

He expected the harder question—*why did you*

disappear in high school? The answer to either question wasn't that simple. "I was at the same firm for six years before realizing it wasn't what I wanted. Mergers and Acquisitions can take over your life. Representing huge companies buying up other companies isn't exactly a people-friendly business. Our clients were faceless entities to me. I did the behind-the-scenes work. The partner in charge did the negotiations and attended meetings. I started to feel like a robot. Doing what I was supposed to do, but not caring why.

"So I gave my notice, packed my bags, and headed here." An abbreviated version of his past should do. "I loved the shore growing up. My mom would take my sister and me for a week every summer. I couldn't get enough of the ocean." He scanned its vast expanse, zeroing in on a big wave gathering force, and he longed for his old surf board. "As I got older, I liked the other seasons here too. The peace, the small-town atmosphere, the beach when no one's on it." He liked that best of all.

"How could you leave the excitement of the city?" Utter shock etched her face.

"The excitement had worn off. All I did was work and sleep. Being stuck in my New York office for eleven hours a day trying to anticipate every facet of a merger that could go wrong got old after a while. And I started to notice the dirt, the decay, the people who didn't care about the millions of others who inhabited the same city." He avoided talk of the one person who'd driven him away. There was no point in bringing her into this conversation. "I was earning a good living, but it wasn't making me happy."

"Are you happy practicing law here?"

"Definitely. I'm making a difference helping individuals. And it feels so good to be out here by the ocean with its salt air and warm breeze." Of course, that wasn't the reason he ended up in Crescent Beach. Sometimes, outside influences sent one on a new path. "Not only do I get to play beach volleyball after work, but I bit the bullet and bought a sailboat a few weeks ago. I intend to take advantage of the summer months by spending as much time as possible on the water."

"What about the museums, the theater, the restaurants?" She kicked at a shell, and it splashed in the water.

"While living in New York, I didn't have time to go. I rarely made plans to see a play, and I never had the patience to call the 'in' restaurant, weeks ahead of time, to get a reservation. I was becoming cynical. And crabby…like you." He chuckled, hoping to add levity to his statement.

She gave him a shot in the arm, then apologized. "Sorry. I told myself I was no longer permitted to hit people."

"Has that become a habit of yours?"

She laughed, thankfully. A beautiful, melodic laugh.

"No. But I did hit you with a volleyball. It was an accident."

"Of course." He nodded.

She stopped short to plead her case. "I didn't realize you were so close. And I didn't know it was you."

"Likely story. You were taking out your aggressions on me for calling you 'lady.' "

Another laugh escaped. "Please. Let's not go

there." She resumed walking.

She was loosening up. Good. Even though they'd known each other in high school, that was a lifetime ago. People changed. He certainly had. And she had too. All those years ago, she'd seemed so *Catholic school*, kind of uptight, always looking out for her girlfriends to make sure they weren't doing anything she wouldn't do. Now she was confident, more outgoing. And a knockout. A warm sensation rushed through his veins, and a smile tugged on his lips. But if he had any hope of spending more time with her, he had to address the whale on the beach. He inhaled for fortification.

"I'd like to answer your question about why I disappeared in high school."

Her brow furrowed in surprise. He surprised himself, since he hadn't started out this conversation with that goal in mind.

"I'm listening."

Her voice suggested comfort, but he hated talking about this. The ugly memory pumped blood to his brain like a poison. But he needed to get it out there so they could move past it.

"Things were bad at home with my father. I'm sure you knew. Everyone knew. He'd given me a black eye the day of Alyssa's party because I played baseball instead of going to work." The twist in his gut stunned him as he recalled the events from so long ago. "I was not in a good mood when I arrived at the party. I was angry about a lot of things and chose to unleash that anger on Carl, who was in my face for being such a wuss with my father. Like I should have punched my father back. In retrospect, I should have ignored Carl.

But I pushed him away from me, the way I wanted to push back at my father. I would have decked him right then and there; I was so steamed. But the guys pulled us away from each other."

Embarrassment wound through him at the retelling of this sordid tale. "You know what went down after that. When it was over, I kept hearing Nicki's words in my head. 'You're no better than your father, using your fists to settle disagreements.' I hated my father. I hated that he used me as his punching bag. I didn't want to become him. In order to make sure I didn't, in my mind, the only thing I could do was get away from him. I didn't want to be one of those statistics where the abused becomes the abuser."

Michael glanced at Sam to see if she was totally disgusted with him. Instead, he saw tears in her eyes.

"Hey." He grabbed her hand. "This is not a sob story. Don't feel sorry for me." He pulled out a smile from deep within. "You wanted to know."

She nodded. "Where'd you go?"

"New York City. I had saved some money and got a room at the Y, a job as a janitor, and did what I had to do to get my high school diploma."

He couldn't tell if more questions were fighting to get out of her mouth or whether he had totally floored her, making her speechless.

"So now you know." He breathed out a sigh of relief. "Let's talk about you. Is your sabbatical working?"

"I guess."

Now there was a non-answer. They walked in silence, as he bided his time, trying to assess how best to re-establish their connection.

"You're one of those people who loves New York." He made it an accusation, suspecting it would prod a response out of her.

"I do. I love the electricity it generates. So many people, so many things to do. But I didn't realize, until you were just talking about your life in New York, that I don't do half the things I live in the city for. Like museums. I never find time to go. When I finally leave work at night, I'm too tired." She sighed. "I work on Saturdays, and on Sundays I lie around in my pajamas and read the paper. Still, if the museums weren't there, I think I would go mad."

"You have to have it, even though you don't use it." He knew the feeling.

"Exactly."

It was nice they understood each other. And he was more than a little surprised to learn how much they had in common; an insight he would never have gleaned from their first few meetings.

As they neared the volleyball court, one of his teammates yelled, "Hey, Michael, did you get lost? The game's over here."

Sam grinned. "You better get going. I think they miss you."

"I guess." He hesitated. "I'm glad you're feeling better."

He ran up to the court, wishing the game had been over so he could continue his conversation with Sam. She intrigued him with her split personality, tough and assertive one day, warm and introspective the next. He shook his head. An attorney in the city. Too bad, since he had more against the city than its dirt and its inhabitants' apathy. Hannah lived there.

He turned to see if Sam was still watching. She was. And more than one of his single friends showed off for their new audience by spiking and pummeling the ball for good measure. Curse words flew around the court with abandon, and bare chests glistened with sweat and sand, as his buddies teased and cajoled each other, arguing over the rules. Sam laughed at their antics, looking gorgeous with those violet eyes and glossy hair. A wave of lust hit him in the gut when she directed that sparkling smile at him.

He brought his attention back to the game and inwardly groaned.

The past had just entered the present.

Chapter Eight

Denise arrived at eight on Saturday, her Honda expertly packed with a duffle bag, sand chair, beach umbrella, and blanket. Early, efficient, cheery, and adorable, that was Denise.

"I can tell you have kids." Sam chuckled as she hugged her friend, then opened the rear car door to help unload. "Nicki would have never left her house at the crack of dawn to drive to the beach. Nor would she only have a small overnight bag."

Denise laughed, but her dark brown eyes lacked their usual glint. "And lose precious alone time? Not me. Besides, I've been up since five. Jennifer woke me to watch cartoons, and Johnny begged for pancakes before I left. Poor Ben's going to have his hands full this weekend with those two. And Bobby..." Her voice caught in her throat, and her eyes filled with tears.

Sam's sensitivity heightened. "What's wrong, Dee?"

Denise let her handbag slip to the ground and covered her face for a few torturous seconds before she responded. "Bobby has leukemia." She inhaled, regaining her composure.

"Oh, my God." Sam's insides screamed. "When did you find out?"

"A few weeks ago. Just after I was here with Nicki and Alyssa."

"And you're only telling me now?" How could she keep such awful news a secret from one of her best friends?

"I know. I'm sorry. I couldn't pick up the phone and share. It was too personal. Too...heavy." Denise's words were buried in angst, and she raised her eyes to plead with Sam to understand.

"I didn't mean for that to come out so critical. I'm shocked, that's all." Sam leveled her tone and went over to Denise, giving her a hug. "You poor thing. Poor Bobby. How is he?"

Denise pulled away and twisted her hands. "He's getting chemo. When that's done, the doctor wants to do a bone marrow transplant." She looked at Sam, then bit her lip. "I know you filed the adoption papers for us, but I need another favor."

"Of course. Anything."

"It would help if we knew the identity of Bobby's birth parents. The records were sealed when my in-laws adopted Bobby. I understand the law has changed since then. Can you do whatever needs to be done to get his original birth certificate? We'll have a better chance of finding a match for the bone marrow transplant." Her eyes were bright with hope.

"Of course, Denise. I'll do everything I can to help."

"You're the best. Thanks. I hate to ask you this after what you've been going through, but if we can find Bobby's birth parents, it might save his life."

Denise's relief underscored her anxiety over asking this favor.

"You're going through much more than I am. I hope you'll never hesitate to ask me to do whatever you need."

Denise's eyes teared again, but this time in gratitude. "Thank you."

Sam led her into the house. "You know there's a chance the birth parents won't want to get involved." She couldn't help herself from pointing out the risk. All clients should be informed of the worst-case scenario.

"I understand. But I refuse to believe they wouldn't want to help." She gave Sam a wan smile. "I have to stay positive and not dwell on any roadblocks. I have faith that any parent will help their child if given the chance. Even if they gave him up for adoption."

Of course Denise was assuming they'd be able to find the birth parents once they learned their names. Obviously, there was no point in going there with her. She didn't want to hear it. And frankly, Sam couldn't blame her. It was Bobby's number one hope of getting well.

"I'm surprised you came to Crescent Beach." Sam swallowed the lump in her throat. "You didn't need to check in on me. A phone call with your request would have been enough."

Denise slid her hair behind her ear. "I have to admit I needed the break. And I wanted to tell you in person about Bobby."

Sam exhaled. "Now that you told me, please feel free to leave at any time. Or stay. Whatever you want."

"Just having a plan in place makes me feel much better." Her sigh was audible and hopefully cleansing. "Anyway, it's good for the kids to have Ben all to themselves. They rarely see him during the week. He's on the train before they wake up in the morning, and they're in bed before he arrives home."

Sam poured coffee for both of them and handed a mug to Denise, as they sat at the kitchen counter.

Denise stirred some sugar in her mug, keeping her eyes downcast. "Will this new issue hold up the adoption process?"

"Not at all." Sam placed her hand on Denise's arm and squeezed it. "It shouldn't take too much longer before we get a date for the hearing. I'll have my secretary call the court on Monday and push them along."

Denise nodded her thanks. "Ben and I are anxious for the adoption to go through before things get any worse. Not that they will," she quickly added.

Their appointment as Bobby's guardians under Ben's brother's will obviously wasn't enough for them. They wanted to be his parents legally.

"We want Bobby to feel as much a part of our family as our own two kids."

"I'm sure he already does. You've been wonderful to him."

"It's just that this is the second time he's being adopted. And now this. He must feel like he has a black cloud over his head."

Seeing the pain so evident in Denise's face, Sam shifted the conversation to something a little lighter. "How are your little guys doing? Running you ragged?"

Denise laughed, the hoped-for effect.

"It's so much harder than going to the office every morning. I didn't realize that until I quit. What was I thinking?" She hit her head with the palm of her hand and gave Sam a comical look.

"Well, I certainly don't envy you. It sounds like a tough job to me."

When Denise had decided to quit her job as a vice-president at an international bank in New York City upon Jennifer's birth, Sam thought she was out of her mind. Denise had worked so hard to get her MBA. Being one of only a handful of women who had broken through the glass ceiling in international finance should have made her stay for the sheer pleasure of competing with the big boys. But she'd given it all up. Not only the extraordinary salary, but a career that was sure to land her in the executive offices on the penthouse floor. Or at least the equivalent by bank standards.

Sam would never understand why Denise chose to stay home to change diapers and wipe runny noses. But every time Sam saw her, Denise appeared happy and content doing the mommy thing. Gone were the days of dressing in designer suits, running a department, juggling business meetings, and hosting power lunches. She had traded it all in for jeans and T-shirts, carpooling, and bologna sandwiches.

Sam smiled at her friend's joking acknowledgement. "You're no worse for the wear. But now that you're here for some rest and relaxation, let's get you settled in. I'm sure you're not going to want to waste a minute." She got off her stool. "I'll show you to your room."

"How are you faring?" Denise asked as they ascended the narrow staircase.

"It depends when you ask. Right now I'm good. Happy to see you and spend the weekend together—if you decide to stay. But when I'm alone, I tend to dwell on my problems. That's why I called you the other night."

Denise had said to call anytime. Unfortunately,

Sam hadn't known about Bobby's illness. She would have never asked her to leave her family for the weekend.

"Sorry I couldn't talk once we made our plans. Seven o'clock is meltdown hour. It's all I could do to get the little ones into the tub and ready for bed. I guess I should have called you back after they fell asleep. I wasn't thinking. But what else is new? I lost my mind when I gained two children. Now three." She chuckled, then turned her focus to Sam's dilemma. "I'm here now, and I have no kids to interrupt."

Denise needed a breather, not an energy-zapping discussion with an emotional wreck.

"Let's go to the beach and read gossip magazines and dish about celebrities. We could both use a break from our lives." Sam infused her words with levity and light-heartedness, but Denise gave her a perceptive look. "We'll talk on the beach."

Before long, they had their chairs positioned just right, facing the sun, with their towels stretched out before them. A sun worshiper from her younger days, Denise had an enviable complexion that soaked up the tanning rays, turning her olive skin to a rich cocoa. A light breeze blew off the ocean, keeping their bodies cooler than the brilliant sun would have allowed.

"Okay, Sam. No more procrastinating. And just so you don't feel obligated, I don't want to talk about Bobby's leukemia the rest of this weekend. I'm now here for you. So start talking." Denise removed her sunglasses to look directly at Sam, confirming this was to be a no-nonsense conversation.

Sam drew in a breath. "I feel like such a failure. And an idiot. How could I not have noticed my husband was having an affair?"

Denise dove in with questions and comments befitting a former banker making a multi-million-dollar loan. Unfortunately for Sam, her in-depth interrogation made Sam analyze the situation more than she ever had, more than she ever wanted.

Finally, she cried, "Stop. I feel like I'm talking to a shrink. Are you sure you don't have your doctorate in psychology?"

"I'm sorry, Sam." She touched her arm and gave her a look of sympathy. "I'm only trying to understand what happened."

"Join the club." Sam sighed.

"Maybe the signs were there. You are both so different. You love the beach; he likes the mountains. You like tropical vacations where you can relax; he likes adventure and sightseeing. You love the ballet; he adores opera. He's a numbers guy; you're all about words."

"Isn't that just superficial stuff? What we like to do in our free time?"

"You have so little free time given your careers. You were frequently going in opposite directions."

"Last winter we went skiing in Colorado." Sam dug deep to find mutual interests to dispel Denise's theory. "Anyway, aren't opposites supposed to attract?"

Denise ignored her last comment. "You hate the cold. You hate to ski."

"I know, but I thought I should try, since Tom loved it so much."

"As I recall, you despised every second of it."

Sam shrugged. "We couldn't always go on vacations where I wanted to go." Her consideration should have given her points with Tom.

"When did you ever choose the vacation?"

Sam looked out over the ocean. "Never, I guess." She still felt the need to rationalize. "But that was because I rarely planned any. I didn't have time. Tom did the leg work, and I was happy to get away."

"Did he ever invite you to go on any of his business trips?"

"No, of course not. I wouldn't have been able to go anyway. I could never take off at the drop of a hat."

Denise paused briefly, seeming to mull over Sam's answer before resuming her interrogation. "Did he ever go on a business trip with Sherry?"

"I don't think so… Wait. He went to California in January. She may have gone. I'm not sure." Why hadn't it occurred to her before? Had Tom been cheating on her since January? This couldn't possibly get worse.

"You don't know?" Denise's eyebrows arched over her sunglasses in total astonishment. "Didn't you talk to him about his trips?"

"No. He didn't want to talk about work at home."

Her answer sounded pathetic. What married couple didn't talk about their day when they got home at night, especially after being apart for several days? And how could she not know whether he had spent his time away with Sherry? Even worse, how could she not know if he was having head-spinning, mind-blowing sex with another woman?

Her stomach cramped and twisted as she pictured the two of them tearing at each other's clothes, lustfully grabbing limbs and body parts until they became erotically intertwined. The thought had her fighting to keep the nausea down. She squeezed her eyes shut to block out the offending fantasy. Had it ever been that way with her and Tom?

Denise cut into her painful thoughts. "Maybe you didn't care enough to ask him about it."

The statement hung in the air between them. Sam burned to shout in protest, but something stopped her. Mere words that she did care could never negate her apathy. It had become clear she'd known very little about Tom's schedule while he was away. If truth be told, she'd liked when he traveled. She could work even later than usual without hearing his complaints. And she hadn't had to worry about getting home in time for dinner. Did that make her as culpable as Tom for the breakdown in their relationship? It was an eye-opening thought. Too eye-opening.

"I didn't hear you," stated Denise.

"I didn't say anything." Sam hung her head and sighed.

"I know."

****

Sam just wasn't liking men much these days.

Nevertheless, the bar at Harry's Irish Pub was packed with them, three to four deep. Of course, there were women too. They were necessary so men could insinuate themselves into their space and try out their best pick-up lines.

"Hi, beautiful. What's the rush?" A smarmy forty-something male leered at Sam as she and Denise passed. "Come on, girls, give me a chance."

Sam was dying to respond with an acerbic comeback. She hated the term *girls* as much as she hated *lady*. And *ma'am*. But she promised herself to keep arguments and angry outbursts to a minimum.

Denise grabbed Sam's arm and pulled her through the crowd. "Come on. The waitress is motioning to us. Our table is finally ready."

"You must have eagle eyes. I can't see a thing past this football team."

A gang of hunky, muscled guys clinked beer bottles and yelled over each other, tactlessly discussing the physical attributes of a well-endowed blonde across the bar. The beautiful people were out in full force tonight.

Denise yanked at Sam again, who was also ready to abandon the noise and crowd of the bar for the comfort and relative peacefulness of a green leather booth in the dining room. Food wasn't a bad idea either.

Once seated, with a glass of Chardonnay easing the pain and their food orders in, Denise sighed. "This is more like it." She sipped her wine. "What a perfect day. The beach was fantastic, and I didn't have to build sand castles. It's too bad Ben and I can't get away like this, just the two of us."

"Why not?"

"What would I do with the kids? My parents don't have enough energy to take care of them for an entire weekend, and my sister-in-law...I mean..." She lowered her voice. "Sometimes I forget she's gone." She fiddled with her napkin. "Anyway, with Bobby sick, we wouldn't even consider it."

"Maybe when he gets better..." Sam was about to volunteer but stopped herself. Who was she kidding? She had never even babysat as a teenager. She knew nothing about children. Any attempt to help would surely lead to disaster.

"Yeah...maybe." Denise stared into her wine, as if

contemplating it. "I don't think Ben would go for it. He sees the kids so little during the week. He wouldn't want to be away from them on the weekend."

"You two are so considerate of each other." Would she have been as considerate with Tom's wishes? Had she been in the past? "It's nice to know there are happily married couples in this world." Sam grimaced at her cynical words.

"I don't know what I would do without him." Denise smiled. "He's the best. And even though I only left this morning, it's funny, but I miss him."

A stab of jealousy pierced Sam's heart as her friend talked so lovingly of her husband. She must have felt that way about Tom at some point. She'd loved him when they married. What happened over the span of three short years to make them grow so far apart?

Her career. That's what.

Sam's sole goal of becoming a partner at her law firm precluded spare time for fun activities. The precious little free time she gave herself centered around Saturday night and Sunday, her day of rest. She thought Tom desired the same thing, was just as motivated. He moved up the ranks of his company and positioned himself as the president's right-hand man. But he had other interests too. He often invited her to a Knicks game or an art gallery show. She was generally too busy. So he went alone. Or so she'd thought.

"What makes you and Ben so compatible?" Maybe she could learn something.

"We both have the same goals I suppose. The kids are our number one priority. That's why I quit my job to stay home and raise them. We both think it's important for at least one parent to be there for them."

"Don't you resent that it was you who stepped off the ladder while Ben keeps going?"

"No. Not really."

"There's a convincing statement."

Denise sighed. "I'm sure no woman feels a hundred percent comfortable with the decision she's made—whether it's to work or stay home with the kids. We're all trying to do what's right for us, for our family. I want to be their caretaker, their guide. If Ben stayed home while I worked, I shudder to think what those kids would be doing on a daily basis. It certainly wouldn't be gymnastics or music or joining in playgroups. Ben would probably have them hunting and fishing. Not that they wouldn't enjoy those activities as well. I just think they need more balance. And forget about keeping the house clean. I could picture mud and dirt tracked everywhere, with all of them saying, 'What mud?' " She laughed at the image she painted. "Things are fine the way they are. And if I decide to go back to work after the kids grow up a little, I'm sure I'll find a place."

For such a professional woman living in the twenty-first century, Sam couldn't believe her friend's naiveté or antiquated gender norms. "But you could never make up the time you lost or the experience you missed. You'd have to practically start over!" It appalled her to even think about it.

"The children are more important to me than my position in the banking world. At home, I'm making a difference. I'm shaping their lives, lives that will potentially benefit others. I can only hope to raise three community-minded, productive citizens who work to make this world a better place."

This idealistic view, although admirable, exasperated Sam even more. Denise was sometimes too good to be true. "Isn't it a vicious cycle? If you raise Jennifer to be a great student, a model citizen, who then goes out into the world to make a difference, what happens when she falls in love and gets married and has a baby?" Her voice rose with her irritation. "Does she then stay home to raise that child and forget all about her goals? Just like her mother did?"

"Why are you so angry?" Denise tilted her head, as if looking at her from a different angle would make her understand Sam better. "It was my choice, Sam. Based on my beliefs. No one forced me to give up my career. Perhaps when you have a baby, you'll make a different choice. Millions of women continue to work, continue their climb. I'm just not one of them."

Denise's calm, rational tone took some of the air out of Sam's blustery argument. Denise wasn't Sam. Nor was she Sam's mother, forced to work to support herself and her child. Sam's vulnerability fueled her anger, a state of being foreign to Denise. Her parents hadn't divorced. They were happy together. Stable. And they had given Denise the security and confidence she now possessed.

But even though Sam recognized this, she pushed. "It doesn't seem fair that women are the ones who have to make the choice. If you give up your career, you're ostracized for becoming a stay-at-home mom. If you keep working, you're deemed selfish because you put your job before your kids. I don't see how women ever win." She had often felt this but never argued the case.

"There's no winning or losing. You pick the road that's right for you."

Although Denise's sound opinion made perfect sense, Sam couldn't give in to its logic. Maybe it was her inbred nature to debate every issue to death.

"I disagree," she said, playing with her empty glass. "What if you and Ben divorce ten years from now? He's making a hefty salary after having put in his time, whereas you now have to go out into the workforce and become a teller making minimum wage because you're a middle-aged woman who hasn't had a job in fifteen years. You don't know the latest technology. You don't know your field anymore." She shouldn't be lecturing her good friend, but didn't Denise worry about this stuff? "Hell, the executives will be the pimple-faced high school kids who grew up down the street while you were raising your babies."

"I certainly hope it doesn't come to that." Denise laughed, cutting into her steak, which had arrived. "I'm sure I can reenter the workforce as something more than a teller."

"You laugh now," scoffed Sam, "but I guarantee, you won't be laughing when you're sending your resume to job search sites with no one responding because it's buried in the thousands of other applications." Her steam had built up again, making her unmerciful, cruel even. But she couldn't help it.

"Sam, I know you're trying to make a point. But I can't imagine being divorced from Ben."

"Fifty percent of marriages end in divorce. A divorced woman who put her life on hold to raise children is guaranteed to have a lower standard of living going forward, while her ex-husband's remains the same or increases. I see it every day, and it's not pretty. I lived through it with my parents. Remember?"

God, she sounded like a preacher.

Denise sighed. "I know you had a tough time dealing with your parents' divorce. And I know I can't put my head in the sand and ignore the high percentage of failed marriages. But what's the point in drowning in negativity and 'what ifs' on the off chance I may get divorced someday? I don't want to raise my family under that cloud. If it happens, I'll deal with it then. And since you'll be my lawyer, I won't have anything to worry about." Denise grinned sweetly before raising her fork to her mouth.

Sam shook her head, then chuckled, glad Denise's optimism was able to break through her doom and gloom. "I'm sorry for being so heartless and preachy. I guess I'm reacting to what happened to me. If I had kids and was a stay-at-home mom, I don't know what I'd be doing now with Tom off in San Diego with Sherry." She stared into her refilled glass of wine. "I hate him for making me feel this way. I hate him for making me so cynical. And I especially hate him for falling in love with someone else." Tears spilled over her lashes and slid down her cheeks. "Why doesn't he still love me?"

Denise grabbed a tissue out of her purse and handed it across the table. "Sam, don't cry. He's not worthy of you. He's obviously an egotist who only cares about how he feels at the moment and gives no thought to anyone else. This thing with Sherry won't last. It can't. In a few weeks, he'll need or want something else, and he'll go look for that. He never even tried to talk to you about his unhappiness. He picked up and left." She patted Sam's hand soothingly before adding, "You don't need someone like that in your life. You need someone to communicate with you, someone to share with you."

Sam sniffed. "How could I have been so blind? How did I miss the signs?" The humiliation, coupled with her stupidity, kicked her in the gut. "Do you have any more tissues?"

Denise handed her some, and Sam attempted to wipe away the pain with her tears.

"I'm sorry. I'm not very good company tonight." She gave Denise a watery smile. "I berate you for making a choice to stay home with your kids, and then I look to you for sympathy. I'm a mess." She blew her nose, then lowered her tear-filled eyes. "I guess I didn't realize until today how distrustful of men I've become. Ben isn't Tom, and I apologize for even bringing up the subject of divorce where it concerns you." She could be such a bitch. Reaching across the table, she held Denise's hand. "Thanks for being such a good friend. And thanks for leaving your family this weekend to spend time with me. Especially given what's going on with Bobby. You're the best." She attempted a lopsided grin.

"Remember how we cried over our boyfriends in high school?" Denise smiled, gently changing the subject. "We spent about one week thinking it was the end of the world, and then things got better."

Sam couldn't help a genuine chuckle over that. "You were with Ben most of high school."

"True. But we had our fights and breakups." Denise grinned. "I don't recall you sitting home on too many Saturday nights, missy."

Sam did have short-term relationships with Don, then Paul, once she'd given up on Michael. But they'd meant nothing. Things were so simple then. But were they? Nicki's father died, leaving her mother in a state of depression and Nicki floundering. Getting pregnant turned her life upside down, forcing her to make the heart-wrenching decision to defer college, have the baby, then give it up for adoption. Michael's mother and sister left town to escape, leaving him alone with his abusive father, which in turn forced Michael to disappear. Sam's father divorced her mother, replacing her with someone younger and richer, leaving Sam and her mother to struggle not only with bills but with a loss of self-esteem.

Although hard to recreate so many years later, she recalled the heartache she'd experienced over those events. Thankfully, the distance of the years softened and muddled the feelings of despair and sorrow she'd felt at the time. Yet she sympathized with the teenaged girl who hadn't a clue how to deal with what life had served up.

Nor did she at thirty-three.

Chapter Nine

"It's a shame it's raining." Sam carried two cups of coffee out to the covered porch. Her painful heart-to-heart talk with Denise last night cleansed and lightened her mood this morning, despite the dreary weather.

A white wicker sofa with blue and white striped cushions sat under an overhang with a matching wicker table before it. Perfect for coffee cups, magazines, and propping up feet while lazing on the couch. And Sam intended to do just that all day.

"I don't mind the rain." Denise kicked off her flip-flops and drew her legs up beneath her. "A cozy cottage, a great front porch where we can watch the showers, and time for myself. I may never leave."

Rich, emerald-green grass covered the front yard, so unlike other shore towns on the Jersey coast. Upon arrival in Crescent Beach, Sam thought the municipality must have had an ordinance compelling its citizens to have manicured lawns, brilliantly colored flower gardens, and just the right amount of shrubbery to keep the local landscapers in business.

A ringing phone disturbed the peacefulness. "I wonder who that could be." Sam pushed herself up and headed through the screen door, searching for her cell phone. A male voice echoed on the other end of the line, and Sam's heart thumped in her chest.

"Tom?"

"It's Ben."

Her heart dropped. "Oh. I...I'm sorry. I didn't recognize your voice." Her face burned with embarrassment. "How are you?" she stammered, placing her hand over her chest in an effort to calm the crazy beating.

"I'm muddling through." He chuckled with ease. "Sorry to call on your phone, but Denise wasn't answering hers. She must be enjoying herself."

"Is everything okay?"

"All good. The kids are a handful, but we're having fun."

"I'm so sorry to hear about Bobby. Please know that I'll start working on getting his birth certificate tomorrow."

"Thanks, Sam. We appreciate your help. How are you holding up? I haven't seen you in a few months. I'm sorry to hear about you and Tom."

The mention of their breakup made her throat clench. "Thanks...I'm okay. I'll get Denise. She's right here."

Her hand shook as she opened the screen door. "It's for you. Ben."

Denise popped up, a huge smile on her face as she entered the house, taking the phone into the kitchen. Even though they'd been married for nine years, Denise and Ben were a beautiful couple, so in love, so attuned to each other's needs.

Sam collapsed back onto the wicker sofa outside, giving Denise some privacy. She took in a big breath and closed her eyes. Her over-the-top reaction in thinking the caller was Tom confused her. Did she even want to hear from him? Blood rushed through her head and rang through her ears, but she could still hear Denise's side of the conversation through the open windows, and it warmed her heart at the same time it pierced it.

"Hi, honey. How's it going? I miss all of you too. Are you managing without me? Good. This place is really nice. And it's been great to spend some time with Sam. I miss my girlfriends." Her voice became lower but still audible. "She hasn't heard from him… You know. She's sad, angry, upset. What you'd expect. But she'll pull through it. She's strong."

It seemed so eerie, so oddly out of place, to hear a third party talking about her pain. She supposed she was the subject of gossip and conjecture in the different circles within which she traveled. If she couldn't handle it sitting on her front porch when a good friend talked to her husband about it, how was she ever going to get through the questioning wonder of acquaintances?

Denise was wrong. She wasn't strong. And she had proven her weakness by falling apart in the restaurant last night. Was Denise saying those words to Ben so he wouldn't worry about her, or did she think it was true?

Denise's voice perked up talking to Jennifer first, then Johnny, then Bobby, giggling with them, telling them how much she missed them and that she would be home later this afternoon. Denise's life was so rich, so full. Even with the trauma of dealing with Bobby's illness. Nonetheless, only yesterday, Sam had picked it apart, trying to make her feel inadequate for not continuing in her career. What was wrong with her? Sam wanted a family too. Not now, of course, but in time. She always pictured herself with two children, maybe even three.

Denise blew kisses to the kids, and before she hung up, she told Ben she loved him. Sam closed her eyes, warding off all she'd lost, as her heart squeezed. The isolation and loneliness of her circumstances punched her in the gut. Would she ever have that kind of love in her life?

Denise appeared back on the porch, a big smile on her face and a gleam in her eyes. Sam blinked to rid her own of any telltale signs of misery.

"You're so lucky, Denise. You have a husband who loves you and three wonderful children who make you smile."

"I am lucky. But don't think it just happens. Keeping a good marriage is hard work. There are times I'm so exhausted from doing things with the kids all day, grocery shopping, laundry, straightening up." She plopped back onto the couch and picked up her coffee mug. "When Ben comes home, I would like nothing better than to disappear into a nice hot bath. But he's tired too. So I wait and have dinner with him after the kids are in bed so we can talk, catch up on each other's day, discuss problems…or anything else."

"I guess that's the step I missed," admitted Sam. "Discussing. I would have disappeared into that hot bath." Had she been too disinterested in Tom's day to stick around and talk about it? Or was she too selfish to give up her alone time to hear about his problems? Either choice made her the bad guy. Another example proving their breakup wasn't all Tom's fault.

Denise shook her head. "But that's not the hard part. Sometimes I'm invited out to dinner with Ben and his business associates because the other wives are going. I then have to listen to their recommendations on the hottest Broadway musicals, or the best stores to shop in, when I'd rather jump into the business conversations and put in my two cents."

"Why don't you? You're one of the smartest women I know. They should be happy to have your input."

"I tried once, and Ben and I got into a huge argument on the way home." A fleeting shadow crossed over Denise's eyes.

"That kind of thing must eat away at you." Sam wouldn't have been able to put up with that.

"It did, until we discussed it more. Ben values my insights and experience because he knows me. But his boss and colleagues—all male by the way—didn't appreciate the interference of a stranger. I had also made the wives uncomfortable. Now that I understand the ground rules, I can live with them. It's all a matter of communication. And compromise."

"I guess I blew that one." Sam stretched her legs out, much more confused than she'd been for the past few weeks. Until her heart-to-hearts with Nicki and Denise, the whole mess had been totally Tom's fault. He was a cheater. An egotistical bastard who had no morals or sense of honor. He had tossed to the wind the commitment he'd made to her on their wedding day.

Denise broke into her thoughts. "Communication is a two-way street. It doesn't sound like Tom was very good at it either. Or else he wouldn't have run off the way he did. He would have talked out your problems—his problems—ages ago."

Sam didn't answer and instead stared out onto the front lawn, sipping at her now cold coffee. She was at fault as much as him. And her actions, or non-actions, were what had driven him into someone else's arms. But why hadn't he said something? Why hadn't he tried to make it work?

"You can't climb under a rock and ignore all of this, Sam. What are you planning to do? Are you going to try to work it out with Tom or take your medicine and move on?"

"I don't think I have much choice. Tom's gone. He didn't want to hash it out." Even though she could now see she was partly to blame, the bitterness returned at his refusal to discuss her shortcomings before moving out.

"I thought you said he was only going to San Diego for the summer."

"Or longer. He didn't know." Sam sighed. This new twist on things made her even more depressed. "But that's not the point. I think he wanted time away from me to figure out if this thing with Sherry is real or not. If it is, it doesn't much matter whether he's in New York City or San Diego. If it's not, I don't think I can ever forgive him for doing this to me. I can't imagine taking him back." Even if his defection was partly her fault.

"Have you called him?"

"Are you kidding? He walked out on me. If I talked to him right now, the venom would leak through the phone and kill him." She couldn't control her smirk. "Not a bad idea."

"Has he reached out to you?"

"No." The pain of his failure to call her was almost worse than his initial betrayal. It was an affirmation of his lack of feelings for her.

"What happens when you leave your little cocoon

here?"

"I'm hoping this time away will help me clear my head enough to return to my life. I'll go back to New York, work sixty hours a week, put our co-op on the market, and hire a lawyer to get me divorced." Oh, but it sounded so—so bleak.

Denise pursed her lips and nodded. "Sam, you know if you need to work through this more, I'm only a phone call away. If you need me in person, I'll pack up the kids and bring them here for a day. Or whatever you want."

"Thanks, Denise. That's sweet of you." Sam put her arm around Denise's shoulders and gave her a hug.

"No, it's not." She chuckled. "I want to bring the kids to the beach for a day. And Auntie Sam can help build sand castles."

Sam laughed at the picture, allowing her friend's humor and love to wash over her. Denise's calm, rational statements, combined with her ability to analyze the needs of her own marriage, made Sam realize life wasn't easy for anybody. Relationships were hard, and both parties had to work at them no matter how happy they thought they were. For a fleeting moment, Sam contemplated returning to New York and resuming her life—this time without Tom.

Just maybe she was strong.

****

As soon as Denise left, Sam headed for the beach. The rain had stopped hours ago, but the sun never made an appearance. Even so, there was still at least an hour of daylight, and the near-empty beach would provide the perfect setting for her to think, to plan. The time had come to file for divorce. What was she waiting for? Her return to New York? Some new revelation? She had been over it all, again and again. Her marriage was dead.

If she was in Crescent Beach to heal, she needed to take the next step. Not dwell on the "Why?" and the "How could this happen to me?" The time for self-pity was over.

Sam walked to the jetty and climbed onto the rocks, where the waves crashed and swirled between them. She thought she would find peace, or even inner strength from the forces of nature, but instead a building agitation rose within her like the angry tide.

Fast-forwarding through her mind was the dream of the house in the suburbs with children, a dog, and even a mini-van. The apartment in the city filled with friends attending dinner parties or Sunday brunches. She—a partner in her firm, becoming more and more well-known as the divorce attorney to the socialites. Tom—taking over as president of his company, the price of his stock going higher and higher. A power couple who had it all. Tears flooded her eyes, and she squeezed them shut to block out the perfect pictures. Everything she thought her future would be, gone.

Where had she gotten that happy fantasy? Surely not from her parents' relationship. Before their divorce, her father had worked all the time running his small business, and her parents did very little together. Her mom had been in charge of Sam and the house, and after work her father would do his own thing at nights and on the weekends. She'd never thought much about it—didn't all dads play cards with their buddies or go out for a few beers after work? Didn't most of them play golf on the weekend? Although her father wasn't always working, he did selfishly put his needs above all else. Damn! Sam had the same qualities as the man she now despised.

She had let her marriage play second fiddle to her career. She had taken it for granted, thinking it would always be there, no matter what. She'd been so naive, given her history, as well as the daily reminders she witnessed at work.

The foam swirled around the rocks, surging closer and closer to her feet. She backed up, angry at the ocean for pushing her away, angry at herself for not standing her ground.

Turning her back on the powerful sea, Sam jumped off the jetty and headed toward home. Odd she could even think of her temporary retreat as home, yet she started running in its direction, anxiety pushing her to find peace there. Her marriage was over, and she knew what she had to do. Bile rose in her throat, and she swallowed big gulps of air in an effort to smother the nausea. She hadn't thought that making the decision to file for divorce would affect her this way. But it did. Her stomach churned, and her heart twisted and cramped.

She threw open the door of the house, taking the stairs two at a time while ripping her shirt off, then yanking the zipper of her shorts. The clothes landed in a heap on the floor. She turned the shower on and immersed herself in the sluicing water, clawing at her skin in an attempt to shed the doom that invaded her senses. Sobs escaped from her mouth and tears streamed down her face. She wrapped her arms around her body, holding herself together for fear that if she let go, she would end up in a puddle on the bathtub floor.

She stayed like that until the warm water turned cool, then cold, shivering behind the shower curtain, willing her hands to unglue themselves from her body, to cut off the offending ice stream. When she could no longer stand it, she turned the faucet off.

Droplets of water slid down her skin as she stood naked in the tub, statue-like. Her mind no longer thought. Her brain had crashed and burned, and now she was numb. Numb to the pain of her decision, numb to the reasons for it.

Only three years of marriage, but a lifetime of hope.

Over.

Chapter Ten

Deeply focused on a commercial lease agreement, Michael barely heard the phone ring on his office desk. "What is it, Karen?" he asked his secretary.

"Can you see Eric's four o'clock client? He's not back from court. It's a new divorce."

He glanced at his watch. It was four ten. Even though divorce wasn't his practice area, he could muddle through the initial interview. Besides, Eric would help him out in a pinch. "Sure. I'll cover for him. Give me a minute."

He shrugged into his suit jacket, adjusted his tie, and cleared the paperwork off his desk. Walking toward the reception area, he stopped short.

"Sam! What brings you here?" His body temperature shot up as he took in her short skirt and strappy heels. Hopefully, she'd dropped by to accept his dinner invitation.

"Michael!" She stood, and the magazine she'd been reading fell to the floor with a thud. Her eyes darted to the hall beyond. No, she was definitely not here for him. As a matter of fact, it looked as if she were about ready to bolt if given half the chance. "I…I have an appointment with Eric Donnelly. What are you doing here?"

His joy at seeing her slipped several notches. "I work here," he explained, hoping to set her at ease.

"I thought you were the town prosecutor?"

"That's a part-time job." He shrugged.

"Your name's not on the sign."

"I know. I haven't quite committed to becoming Eric's partner."

"Oh." She bobbed her head, looking painfully uncomfortable.

He inhaled, dreading his next statement. "Unfortunately, Eric's not back from court. I was going to take over his four o'clock appointment." He quickly added, "But of course, if you don't want to meet with me, that's fine. You can wait for Eric. Or you can reschedule."

He felt as awkward as she looked, standing there with her mouth open. If he could rewind this scene and disappear back into his office, neither of them would be worse for the wear from not having seen each other.

She didn't respond.

"Sam?" he prodded, pushing her to make a decision—hopefully to leave.

"Fine. I'll meet with you, then." She inhaled, picked up the magazine, and placed it on the table.

Damn! He forced a smile. "This way." He led her down the hall and into his office. She stood near a client chair, not making a move to sit.

Michael glanced at her, and his mouth went dry. She looked amazing in a pink skirt and top, the color setting off her newfound tan. The skirt, several inches above her knee, showed him too much of her long, gorgeous legs, the legs he had fleetingly thought of wrapped around his body. Her dark brown hair, highlighted by the sun, fell over her shoulders, shiny and soft, and he itched to wind his fingers through it.

Cramming his hands into his pockets, he fought for control.

He cleared his throat. "Have a seat."

She sat and crossed her legs. Very dangerous. Her skirt inched up higher on her thigh, and he had to drag his eyes back up to her face. "So you're here to discuss divorce."

"Yes." Her voice was even, determined.

"I didn't think you were married. You said in the coffee shop that you didn't have a husband." He bit his tongue. "I mean, that's what I thought you said. I must have misunderstood." He was making it worse.

"I did say that. It sort of fell out of my mouth, unchecked." She hesitated. "My husband left me for another woman. He doesn't feel like my husband anymore. That's what I meant."

"Oh." Who in the world would leave her? She was smart, beautiful, and once he'd gotten past her initial aggressive outbursts, quite nice. Now he understood the reason for her anger.

Although it wasn't in evidence now. Instead, her face had frozen into a mask, and her voice was calm and cool.

"Anyway," she continued, "as you know, I took a ten week leave of absence from work. What a joke!" She chuckled, apparently trying to lighten the mood and set him at ease. "I'm still working fifteen hours a week."

"He must be a fool." The second the words slipped out, he lowered his eyes, not wanting to see the shock on her face. He was becoming much too personal—and unprofessional. He should know better. "I'm sorry." He searched her face to see if she took offense.

A sigh escaped. "Thanks for the vote of confidence."

"So you want to file a Complaint for Adultery?"

"That sounds accurate." Her tone remained matter-of-fact. "In New York, obviously. I noticed Eric has his New York license. And of course, you do too. I don't want to wait until I go back in August."

Michael nodded, trying unsuccessfully to keep his head on the matter at hand and not on the V of Sam's shirt. "I'll need some background information. What's your husband's name?"

"Tom…Thomas Burton."

"Address?" He held his pen over his pad, ready to take notes, but he couldn't seem to move his eyes from her face.

"We have a co-op in New York, but I honestly don't know where he is right now. In San Diego somewhere. He went there for business for the summer. With the office comptroller…his girlfriend."

The slight hesitation suggested she felt something about her husband's defection, but he couldn't be sure whether it was sadness or pure embarrassment in sharing this very personal information with him. He sat back in his chair and placed his pen on the desk. "Do you want to wait until he gets back to New York before we serve him?"

"No. I want to get started now. I want to get this over with by the time I return to work."

"You're the expert in this field, Sam. You must know this could take a little longer than a few weeks."

She sighed. "I know. I'm trying to be positive."

"You'll have to find out his address in San Diego."

"I'll have it for you tomorrow."

A no-nonsense woman with a goal. So calm, so unaffected. Was it an act or did she just not care? "To file for adultery, I'll need the name and address of his…paramour."

"Paramour?" She laughed, all humor absent. "I love that word. Sherry Trugman. She was a friend of ours. I guess she was more a friend of his." She shook her head. "You can't trust anyone these days." The words tumbled out with the expected sarcasm, but missing the expected hostility. Shifting in her seat, she admitted, "I didn't mean to share all that with you."

"Since I'm your lawyer, Sam, you're going to have to tell me everything." He thought her eyes watered for a moment, but she blinked and sat up straighter.

"This is all so embarrassing." Her fingers intertwined and then unlocked as she bowed her head to study them. "What else do you want to know?"

Her voice was low but composed. She sat quietly, elegantly. Not at all the Sam he'd known as a teenager, tall, skinny, shy.

"Let's go through the marital assets. That should be easier." He slid a packet over to her. "I'll need you to fill out these forms."

They spent the next forty-five minutes discussing equitable distribution of their marital property and debts. Alimony was not an issue since she and her soon-to-be ex-husband both made comparable salaries.

Michael looked up from his notes. "This should be an easy divorce, since it's only a matter of a property settlement. The hardest part will be filing the Complaint and having it served. Are you sure this is what you want to do?"

Where did that question come from? Nothing in

Sam's demeanor gave him cause to think she wished to stay married to the cheater. It wasn't his place to get into the psychological reasons behind his clients' decisions. Unfortunately, in this case, he was dying to know. He needed to know.

"I'm sure." Her definitive statement left no room for conjecture. "I'll get you the information you need and fill out these forms by tomorrow." She stood and held out her hand to shake his. "Thank you for your time. Do I leave the retainer check with you or with the receptionist?"

Efficient and to the point. Everything had turned so formal between them. Only a few days ago, they had walked on the beach and shared some personal information. In retrospect, Sam hadn't shared much at all. He hadn't known she was married or contemplating divorce. All she'd told him was she was taking a break. He'd thought she needed time off from her stressful job.

Mimicking her formality, he shook her hand. "You can leave it with the receptionist. Why don't you stop by at six tomorrow night with the completed forms?" By that time, he would be winding down, and perhaps he could coax her into having a quick drink with him. Maybe even dinner. "I'll give my notes to Eric, and he can handle it from here." There was no way he was going to keep this case. He was much too interested in the lovely Samantha Winslow. Besides, she would only be here for another six weeks.

Hardly enough time at all.

****

Sam awoke to the shining sun pouring through her bedroom window. She rolled onto her back and laid an arm across her eyes to shield them from the brightness.

Her body ached from lying in the same position all night. The events of the day before came hurtling back at her, but she pushed them away.

The strength she'd felt returning days before had been temporarily zapped when she'd taken the first steps in the legal process of divorcing Tom. But that was yesterday. Today was another day. A better day. A day to celebrate a new beginning. At least it sounded good.

Sam padded downstairs to make coffee, then thought twice. Maybe she would go to the coffee shop. Seeing other people would do her good. For a fleeting second, she tingled at the thought of seeing Michael there, but she didn't really want to see him.

He was a series of conflicting personas—the man who'd witnessed her temper and called her on it, the lawyer who prosecuted her and counseled her, the guy on the beach who shared a little piece of himself while trying to get her to do the same, the unhappy teenager who'd left town fifteen years ago hoping to outdistance his past.

She was far too attracted to him for her own good. An obvious stray feeling from those high school years. A romantic fling was out of the question. She was still married and he… She didn't know his relationship story. Although he didn't seem to be attached to any one particular woman. The "cheerleaders" at the volleyball games were interchangeable. But so what? Her marriage was over. She should take a page out of Nicki's book and have fun. With no attachments of course. She wasn't about to get involved. Now or ever. She would never put herself in a position to be vulnerable again. It might do her a world of good to have a "thing" with Michael. Help her get through this difficult period.

As she debated the possibility, she donned a pair of cut-off jeans and a red halter top, then ran a brush through her tangled hair before tossing it up in a ponytail. She grabbed her purse and headed out the door, her decision made.

****

The coffee shop's stools were filled with the regulars. As Sam scanned the occupants, her buoyancy slipped. Michael wasn't one of them. Maybe fate had stepped in to protect her from her foolishness. She had been saved.

"Good morning, Flo. The usual, please." She smiled at the waitress, as she sat at an empty table. She was starting to feel like a local.

Sam read *The New York Times* as she drank her coffee and nibbled at a blueberry muffin. Unfortunately, every time the door opened, she looked up, hopeful, then dejected. This was ridiculous. She vowed to concentrate on the article in front of her, but by her fourth reading, she folded the newspaper and pushed it aside. She had a meeting with him at six o'clock tonight anyway. He was probably in court now. It was Tuesday morning, and he did have a job.

So Sam modified her plan and got to it. The grocery store and an hour or two of work. By one thirty she was perusing the beach, sand chair in one hand and tote bag in the other. She found herself near the ocean between a mother with four children to the right, and a teenage couple making out on their blanket to the left. The contrast amused her, interjecting romantic fantasies upon life with children. The irony couldn't be ignored.

One assuredly led to the other.

Intermittently, Michael insinuated himself into her thoughts, playing volleyball, retrieving her change on the floor of the coffee shop, prosecuting her case in municipal court, apologizing to her about the broken meter. Smiling at her. Electricity zapped through her body.

Unacceptable.

She warned herself, she advised herself, she cautioned herself. *Stay away from him.* She didn't need any complications in her life right now. He was probably a player, out to have fun with as many women as possible. But still, she flirted with the idea of a fling. It might make her feel better, desired, wanted. Tom had done such damage to her ego that Michael's mild flirtations with her, at the very least, had taken her from the gutter to the curb. She was now ready to stand. What harm could it do to lean on Michael as she found her balance again?

And it wasn't like she'd be flirting with a stranger. In some weird way, she felt safer, more secure with the idea of seeing Michael because she'd known him in the past. Still, something niggled at her, attempting to thwart her idea.

Restless, she headed for the ocean. That first feel of its icy splash almost convinced her to back away. But she turned it into a dare. If she dove in and swam for at least five minutes, she would give herself permission to take the plunge with Michael. If she chickened out and walked back to her chair, she would steer clear of him. Sam took a few more steps, allowing the waves to crash around her thighs, spraying her midriff with its frosted droplets. Her heart pounded as the coldness shocked her overheated body. She held her breath, counted to three, and dove in.

Breaking through the surface of the water, her body quivered from head to foot. She glided into a freestyle, concentrating on positioning her arms perfectly to slice through the water and give her momentum. The difficulty in swimming over roiling waves exhilarated her, giving her purpose. The current helped as she measured distance by the lifeguard stand. The initial frigidity of the ocean tempered, and her muscles warmed with the grueling exercise.

Electrified blood hummed through her body. She felt alive. She had taken the plunge that made a decision, and she laughed out loud at the game she had just played.

And won.

Chapter Eleven

Sam stood before her closet far too long deciding on an outfit. She didn't want to be overdressed, for she was only dropping off information at Michael's office. But too casual didn't work either. She needed to look good if she planned to entice him.

Sam glanced at her watch and gasped. It was already five thirty. She grabbed a pair of white slacks from their hanger and rummaged through her drawer for a black sleeveless top, coming across at least ten in different styles and materials. Groaning, she hastily tried them on, discarding them one by one, until she found the perfect fit—as if there were any difference.

Her afternoon at the beach had provided her with a deeper tan on her body and a rosy glow on her cheeks. She brushed on one coat of mascara and dabbed some gloss on her lips. Her hair was still damp, so she quickly braided it and stepped into a pair of white sandals. After all this, he better give her more than the minute it would take to provide the information and forms she'd completed.

Arriving a few minutes past six, Sam walked into an eerily quiet office. No receptionist sat at the front desk, and no ringing phones or muted conversations echoed from the hall.

"Michael?" she called out, not wanting to head to his private space unannounced. The rustle of papers caught her attention, and a man in his fifties with thick graying hair appeared out of the office to the left.

"May I help you?" he asked cordially.

"I'm Samantha Winslow. I came to drop off some information with Michael for my case."

"I'm Eric Donnelly." He stuck out his hand to shake hers. "I'm sorry I wasn't here yesterday afternoon to meet with you, Ms. Winslow. I was tied up in court. Michael told me you would be stopping by tonight. Why don't you come into my office and explain what you have? I understand you'd like the Complaint to go out this week."

Sam's heart plummeted as she followed Eric into his office. She wanted to see Michael. Even if only for five minutes. She never thought she'd be meeting with Eric. But maybe this was another sign.

Maybe fate, for the second time today, was stepping in to protect her.

"I have my husband's temporary address. As well as Sherry's. I assume they're together. We had talked about filing for adultery and extreme cruelty, so I wrote out some information for the Complaint right here." She handed Eric the financial forms as well as Tom's current address scribbled on a scrap of paper. "I hope you can read this."

He glanced over the papers. "I've heard you're a high-powered divorce lawyer in the city. You could be handling your own divorce. But I guess it's true what they say, 'A lawyer who represents himself has a fool for a client.' " He chuckled at his quip. He had a nice smile.

"I'm sure it's true. And I know I can't be objective." She sighed, letting out the disappointment over her circumstances.

"For what it's worth, I'm sorry you're in this position." His eyes held compassion, and Sam decided she liked Eric Donnelly.

"Thanks." There was nothing else to say.

"This looks fine. I'll have the Complaint ready for you tomorrow, if you want to drop by to sign it."

"What time?" She couldn't seem to muster up any enthusiasm.

"Does this same time work for you?"

"Sure." She rose and shook his hand. "It was nice meeting you, Eric."

"Same here, Ms. Winslow."

"You can call me Sam." She attempted a smile, then turned to leave.

Once out the front door, she stood there for a moment, looking down at the sidewalk as if the answers to the two most important questions on her mind would be there. Why hadn't Michael met with her? Why did she care?

The walk back to her house took longer than usual. She had no spring in her step, no purpose in arriving at her destination quickly. When she did bang through the front door, she threw her purse on the couch and headed to the kitchen. In no mood to cook, she grabbed the container of leftover chicken lo mein and poured herself a glass of wine, taking both to the front porch. Things happened for a reason. Not meeting Michael tonight was a definite sign. A sign that—

"Excuse me, miss," a voice said politely. "Is this the Winslow residence?"

Startled, she looked up. "Michael! What are you doing here?" Her heart somersaulted in her chest.

"Is that any way to greet a guest?" He smiled. One of his dazzling smiles.

"I'm sorry," she stammered, blinded by its brilliance. "I didn't see you come up."

"You look like you're off in outer space. Am I interrupting?"

"I could use the interruption," she admitted.

"Oh? Any problem I could help with?" His blue eyes flashed mischievously.

Yes. You could take me in your arms and make love to me like I'm the most beautiful, sexy, wonderful woman on earth. You can make me feel whole again. Be my rebound relationship, my fling. A means to an end.

Instead she answered, "No. I'm good. Would you like a glass of wine? I don't have anything else."

"Sure. Thanks."

Sam went into the house, pinched herself, then poured his wine.

"What brings you here?" She stepped back out on the porch and handed him his glass.

"I wanted to apologize for not meeting with you earlier. I got a last-minute call from a client who needed me at a meeting. I tried to get back in time, but I had just missed you."

The heaviness lifted from Sam's shoulders, and she felt like flying. No attorney would track down his client's residence to apologize for missing a meeting unless there was more to it. Besides, she wasn't really his client.

"Thanks for your apology. But it wasn't necessary." She hoped he couldn't hear the glee in her voice. "I met Eric Donnelly and dropped the information off with him. He said he'd have the

Complaint ready for my signature by tomorrow."

"Good. Then it's official. I'm no longer your attorney." The corners of his mouth turned up in a sexily wicked grin.

Sam couldn't help but laugh, even as she felt a tingling at the back of her neck. Was it a warning or excitement? "And why is that good?" she teased.

"Because now we can catch a movie or I can take you to my favorite Italian restaurant." His smile faded, and he looked even better serious.

"What makes you think I would want to do that?" She took a sip of wine to calm the butterflies in her stomach. If he only knew she'd longed to make out with him in a darkened movie theater since she was eighteen.

"Eric told me you looked disappointed when I wasn't in the office to meet with you."

Damn. She didn't think Eric would notice, much less squeal on her.

"It wasn't that," she fibbed. "I was down about the whole divorce thing."

"Oh." Now Michael seemed disappointed as he placed his glass on the table.

"But I'm glad you're here," she added quickly, not wanting him to think he'd made a mistake and leave. "I was about to eat dinner." She pointed to her box of leftover Chinese food. "Would you like some?"

"Cold Chinese?" He winced.

"I have chicken or salmon. But I wasn't in the mood to cook it. Now that I have company, I'm sure I can figure out how to work the oven."

"Do you have a grill?" He turned, inspecting the front yard.

"It's around back."

His suit jacket was off, hooked on a finger and slung over his shoulder. He tossed it onto the chair before he rolled up the sleeves of his white shirt, uncovering bronzed forearms with hairs bleached by the sun. Those beautiful hands loosened his tie and unbuttoned the top button of his shirt. She swallowed hard as if watching an erotic striptease. She silently begged him to release more buttons and give her another glimpse of his broad chest and flat stomach.

"I'll start the grill," he said.

She snapped her gaze from his chest to his eyes.

"Why don't you get the salmon ready?" A little smirk crossed his lips, advising Sam she'd been caught staring.

A flush burned her cheeks. "Fine." She pushed herself up off the chair and scurried into the safety of the kitchen.

She didn't know the first thing about cooking. In New York, they usually brought something in from the local Chinese restaurant or Italian trattoria. When she bought the salmon at the grocery store, she'd intended to put it in the oven as is. How in the world did one get salmon ready? Wouldn't they just throw it on the grill? She removed the fish from its paper, washed it off, and placed it on a dish. Then she stood there looking at it.

"How's it coming?" asked Michael, entering through the squeaky screen door and dropping his suit jacket in the living room before joining Sam at the kitchen counter.

"What else am I supposed to do with it?"

At least her question brought a chuckle. "Do you have aluminum foil, a lemon, some butter?"

She found what he requested and handed the items to him. Without comment, he did the rest. While he cooked on the grill, she set the table, made a salad, and splashed more wine in their glasses. A few fresh flowers in a vase acted as the centerpiece, and the warm colors of the cloth placemats and napkins she found in a drawer made the dining room table look homey and inviting.

In less than fifteen minutes, they were sitting down to their feast, and she felt infinitely better than she had an hour ago. And all because of the man sitting across from her. His easy smile and aqua eyes made it difficult to stop staring, but she made a concerted effort to act normal and eat the wonderful fish he had prepared.

"So how was your day, dear?" Michael asked.

Sam laughed at the cliché. "It was good. I went to the coffee shop, read the newspaper, went grocery shopping, worked on an agreement, and went to the beach. It was actually a perfect day." With the exception of Michael not being at his office at the appointed time.

"And yours?" She lifted her fork to her mouth and savored the morsel it held.

"Busy. At the courthouse all morning. Then a lunch meeting with the mayor and town council about some pending regulations relating to the cost of beach badges. Then office appointments all afternoon until I was called out at four."

In her attempt to avoid his eyes, she focused on his hands. Beautiful, long fingers cradled his wine glass, and she wondered what those hands would feel like moving over smooth skin. A thrill rushed from her head to the pit of her stomach at the thought.

"Do you like the life of a small-town lawyer?" Her focus moved from his hands to his lips, and she felt herself biting hers.

"It's different. More laid back than working in the city. More people oriented. I like that. But it's also more political. In order to get business, I have to be out and about, meeting government officials, business owners, police. I guess when it comes right down to it, I like that as well. I've been thinking of running for town council next November, but I'm not sure if I want to make the commitment."

"Sounds like you're planning to stay."

She watched him watch her, before his gaze slid down to focus on her mouth. A slow burn traveled through already heated blood, and she licked her lower lip, secretly wishing it was his tongue taking that path. His eyes refocused on hers, and she swirled into their depths, so serious, so solemn. She begged herself to break the connection, to stop the ember from sparking. Her hand obeyed, and she lifted her glass and took a sip.

"I don't know what my plans are." His voice was husky, raw, and very, very sexy. Was he responding to her last statement or some unspoken, subconscious plea?

"Is there someone special here helping with your decision?" She inwardly cringed at this personal—even nosy—question, but she had to know before further considering her vague plan.

"No." He arched an eyebrow. "No one special." His grin played at the corners of his mouth as his eyes held her captive in a much more serious connection. "Not yet." His chair echoed against the floor, bringing her back to reality, back to her senses. "I'll help you clean up."

He carried his plate into the kitchen, and she followed, accidentally brushing against his arm as she put her plate in the sink. The crackle of electricity between them should have been audible. When she turned, he stood within inches. Her gaze moved from his lips to his eyes, those gorgeous blue-green eyes, those Caribbean Sea eyes. Sensual fingers touched her cheek, and she quaked under that simple gesture as he slid his palm behind her head and pulled her toward him, his lips close to hers. In the second it took for him to lower his head, a flash of desire coiled through her with the intensity of a lightning strike. His mouth met hers, and an electric current swirled and enveloped her.

Desire hummed through her body, pulsing to all extremities. In three small steps, he backed her against the refrigerator, hungrily sliding his tongue inside her mouth, giving Sam what she'd yearned for all evening. Hot passion scorched her from the inside out, her urgency shocking. Sliding hyper-sensitive arms around Michael's neck, she leaned in closer, pressing female to male; softness to hardness. His kiss was like a drug, sending euphoria through her bloodstream, addicting her with its power.

Strong arms braced against the refrigerator door as he pushed back, giving her some space—space she didn't want—but still jailing her with his body.

"I didn't mean to come on so strong. You just do something to me."

Trailing fingers caressed temple, cheek, and jaw, flitting to the delicate skin of her neck, making it next to impossible to respond. His eyes penetrated hers, searching.

"I'm glad," she rasped, giving him permission to continue.

His intense gaze looked deep into her very soul. She lowered her lids, trying to hide unwanted feelings. He kissed them fleetingly. "You have beautiful eyes," he whispered.

She looked back into his, lust skimming their surface, and all vulnerability faded. She lifted her lips toward his, and he captured her mouth again, teasing it open with his velvet tongue, hot and insistent, driving her crazy. Hungrily sliding from her swollen lips, he licked a delicate earlobe, eliciting a tremulous sigh of pure pleasure. His tongue traveled to her neck, and she stretched it out, swan-like, inviting him to do more. And he obliged. His musky scent intoxicated. His liquid movements excited every nerve in her body.

His warm palm slid under her top, spreading tingles and fire up her torso, before stroking her breast. Unintelligible words spilled out in gasps as she spun into a whirlpool of erotic sensation. Before she knew it, her top had miraculously disappeared, and he inched her bra strap down over her shoulder as she shamelessly arched her back, begging for more contact. Shock waves tore through her system as he brushed his thumb over her hardened peak before fastening his mouth where his fingers had been.

Her head swam. Her body sizzled.

A ringing cell phone in the distance broke through the haze, and she surfaced, reality setting in. *What am I doing?*

"Stop. Please stop," she rasped, pushing his head away.

"What's wrong?" He looked dazed, confused.

"I can't do this. Not here. Not now."

"We can go to your bedroom," he reasoned, not understanding her plea.

She exhaled, a combination of frustration and regret. "No, I don't mean it's the wrong place. I mean… I don't know what I mean. I have to think this through. I need some time."

She sounded irrational. Here she was in the throes of pleasure with the most gorgeous man on earth, following her plan to have a fling. And she stopped the action.

"I'm sorry, Michael. I truly am." She shook her head. "I…" She wanted to say she needed to make sure she was doing this for the right reason. But that sounded like she expected a relationship. "I can't." She hung her head.

He cupped her cheek in his hand, then tilted her chin up, forcing her to look at him. "It's okay. I understand. You're going through a lot right now. I didn't mean to rush you." He breathed in. "You're just so damn sexy."

She melted with his words. If she hadn't made such a scene, she would have leaned back into him and given him the kiss of a lifetime. He made her feel so desired. Yet the gentleman in him offered kindness and understanding. She wanted to cry.

Sam closed her eyes. "Thank you. You can't know how good you are for me."

He stepped away and handed her the top he had deftly removed. She shrugged into it and smoothed her hair.

"Thanks for dinner." He flashed her an awkward

smile, then headed to the living room and picked up his suit jacket. "I think I better go."

She bit her lip to ward off stray emotions. "Yes."

After the door closed behind him, Sam slunk back to the kitchen to wash the dishes. But every time she looked at the refrigerator, her heart pounded and her breath caught in her throat. She pictured herself pinned against the door, Michael's mouth devouring hers before moving to her neck, her breast. Flames flicked within and burned her skin with the memory. She ached for him. Now. Then. But something had stopped her. Made her put an end to the ecstasy.

Why couldn't she be like Nicki? Do something without thought, for the pure fun of it. No strings. No commitment. Just sex.

Sam pressed her lips together and hung her head, her soapy hands still dangling in the sink. A tear slid down her cheek with the realization that she couldn't, because she already felt something for Michael.

God, she hoped it was just lust.

****

The next day mimicked the day before, only this time she didn't spend an hour figuring out what to wear to her lawyer's office. Shorts and a tank top would suffice for this meeting.

"Hello, Sam." Eric cordially shook her hand. "Here's your Complaint. Why don't you read it in the conference room, and if it's okay, sign it. I'll send it out tomorrow."

As he led her through the hall, she glanced toward Michael's office. It was dark. Good. He wasn't here. Now she wouldn't have to make polite small talk with him in front of Eric, while dying inside about her decision last night. The swirl in the pit of her stomach settled, yet she felt oddly disappointed.

"It will only take me a few minutes to review this. I'll be out of here in no time. I don't want to hold you up. I'm sure you'd like to go home," she babbled, keeping her voice light and her body language upbeat. She didn't need Michael hearing about how glum she looked.

She sat at the head of the conference table, the quiet room illuminated by cylindrical fluorescent bulbs. Alone. Before her sat the Complaint, a few pages of legal jargon printed neatly on pleading paper, double spaced, so easy to read. But she couldn't get past the caption: "Samantha Winslow, Plaintiff versus Thomas Burton, Defendant." She was here to begin the process of ending her marriage with the stroke of a pen.

This happened to other people. Not her. She should have still been feeling the bliss of the love and commitment they'd promised each other on their wedding day.

But she didn't. He didn't.

Now she was sitting in a strange law office reading a Complaint for adultery and extreme cruelty against the man she had vowed to love and honor forever, and who had made that same promise to her. When had those promises become void? When did their love fade away, dissipated by career goals, opposing views on free time, and lack of communication?

Sam took a deep breath, then moved her pen over the signature line.

That was it.

She rose and crossed the hall to Eric's office. "Here you go." She practically sang the words as she pasted a smile on her face. *Let's not overdo it, Sam. Eric might tell Michael you're manic depressive.*

He looked up from his desk and gave her a sympathetic nod. "Your husband should have this by the weekend."

"Fine." She took a shallow breath and backed into the hallway. "Call me if you need anything more."

"After he's served and responds, we should send him a settlement proposal. I'll let you know when we hear from him."

A knot formed in her stomach, and the air felt thick and stifling, threatening to suffocate her if she didn't escape immediately. She turned quickly and said over her shoulder, "I'll talk to you then. Bye."

She pushed on the door, which flew out and banged on its hinges. "Sorry," she called as she propelled herself out and onto the sidewalk. At first she walked quickly, but her steps became a jog and then a run. She headed to her haven, the beach, gulping in big breaths of air as she went. By the time she reached the boardwalk, she was gasping and her side ached.

Forcing herself to walk, Sam tossed her sandals under the wooden steps descending to the beach where she headed north, slanting toward the ocean. The sea breeze blew life into her, along with serenity, and she breathed in its salty tang, allowing the familiar scent to soothe her. By the time her toes felt the cold fingers of the tide washing over them, she had taken back control.

Shouts and laughter from a nearby volleyball game entered her consciousness, and she gazed over to the group of young men with their admiring cheerleaders in tow. The court was never empty. During the day, teens battled it out, sometimes boys, sometimes girls, sometimes both. But the evening belonged to the men. Her eyes moved over the group and like magnets settled on Michael, who was serving the ball for his team.

"Go, Michael," a young woman in a string bikini yelled from the sidelines, standing with three other clones. They could have been models with their perfect bodies and long straight hair.

Sam kept walking, head down, hoping not to catch Michael's eye. She strolled in the surf for at least a half hour before turning around and heading back. Questions bombarded her from every angle. What would it be like to be a single woman again, living in Manhattan? Although she had only been married for three short years, she and Tom had been a couple since she graduated from law school. She couldn't quite remember her carefree, independent days of going to happy hour or dancing the night away. Would she ever be able to do that again? After working a twelve-hour day, she doubted she'd have the energy to even think about it.

She was doomed to be alone with nothing but her career and a handful of friends. Even so, she had done the right thing, despite the fact she might turn into a lonely old spinster.

Dwelling on her future took the better part of an hour. Finally tired of her own musings, she thought about stopping by the volleyball court to say hello to Michael. She could be a groupie too. Maybe she'd meet some new people, have a gang of newfound friends. She could certainly use the distraction.

But when she arrived back, the court was empty, eerily silent. Only footprints in the sand remained, along with a lone volleyball, which someone had left behind. Sam picked it up and tossed it over the net.

"You need more than one player if you want the ball returned." A voice behind her sent a tremble through her system.

She turned, and the melancholy that surrounded her dissipated with his smile.

"Michael. You're still here."

"I forgot my ball."

Sam ducked under the net and picked it up. She held it out to him, forcing him to come closer. Her heart beat wildly, and she tried desperately to come up with something to say, but her tongue tied.

"Michael! Are you coming?" An impatient cry echoed from the boardwalk.

Both Michael and Sam looked up. It was one of the models, the one with the red bikini. Sam's hope for some time and conversation with Michael evaporated like the mist from a crashing wave.

"I'll meet you there," he called.

"Okay." She pouted. "But hurry. We're all starving."

Michael turned back to Sam. "Would you like to come and get something to eat with us? We're going to Bill's Ale House."

What had seemed like a wonderful plan during her solitary walk on the beach, now seemed awful. She didn't want to make idle chitchat with rowdy strangers, vying for attention, having to scream above the other voices to be heard. Besides, she wasn't in the mood to compete with the clones.

"Thanks. But I don't think I'd be very good company tonight."

"Did you sign the Complaint?"

137

"Yes, but…" She was about to say that wasn't the reason for her glumness. She shook her head. "Yes. I signed the Complaint."

"Would you like to talk?" His empathetic voice curled around her and warmed her heart.

Not about that. "No, thanks." She blinked and looked back up toward the boardwalk. "Your friends are waiting for you. You should go."

Her walls inched up. She was pushing him away, not permitting him to see her vulnerable side.

"If you change your mind, I'll be at Bill's."

"Thanks, but I won't." She watched his back as he headed toward his friends.

Sam kicked at the sand, then smoothed it, wondering if she was stepping on Michael's footprints, yearning to take back the words that made him leave. He had offered to stay and talk, but she had stubbornly refused his proposal, even though she'd wanted to spend time with him more than anything. Only she didn't want to talk about the demise of her marriage, or her feelings about filing for divorce. She wanted to talk about his day. About how many points he'd scored in the game, or what his plans were for the weekend. Michael had offered consolation. She needed distraction. And maybe even excitement, which she felt every time she laid eyes on him.

She longed to forget about her divorce when with him. The two were mutually exclusive. Michael made her feel alive, confident, sexy. Yet she felt guilty over her attraction toward him.

Last night she had melted like liquid gold in his arms, desire washing over her with every touch of his lips, his hands, his tongue. Her blood pulsed merely thinking about his body pressing into hers, the evidence of his lust straining against the clothes she had ached to rip off. And she had been halfway there, her shirt discarded in a heap on the floor as his hands and tongue awakened every nerve, every synapse, along their route. She wanted him. And he wanted her.

But some misguided sense of moral behavior had made her stop. It wasn't because she was married. That was in name only. Was it because of the possibility that Michael dated around and she didn't want to be one of many? That shouldn't bother her. She was leaving in a month and a half anyway. Hadn't she previously attempted to convince herself that a fling was what she needed to move on? And Michael was the perfect candidate. The only candidate.

She knew the answer. She just didn't want to believe it.

She was afraid of getting hurt.

Again.

She was afraid she could care about Michael. That her fling to get over the remnants of her failed marriage could turn into a romance that would do more damage to her than good.

Sam walked toward her house. She needed a friend to talk to. These conversations with herself were getting her nowhere. Thankfully, her Sworn Sisters were only a phone call away.

Chapter Twelve

The ringtone on Sam's phone drifted out onto the porch. She ducked through the screen door and located her cell.

"Hey, Sam. It's me." The familiar voice tangled her stomach and chilled her skin.

"Tom." She dropped into the living room armchair before taking a breath. "How are you?" Not that she cared, but she didn't know what else to say.

"Not good." His voice sounded strained, clipped. "I got your Complaint for Divorce yesterday."

"Oh. My lawyer said you would probably have it by the weekend."

"What's the rush, Sam? I thought we would be apart during the summer. See how things went. I didn't expect you to file for divorce."

Anger bubbled up inside, pressing on her chest like heartburn. "Are you kidding?" Her voice escalated. "I was supposed to sit back in New York while you flew off to have an affair for the summer, and you thought I would then want to discuss how it went in September? You must be joking."

"I know you're hurt, Sam, and I'm sorry. But our marriage wasn't working. I thought if we gave ourselves time apart, we could then come back and either try to fix it or decide jointly to move on. I didn't think you were going to make this decision unilaterally."

She controlled her voice by taking a deep breath. "I didn't make a unilateral decision. You did when you moved to San Diego for the summer with Sherry. I had nothing to do with that decision. You didn't ask me. You didn't discuss it with me. You didn't even give me a chance to respond. You packed your bags and left. And I might add, you never once picked up the phone over the last two months to call and see how I was doing."

"I did, Sam. Or I tried. But every time I dialed your cell number, I hung up. I didn't know what to say."

"If you think that's a good excuse, you're wrong." Fury burned deep in the pit of her stomach.

"I can tell you're still angry. And I understand. But Sam, please don't be hasty." His smooth, calm words rolled like silk off his tongue. He had called upon his most convincing—or was it manipulating?—manner. "Why don't you withdraw your Complaint? I'm coming back at the end of August. Let's sit down and talk. Maybe go to marriage counseling."

"So now you want to talk?" She bit back the sarcasm, but no matter how hard she tried to sound as cool and smooth as he did, she couldn't pull it off. "You didn't want to talk when you were packing your bags to run off to California. Instead, you slammed me with your news. I was in shock. As far as I was concerned, your defection came out of left field. I had no answers. I didn't even know what the questions were." Raw emotions erupted and flooded her surface, refusing to be tamped back down. "I never felt so out of control in my life. You did that to me. And I hate you for it." There. She said it. And she felt lighter, freer.

"Sam, I'm sorry. How about if I fly home next weekend? We can go away for a few days. We'll talk. I know we can fix this. Let's try." He was pleading now. How amusing. He no longer felt above it all. That he could act with impunity and nothing would touch him. That he could make it all better in the space of a few persuasive words.

"What happened? Did your affair with Sherry fizzle out?"

"No...I don't know. I keep thinking about you. I miss you."

"You know what, Tom? I don't believe you. But it doesn't matter. I will not open myself up to you again. You hurt me. Really bad. And I can't forgive or forget. Not now. Maybe someday. But not now."

"Can't you at least hold up on the divorce? Maybe in a month or two you'll feel differently. Maybe you need some time. What are you doing in Crescent Beach anyway?"

"How do you know where I am?"

"Your secretary told me, after I left several unanswered messages for you at work."

Sam had told Carol not to give her any messages from Tom. Apparently, she should have gone further and instructed her not to share information about her whereabouts.

"I took a leave of absence. I needed to get away."

"That's not like you."

She sighed. He just didn't get it. He didn't understand how much damage he had done. "No. It's not." There was no use in explaining it.

"Sam, please reconsider. Don't throw it all away so fast."

She didn't respond. She had already said it all.

"Would you at least think about withdrawing the Complaint for now? Give it a few months? You could always refile."

"Goodbye, Tom." She didn't wait for him to reply before she hung up.

She sat in the armchair unable to move. She should feel something. Sorrow, pain, happiness, smug pleasure, relief, something. But even though she reached deep down within herself to pull an emotion out, there was nothing. The still air of the house blanketed her in a heat that left her lethargic, her energy gone, dissipated by the few but intense words spoken to the man she'd only thought she knew.

It would take all of her energy to focus on the future, the new life she would carve out for herself, leaving the hurt from the past behind. Leaving Tom behind.

The haze in her brain swirled and dissipated, making it clearer, brighter. Her lips quirked up into a smile as she pushed against the arms of the chair and propelled herself to her feet. *I need a change of scenery. It's time to go to the beach.*

****

"Morning, Flo. Has Sam been here yet?" Michael straddled a stool at the counter.

The haggard waitress glanced at the clock on the wall. "It's only eight thirty. She doesn't come in till nine, nine thirty. Sometimes not at all. Coffee?"

He nodded, and she hastily filled a heavy-duty ceramic mug and set it with a thump before him.

On this particular Monday morning, Melanie's Coffee Shop looked like a different place. An informal line of vacationers waiting for a table had formed out front, there being no room to wait inside. With the first week of July came families with children who were now out of school. The atmosphere screamed more than hummed, and it was hard not to notice the difference a week could make.

For the next fifteen minutes, Michael alternately sipped his coffee, looked at his watch, and studied the door, hoping Sam wouldn't disappoint him today.

He hadn't seen her since Wednesday night on the volleyball court. The night she had signed the Complaint for Divorce. He'd noticed the sadness in her eyes, the sadness that was missing when she had met with him to discuss her divorce. That day she'd been so matter-of-fact. As if she didn't care. But he had caught her off guard Wednesday night. No time to put on her mask and pretend her marriage meant nothing to her. He had contemplated wrapping her in his arms and hugging away the pain, the pain he knew so well.

Instead he left her standing in the middle of the volleyball court, alone and melancholy, and it had eaten a hole in his gut.

He hadn't wanted to leave. But he didn't want to push, either. He had pushed her Tuesday night and then felt like a heel. Despite his lapse in judgment, every time he replayed their kitchen scene, his blood heated and his heart raced. He'd wanted her, and if she hadn't stopped him, he probably would have taken her right there on the kitchen floor. She had wanted him too. Her sighs and moans still reverberated in his head. He could feel her hands sliding around his neck, pulling him closer, her sweet, warm mouth opening under his to let him in.

His head swirled, remembering the feel of his palm against her smooth skin as he inched up her torso to her breast. She'd begged him for more with her body, driving him crazy as her nipples hardened under his touch, her hips pressing into his, straining to get closer. He yearned to be back there now, against her refrigerator, against her body.

But she wasn't ready. Not yet.

He glanced back toward the door. No Sam. Calling her wasn't an option. His invitation was meant to seem casual, unplanned. But nothing Michael ever did was unplanned. He was busy working on plan B when she breezed through the door.

Dressed in red shorts and a white tank top, her hair pulled up on the sides, she looked fresh and young as she slid through the crowd and headed for the counter. He waved to get her attention.

"Michael. How are you?" Surprise marked her face as she took the stool next to him.

"Good morning, Sam. I'm great. How's it going with you?" His smile erupted from within.

"Fine." She peered at his clothes questioningly. "You don't look like a lawyer this morning. Is that what you wear to the office when you're not in municipal court prosecuting the innocent?"

He shook his head and chuckled. "They are not so innocent. Including you." Picking up his coffee cup, he nodded to Flo for a refill and a cup for Sam.

A sweet blush rose up on her cheeks as she sat beside him.

Her melancholy mood of the other night on the beach had miraculously vanished, as had the anger and irritation that had governed their first few meetings. She seemed almost jovial, as if the depressing aura of her divorce had lifted and melted away. Her violet eyes were bright and clear, without the hint of a shadow that had so often clouded over them the past few weeks.

It was the perfect time to ask. "How'd you like to go sailing today?"

"Sailing! But today's Monday. Don't you have to work?"

"Nope. No municipal court today. And no appointments. So I took the day off." He hoped his carefree attitude was catchy. "It's eighty degrees, sunny, breezy. A perfect day for a sail. What do you say?"

"Well, I…I usually work for a few hours each day. There's always emails to respond to."

"Couldn't you let them go until tomorrow?" Disappointment welled up inside him as he saw his plan slipping away.

"I suppose I could." Sam's hesitant speech was not a resounding yes. "But I should at least check to see if there's any emergency. I'm also waiting for a decision to be made on an application to unseal the birth certificate for Denise's adopted son, Bobby."

"Okay." Hope returned. Now all he had to do was get her to relax and buy into his playdate. "Why don't we order breakfast, then you can go home to check your email. But if there's a needy client, pretend you didn't notice." He smiled and winked at her, making her part of his conspiracy.

They ordered eggs and drank coffee, talking like old friends about the practice of law, the summer crowds at the beach, and their favorite restaurants—in the city and out. Michael felt like a kid playing hooky, so decadent was it to spend more than fifteen minutes eating breakfast and talking to a dynamic, intelligent, beautiful woman who shared his love of the law.

"You must have had a great weekend," he commented, hoping for some insight into her lighthearted mood.

"I did. You remember Nicki Reading from high school, don't you?"

He nodded, as a twinge of regret spiraled through him. They'd been good friends back then. He kept his eyes on his toast as he buttered a slice.

"She visited, and we hung out together. Walked on the boardwalk, went out to dinner."

"How is she?" His voice caught in his throat as he remembered how they'd shared their painful stories while giving each other a shoulder to lean on. And a little more.

"Good on the surface. She's also going through a tough time due to a break-up. She pretends otherwise, but I could tell."

"That's too bad. She was an amazing friend to me senior year." He left it at that. No good ever came from reliving the past. At least not his past. "Where is she working?"

"At Snow Leopard Music in Philadelphia. Marketing and public relations. Moving up the ranks."

"It's nice that she's close enough to visit."

"She's been a godsend during my little sabbatical. Denise Nelson, Rossini back in high school, and Alyssa Banks too. They've all been so supportive, coming to visit for a weekend, here and there. A little getaway for them. And I get to have my Sworn Sisters around. Unfortunately, they've had to deal with my…" She stopped and smiled, a brilliant, beautiful smile which confirmed she had the ability to tease herself. "I've been such a broken record. And a bore."

"They've been your friends forever, Sam. I'm sure they don't mind." She would never bore him.

Michael watched her long, elegant fingers fish a packet of grape jelly out of its dispenser. As she peeled back the foil, his mind wandered to visions of what else those graceful fingers could be doing.

She glanced over at him, her eyebrow arched, as if questioning his trance-like stare. With effort, he brought himself back to the conversation. "I'm sorry, did you say something?"

"I was saying that I've been analyzing my friends to try to figure out what they did to achieve satisfaction in their lives. But everyone's vision of happiness is different. What's right for Denise or Nicki or Alyssa isn't necessarily right for me. I need to map out a new route for myself that will make me happy."

Her casual analysis held no sarcasm or even self-pity. She seemed more accepting of her fate after having viewed it through the lives of her friends.

"Sounds like you've had your own personal therapists visiting. You seem infinitely happier than when I first saw you this summer."

She laughed, grabbing a piece of toast and smearing it with jelly. "Oh. Please don't bring that up. I'm so embarrassed."

She nibbled at the bread, and a bit of jelly clung to her top lip. Her tongue slowly ran a path across it, putting him in a stupor as he focused on those full, soft lips. His tongue had been in that very spot a few nights ago, a night not soon forgotten. His blood pressure rose every time he thought about her in his arms. He ached to be back there, tasting passionate lips, gazing into jewel-colored eyes, feeling satin skin melting like hot liquid beneath his touch. He had trouble taking a breath. How had he not noticed her in high school?

"Let's get going." His voice sounded husky and rushed, but he wanted her alone, on his boat. As soon as possible.

"I'll run home to do what I have to do. Besides a bathing suit, what else should I bring?"

"A towel, a pair of shorts, and a sweatshirt in case it gets breezy later. I'll have everything else we need. How about I pick you up at noon?" Sooner would have been better, but she made it clear she needed some time to work.

"I'll meet you at your boat at noon."

He grinned. "You're being overly cautious, aren't you?"

"One of us has to be sensible. What if we get on each other's nerves after a few hours? At least after we dock, I could ride off into the sunset without having to make an excuse."

He couldn't help but laugh. She was refreshingly honest and to the point. Even more so, he loved the ease of their conversation and the familiarity they shared, even though they'd been mere acquaintances in high school. Her ability to laugh at herself and acknowledge her problems chipped away at his hardened heart.

Still, he wasn't looking for a soul mate. Just the opposite. He had convinced himself that if he spread himself thin, dating different women along the way, he could avoid commitment. If he'd learned anything from the past, it was that he couldn't count on others to be there for him. His parents, each in their own way, had proven that, as had Hannah. He now knew to refrain from getting too close. He wasn't about to get hurt again. That was his game plan, and he intended to stick with it.

"Okay. I'll meet you there. Do you know where the Crescent Beach Marina is?" When she nodded, he continued. "My boat's in slip forty-two."

She slid off her stool, gave him a sailor's salute, and glided toward the door.

His gaze moved up her long, shapely legs, and his mouth went dry when they settled on her firm, round butt.

At least one of them was thinking straight.

Chapter Thirteen

Michael noticed the top of her lime-green bikini before her gorgeous smile. A pair of hip-hugging white shorts covered the bottom of Sam's bathing suit, but the low-rise waist showed him plenty of midriff. Enough to make his fingers twitch. He swallowed and sent up a quick prayer. "Please don't let me do anything to piss her off today."

"Hey, sailor!" she called down the dock. "Could you use a deck hand?"

Could he ever. "Glad you made it. Welcome aboard."

He straddled the side of the boat and held out his hand. Her fingers sent jolts of lightning up his arm and down his spine, and he bit the inside of his lip to focus attention on something other than her body. No use. Long tan legs jumped from the dock over the life lines and onto the boat deck, putting her chest within inches of his. His eyes wandered over her with lust-filled thoughts. He shook his head to dispel the images. Now was not the time or the place.

Instead he busied himself unwrapping the sail cover—a much more productive task, and less likely to get him in trouble. He intended to respect Sam's feelings about a sexual relationship, no matter how hard it became. She needed to make the decision. But that wouldn't stop him from trying to change her mind.

"How can I help?" she asked.

"Why don't you bring up the cushions from downstairs to cover the benches?" His goal was to get through the preparations quickly so they could set sail and relax. "Then you can unpack the picnic basket in the galley."

"This is a beautiful boat," she called from below as she placed the food and drinks in the refrigerator. "What kind is it?"

"A Catalina cruiser." He was very proud of his baby.

"It looks brand new."

"New for me but she's a few years old. In great shape though." An expensive luxury meant to repair the hole in his heart.

"I noticed you named her 'Emotional Rescue.' Why?"

He should have known Sam would pick up on that. And he should have had a ready answer. "Uh...I like that Rolling Stones song?" *What a stupid response.*

"I thought people named boats for more meaningful reasons." Her eyes sought his as she came back on deck.

"They do." And he had one hell of a reason. He just wasn't ready to reveal it.

Her brows shot up, but thankfully she let the subject drop.

For the past ten months he had sheltered himself by working hard, playing hard, and dating casually. The women he met during the summer were here to have a good time, living in seasonal rentals and commuting to their jobs by day. He met most of them on the volleyball court, twenty-something college grads who made it easy to connect. He could travel in crowds or not, depending on his mood.

The other seasons had proved sedate. A great time to catch up on sleep, reading, and the law. The stillness and ennui of this past winter allowed him to work through his recent anger, feelings of inadequacy, and loss of connection. He had redefined his expectations of others. In fact, he decided it was best not to have any. Instead, he changed his priorities, spent time on simple pleasures, and smiled more.

Unfortunately, Sam had shown up, inadvertently causing him to question his philosophy. Yet she was the last one who should make him think twice. She'd recently filed for divorce and probably didn't even know whether she'd stick to her guns if her husband appeared on her doorstep.

This was not the ideal time to meet up again with Samantha Winslow.

He released the lines attached to the dock, put the boat in gear, and pushed the throttle. The engine hummed as he steered out of his slip, through the inlet, and toward the ocean. "The conditions are perfect today," he called over his shoulder from his place at the wheel.

The inlet wasn't crowded since it was already noon. The commercial and party boats had left hours earlier, so it took only ten minutes to pass through the narrow opening cradled by rocks, signaling entry into the ocean. Michael pulled on the halyard to raise the main sail. The white sheet rose up the mast, thundering and billowing in the wind until it stretched to its potential. He then secured the line, set the jib, and cut the engine.

A familiar euphoric release spread through his body as the sea breeze and sunshine surrounded him. This was life—pure and simple—to be enjoyed so much more because of the hours he put into his career.

"Here, Sam. Why don't you try your hand at steering? I'll get us something to drink." The boat was heading south, and there was nothing but smooth sailing ahead.

"I don't know how to control this thing," she protested, a hint of fear in her eyes.

"See that fishing trawler out there?" He pointed. "Head in that direction. It's like driving a car. Only easier. There's no one near us, so you can't mess up. I'll show you."

Standing behind her as she took the wheel, he coached her for a few minutes. The scent from her hair, flowery and feminine, swirled around him in the breeze. Her tawny shoulders gleamed in the sun from tanning lotion, and the string from the top of her bikini hung down her back, into the hollow of her spine. He ached to run his finger down that path. Yearned to lean over and trail kisses on her neck. Craved to slide his hands over the smooth curve of her hips. Closing his eyes, he inhaled.

"How am I doing?" Sam's words broke the spell she had unwittingly cast over him.

"You're doing fine. See how easy?"

She turned her face to him and smiled—a glorious, bright smile that turned his insides upside down. If he had any hope of playing this cool, he needed some distance.

"I'll get the wine."

He backed away from her, then stepped down into

the galley. Having located the Chardonnay, he uncorked the bottle and grabbed two glasses.

"You can let the wheel go." He flipped a switch when he came back up on deck, then sat on one side of the helm. "I turned on the autopilot."

He watched her as she breathed in the salty sea air and lay on the bench opposite him, raising her face to the sun.

"This is the life," she purred, stretching her body like a cat, then placing her head on a rolled-up towel as she closed her eyes and smiled.

Michael stopped mid-pour, gazing at the slinky woman lying so near, green bikini covering the essential parts but awarding him an eyeful of soft, bronzed skin extending over very long limbs and a curvy torso.

She reached out a graceful hand and said in a way-too-sexy voice, "Is that for me?"

He looked down to see he had poured half a glass of wine before going into a coma. "Yes." His voice sounded frog-like, and he hurriedly finished pouring her wine and handed her the glass.

His resolve was dissipating.

****

Sam sipped her wine as she watched Michael through lidded eyes—the god of light. His skin was the color of caramel, and his chestnut hair was feathered with blond highlights streaked by the sun. She hadn't been able to stop gawking at his muscled biceps as he unfurled the sails, pulled the ropes, and worked the winches. A masterpiece in motion. And now, as he sat in repose leaning against the rail, one leg up on the bench contemplating the sea, he could have been on the cover of *Yachting News.*

"So Michael. You're still a real mystery man. I can understand your wanting to get away from your father all those years ago, but I still don't understand this more recent move from New York City. It can't only be about the ambivalent residents and crowded streets."

He turned to look at her, the sun tinting his aqua eyes a lighter shade of blue. A smile curved his lips. "This is the place to be." He answered with a non-answer.

So she got more specific. "Why did you move out of the city? Why here? Why did you name your boat 'Emotional Rescue'? Which volleyball groupie is your favorite?" She hadn't meant to add this last question, but it lay out there now like a neon sign.

He laughed, and his smile competed with the sun. "Is that all you want to know?"

"For starters." She'd get to the rest later.

"I told you a little about why I left New York. But you're right. There's more." A shadow crossed his face and dulled his eyes. He took in a breath as if to fortify himself before going on. "I was living with a woman named Hannah. She was an assistant curator at the Metropolitan Museum of Art. The love of my life. At the time." He paused, and a bittersweet smile crossed his lips, then disappeared. "One day, I forgot I had a fundraising dinner after work, so I went home at lunch to pick up a clean shirt and different tie to change into at the end of the day. I found Hannah in bed with another man."

Sam sat up, the shock of what he'd shared propelling her forward. "Oh, Michael. I'm so sorry." She didn't know what else to say.

The pain surfaced on his face before he covered it up with a tight smile and a shrug. "That was a year ago. A lifetime ago. I moved out of our apartment and into a hotel. But I needed to get away from the city. It was a constant reminder of her, of everything we did together. So two months later, I gave my law firm notice I was leaving and bought a house down here."

She longed to reach out to him, lay her hand on top of his, an inadequate gesture of consolation. But he was across the deck, unreachable.

"Did she ever explain why?"

"Sure. She blamed it on me." Defeat flashed over his face. "She said I wasn't around enough. That I wasn't willing to commit to our relationship. I was always working. She wanted a true partner in life." He gazed out over the ocean, his jaw tensing with the acknowledgment. "You know the story."

Unfortunately she did. And his words cut into her as if Tom had been sitting next to her, forcing her to relive her sins. She battled back to the present and posed the logical question. "So are we two workaholics doomed to be alone in life because our priorities are in the wrong order?"

He turned back to her, and the hint of a grin brushed over his lips. "I don't know about you, but I'm working on that. That's why I moved here. A better quality of life. Slower pace. It gives me time to enjoy the little things. I smile more. I'm happier."

"Have you talked to Hannah since you left the city? Did you ever try to work it out?" She didn't know whether she asked these questions because she was curious about Michael and Hannah or because she questioned her own decision.

"Hannah wanted to get back together. She apologized daily. She finally took some of the blame and said her little affair didn't mean anything. She still loved me. But I couldn't get past it. I knew I would never be able to trust her again."

"Do you still love her?" Her voice cracked.

"No. It's gone."

The sadness in his voice made her want to cry. For him. For her. For lost love. She bit her lip and looked out toward the ocean, trying desperately to keep a tear from spilling down her face.

Michael moved across the deck and sat next to her, slipping his arm around her shoulders. "I'm sorry," he whispered against her ear. "I was only answering your questions. I didn't mean to make you think about your circumstances."

She turned her face away so he couldn't see the moisture in her eyes. She didn't want him to get the wrong impression that she wanted Tom back. But words to describe her emotions deserted her. After a few seconds, she tried for clarity. "Hearing your story brings it all back. My mistakes. My focus on career. My failure."

"It's good to let it out. You've been trying to bury your feelings so no one can see the pain. When you came to see me in my office that day to discuss divorce, you gave the impression you didn't care about your marriage. There was no emotion. It wasn't until I ran into you at the beach the other night that I saw a glimmer of the grief you've been hiding so well."

Sam breathed in, hoping to push it back down. She nodded. "That was a tough night. I had signed the Complaint, and the finality of it all hit me. My marriage, which I thought would last for the rest of my life, was over."

"Are you sure it's over?" His piercing gaze looked for the answer in her eyes.

"Yes. Tom called the other day. He suggested that he come home and try to work things out, but I can't. I don't want to. He hurt me too badly to forgive and forget."

"That's the way I felt. But the good thing is, you will get over it. And move on. It takes time." He placed his hand over hers on the bench between them.

"Have you moved on?" She searched his eyes for the truth.

"Of course. Can't you tell?" He grinned.

"Absolutely. You have your pick of the twenty-something volleyball fans. It must be difficult to choose—they're all gorgeous."

His grin faded. "No! That's not what I meant. I meant—"

"What?" She poked him playfully in the ribs.

"I meant that I'm not stuck on past mistakes anymore. I'm free. Maybe I'm even open to starting another relationship. If I find the right woman." A frown furrowed his brow as if he'd stumbled upon the elusive insight he'd been seeking. Or perhaps avoiding.

They sat together in silence for a moment, as they sipped wine and enjoyed the calmness of the day.

"What about you?" asked Michael, breaking the silence. "Why do you work so hard?"

"I want to become a partner." The words, said so often, tumbled out as if by rote.

"That's not the real reason. One thing I've learned is that unless you delve deep into the reasons why you put your career first, you'll never be able to change your ways. Why is becoming a partner your goal in life?"

She thought for a minute. "I suppose it's the usual—money, prestige, power."

He frowned. "Why do you care about those things? You can make enough money to live comfortably without working twelve-hour days, six days a week. Prestige means you want to impress someone. Who? And power is self-gratifying. Or do you need to feel an enormous amount of control over others?"

She glanced at him to see if this last question was meant to be a joke, but he wasn't smiling. She looked down at the deck, avoiding the intensity of his eyes. Precluding him from reading hers. She couldn't unravel herself here and now.

His warm hand covered hers again. Strange, wonderful sensations moved up her arm and down her body.

"I'm not trying to make you uncomfortable, Sam. You don't have to answer my questions. The answers are none of my business. But you have to deal with them honestly before you can move on. Your marriage broke up because of your sole focus on your job. If you want to avoid a similar disaster in the future, you're going to have to come to terms with what you truly want." He ran his hand through his tousled hair and sighed. "I don't mean to sermonize. But I went through the same thing you're going through, and I would have gotten through the worst of it much faster if I had faced what drove me sooner."

His concern for her was engraved on his face, and it warmed her heart.

"It's not that I don't want to talk about this. It's just so personal."

She bit her lower lip, considering whether to share what really drove her. She'd already bared most of her soul. Why not the rest? If she had learned anything from this journey, it was to communicate, be more open. Now was as good a time as any to start.

She began tentatively. "You may remember that my father divorced my mother when I was fifteen. I felt like he divorced me as well. I watched my mother struggle every month to pay the bills because he was constantly late with the little support he agreed to pay." She traced a spot on the deck with her toe, avoiding Michael's eyes. "My mother worked hard, but she only had a high school diploma, so her salary wasn't enough. My father owned his own business—a box manufacturing plant. It's not like he had a lot of money, but he could have helped out more, especially once he married a very wealthy woman. Instead, he fought my mom every step of the way until she gave up and took what he offered."

"Did your mother have a lawyer to help her?" Michael's eyes showed clear concern.

"No. She said she couldn't afford one. I think my father convinced her to go along with his settlement proposal by giving her the house, which she wanted to keep for me. Unfortunately, she gave up alimony in exchange for it."

Sam looked past Michael to the ocean, so calm and glassy in the mid-afternoon sun. Yet her insides flip-flopped as if they were sailing on a stormy sea with ten-foot swells. Anytime she thought of her father's selfish nature and what it did to her and her mother, she felt physically ill.

"I remember the day he walked out the door like it was yesterday. Although he was at fault—having had an affair—he was angry that my mother had kicked him out of the house. He thought he should be able to continue his life with my mom and me at home at the same time he was seeing her. He told us we couldn't take care of ourselves and we'd never get anywhere without him." Although his angry tirade had been mostly directed at her mother in the heat of the moment, Sam had felt the stab of rejection and the fear of insecurity seep around her very soul.

"What an ass." Michael's response forced her back to the present.

She couldn't help but think that his father was even worse. She'd never thought about their family similarities in high school. Although she wanted to push the horrible memory of her father from her mind, she continued. "Even though my mother was strong, I felt a huge weight on my shoulders. But I also felt the challenge. I didn't just feel it, I embraced it. I was going to show my father I could succeed without him. I was going to college, then law school, despite his lack of financial help. I was going to become independent and strong. Of course this had two attractions. Proving to my father he was wrong and being able to rub it in his face. But I could also help people like my mother against verbally abusive and controlling husbands like him. I could fight the battle they couldn't. I could be their mouthpiece. Their gladiator."

Sam's chin quivered, but she inched it subtly higher, embracing and validating her purpose. "And I vowed I would always be able to take care of myself. I would never have to rely on a man to make me feel secure."

Silence hung between them like a vacuum. Why had she poured out such a personal story to Michael, a man she was just getting to know? She probably scared any response right out of his mouth. She must sound like a man-hater.

But sharing these intimate details of her life felt incredibly liberating. She hadn't even told her friends most of the gory details. All they knew was that her parents had divorced and she stopped speaking to her father after he married again. The raw facts had been stored safely away. And although she knew, intellectually, it wouldn't change the way people saw her, she was still afraid, at least emotionally, that her past would somehow expose her as flawed. Here she had been given a chance to expose it herself—at a time that seemed right. To someone who may even understand.

Michael broke into her thoughts. "I admire you. You did what you set out to do."

"Almost." A bittersweet smile crossed her lips. "I'm up for partner in September. But I don't know how this little sabbatical is going to affect my chances. Until a few months ago, I was a shoo-in. Now, I don't know."

"Everyone has issues in their lives at one time or another. I'm sure the partners at your firm aren't immune from personal problems."

"True. But I don't know any who needed a mental health break. Or even if they needed it, no one ever took it. I tried so hard to remain on the fast track. I was doing so well too. Until this came along."

He brushed his fingers down her cheek. His tenderness and compassion reached into her heart, and she felt herself falling hard and fast. He had delved deep into her psyche and encouraged her to verbalize her motivations, allowing a sense of freedom to replace the memories chained to her heart.

She turned away from him, gazing at the ocean, needing some distance, some breathing room. Or at least she thought she did. Until he lounged back on the bench and pulled her against him. Slowly, she relaxed her head against his chest, and his strength surrounded her as she closed her eyes, exhausted from her therapy session.

Now all Sam could hear was the rhythmic smack of the waves against the hull. All she could smell was the moist salt air, so fresh and natural. All she could feel was the warm ocean breeze against her skin. And the strength of Michael's arms holding her close. She hungered to stay in this cocoon forever. The pain and anguish, so vibrant moments before, dissipated into thin air, replaced through soothing words and gentle touches. And the tingling of having him so near. Her heart not only thumped against her ribs, but in her throat, pulsating with life, with excitement.

She turned her head against his chest to look up into his face. She could no longer resist seeing those eyes, that mouth, those lips. And as she took in the features that were imprinted in her mind, her heart stopped as he leaned over and covered her mouth with his. The soft kiss became languid, and she parted her lips to welcome him in, tasting the tang of the wine, feeling the spark of his tongue joining with hers.

He eased down the bench, pulling her onto him,

sending shivers down her back as tickling fingers caressed her spine. She flattened her palm against his chest, feeling the smooth hardness of his muscles, reveling in the tiny spasms caused by her wandering hand. The string of her bikini loosened around her neck as deft fingers pulled at the fabric until it was gone, replaced by warm hands, then his awesomely wicked mouth, covering her naked breasts with flickering heat. She straddled his hips and ground her pelvis against him, feeling his passion, hard and pulsing. Delirious with pleasure, she was barely aware that they were not exactly in the privacy of a bedroom. He groaned as she pressed harder, licking the lobe of his ear, his neck, his mouth.

Then he placed his hands around her waist and lifted her off as he sat up and sighed heavily.

"I think I need to sail this boat. The wind's changing direction. We don't want to end up on shore." He picked her top up off the deck and handed it to her. "Do you need help?"

Embarrassment flushed her face. "No, thanks."

She grabbed it and headed into the aft cabin to pull herself together. His abrupt end to their interlude left her off balance. Her head spun. Why did he stop? He clearly wanted her. She saw it in his eyes. Felt his ardor, intense and passionate. And she wanted him too. A flicker of doubt surfaced.

She tied her top back on, smoothed her hair, molded her face into an unreadable mask, and headed on deck. She refused to show any reaction to his decision.

And Michael apparently had chosen the same approach. He was all business as he steered the boat, explaining their course, as if she needed to know. "We're making a triangle." He motioned with his arm. "We'll head in this direction for a while, then turn southwest before heading north."

After a few minutes of silence, he asked, "Would you mind getting the food from the refrigerator?"

"No. Not at all." She managed a smile, despite the frustration that ate at her being.

How could he move from the need for intimacy to the need for food so quickly? But if he didn't want to acknowledge what had just happened, she certainly wouldn't bring it up. She could be all business too.

She laid out the feast he had so thoughtfully packed on the bench across the back—chicken salad, grapes, apples, and cheese. She poured more wine into their glasses and sat to his right, slowly nibbling on a grape—her appetite gone—waiting for him to sit and eat.

"The sea air always makes me hungry." He eased down next to her and kissed her temple. "I'm sorry about before. Things got out of control." He looked directly into her eyes, his open and honest apology there for her to see. "You drive me crazy, Sam. I want to be with you, but I know you're not ready."

She breathed a sigh of relief. "You stopped because you thought I wasn't ready?"

"Yes. You made that clear the other night."

She groaned. "I thought maybe you changed your mind. That I'm too much of a hot mess right now."

"Maybe you are, but you're a beautiful mess." His teasing smile lightened her mood.

"I've been regretting my decision to stop the other night, for days."

"Glad to hear we're on the same page." He put his arm around her shoulder, hugging her to him. "Because every nerve in my body jumps to alert when you're near." His dazzling smile warmed her heart, and a current sped through her blood. She wanted to leap through the air, but the allure of his embrace kept her rooted to his side.

At least until he said, "It's time to head north. I'll show you how to jibe." He stood to take the wheel. "When I turn the boat and you release the sail, the boom will swing across the deck, so duck, or you'll get knocked out." He steered as he directed Sam through the next few steps. Within minutes, the sail puffed in the wind until it became taut, majestic.

"Great, Sam. Now you're a real sailor."

She laughed. "I think I'm still a novice deck hand. But at least I feel useful." Michael's easy direction gave her confidence, and she discovered it was fun to sail a boat. "And I've learned a whole new vocabulary," she continued, very proud of herself.

The trip had sparked a series of emotions, which at times had her reeling from their impact. She would remember this day for a very long time. Michael had brought her to tears with his tale of betrayal, had sparked her to delirium when he practically made love to her, had sent her into a tailspin when he pushed her aside, then sprinkled her with joyous relief when he acknowledged he wanted her. Finally, their friendly camaraderie put her on an even keel.

He steered the boat in the direction of the inlet at around four, stowing the sails and starting the engine as they passed through the rocky formation toward their destination. The traffic had tripled from the time they'd set out, and commercial fishing boats vied with party boats as well as other recreational vehicles, all heading in the same direction. As they neared Michael's slip, he pulled up a boat hook and grabbed a line on the dock, instructing Sam to secure it around the cleat. He cut the engine, and their work began.

As he hosed the salt off the boat, he made small talk. "What are your plans tonight, Ms. Winslow?"

Her heart sank. She hadn't wanted this day to end despite the trauma of emotions. "I guess I'll get to the work I didn't do today."

"Any rush?"

"No. Nothing that can't wait until tomorrow." Measured hope returned.

"Good. How'd you like to come over for dinner? I have some steaks for the grill."

Sam's guardian angel was working overtime. "I'd love to. Though I need to go home and shower first. I feel like a salted fish."

"You don't look like one, although you do look good enough to eat." He wiggled his eyebrows, and she laughed in spite of his corny joke.

And the fact that she hoped he wasn't joking.

Chapter Fourteen

Sam's skin prickled as she pushed in the doorbell and held her breath. Her long, silky wrap-skirt blew in the breeze, producing a shiver even though it was still warm and humid. When the door opened, she slowly exhaled. Michael stood before her in blue jeans and a black T-shirt, its sleeves gripping the muscles of sculpted upper arms, his hair still wet from a shower, his feet bare, and a smile lighting his face.

"Come on in." He moved back to allow her entrance, but she stood rooted on the porch. Although she'd initially considered a fling with him—even convinced herself of its merit—she now wavered. He was no longer an old acquaintance she barely knew. Their personal conversations changed everything. She was beginning to care about him. A huge problem.

"Is something wrong?" His smile dimmed.

"No. Nothing." She urged herself to take control. "I brought some wine."

He took the bottle, then her hand and drew her in. The warmth of his fingers simmered through her blood and displaced her temporary nervousness.

She looked around the spacious living room, taking in her surroundings. "This is beautiful." Floor-to-ceiling windows let in the light and a breathtaking view of the ocean. "I didn't realize you had a house on the beach."

"It's the only way to live here. If you can. I know

some people don't want to hear the pounding of the surf twenty-four hours a day, but I'm good with it. It's like having company without having to talk." He moved beyond the living room into a large kitchen, also with views of the beach. "I'll finish the salad, then we can sit on the deck."

The easy familiarity she'd felt working together on the sailboat had curiously evaporated, and in its place, an edgy buzz hummed through her brain. Like walking a tightrope, she could stay the course with rigid control and make it to the other side of the night without incident, or she could intentionally step off the rope and feel the rush of the free fall before landing in the hazard zone of Michael's arms.

The ultimate choice was hers. Michael had made that very clear on the boat. And she knew what that choice would be despite her misgivings.

An aching need pooled between her legs at the thought of his hands roaming over her naked flesh. She shivered. *Get your mind off your fantasies, or you'll never make it through dinner.* She forced herself to focus on Michael's kitchen prowess.

He utilized a serrated knife to slice through the skin of a deep-red tomato, and juice oozed onto the cutting board as his left hand held its ripe body. That same hand had maneuvered over her breasts a few hours before. Her nipples hardened at the thought. His long fingers moved to a cucumber, encircling the long, hard vegetable. She swallowed and clasped her hands behind her back. It wouldn't be polite to do what she craved to do right now. Instead she needed a mundane task to take her mind off his skilled hands…his expert fingers…his…

"Would you like some help?" A strange huskiness took over her voice.

"Why don't you pull up a stool and talk to me? I'm almost finished. Besides, I've seen your talent in the kitchen." He laughed easily. Apparently, his mind wasn't in the gutter with hers.

"Very funny. I know I'm not Emeril, but I can cut tomatoes."

"You can pour the wine." He nodded toward an open bottle of red on the counter. Two crystal wine glasses stood next to it, their sides touching in a kiss. She looked around, needing a distraction. Fast.

"You're very...neat." She took in the light, airy kitchen, and although he was making dinner, everything was in its place.

"I don't know whether that's good or bad. I may have a touch of OCD. Or maybe I'm just organized."

His smile inched up into his eyes, and Sam fantasized about reaching over and stroking his face. When he caught her staring, she quickly turned back to pour the wine, hoping he didn't see the red splotches surely marring her cheeks.

"Do you entertain here often?"

"Usually on weekends. I invite the guys I play volleyball with and whoever else is around."

Probably the groupies who hung by the volleyball court. The cute, adorable women-girls in bikinis. God, she hoped he wouldn't compare her to them.

"What do you do during the other seasons?"

"Read a lot. Work more. Hibernate." He shrugged.

"How do you find women to date in the winter?" She bit her lip and cringed at the question.

He laughed, thankfully. "You make it sound like

I'm a player, a different woman every week."

"Well, aren't you?" She clearly couldn't let this one go. If she weren't careful, she'd be tossed out on her ear in no time.

"I have a lot of women friends, that's all." He sounded tentative, not wanting to go where she was leading. And she didn't blame him. This conversation thread would get them nowhere.

Sam strolled to the sliding glass doors overlooking the beach. Perhaps innocuous conversation wasn't a good idea, since she couldn't manage to behave herself. So what if he moved from woman to woman in his quest to fill the huge gap left by Hannah? She could be one of those women. She quietly sighed, knowing deep down she really couldn't. While it might have seemed like a feasible option when considering Nicki's approach, it wasn't her style. So why even start something with Michael? Before she knew it, she'd be back in the city, working sixty hours a week, back to her workaholic self—at least until she figured out how else to run her life.

Michael walked over to her. "Cheers." He tapped her glass with his.

"Cheers." She looked up at him and smiled. "I'm sorry I questioned you about other women. It's none of my business. I don't know what got into me."

"It's fine. I'm not offended..." He trailed off before changing the subject. "Are you hungry? Should I start the grill?"

"I'm famished. It must be all that sea air and sun."

"The grill's out on the deck. It won't take long."

Sam followed him outside and stood by the rail overlooking the ocean, letting the rolling waves mesmerize her, clear her mind. A meditation of sorts. Upon first arriving in town, her sole goal was to get back to the place where she felt comfortable, back to her old self. Now that it loomed within striking distance, she wasn't so sure that was all she wanted. She had learned to relax, to walk on the beach, to sail a boat, to spend weekends with friends. And to kiss another man.

"Did you have a good day?" He joined her while the steaks sizzled.

"A great day." She beamed from within. "I loved sailing. It was perfect. Beautiful."

"Now do you understand why I don't want to go back to the city?"

"I can see how a day like today would never happen there. In a way, I envy you. It's nice to be able to take a day off and relax."

"It's my way of changing my priorities. Losing Hannah opened my eyes to the life I had created. It wasn't healthy. Not for me, or for the person I was involved with. It's a shame we learn from our mistakes too late. But I'm not going to let that happen again."

"So you've found your life in Crescent Beach." She kept the incredulity from her voice.

"I know you think it's odd that I could give up the excitement of the city. I didn't think I would last here either. At first it was a temporary reprieve. A place to get back to myself. To get over the anger. When I did, I found I was happy here." He looked out over the ocean, a seeming serenity enveloping him. "This place is my refuge. It allows me to think, to be with myself. But I also love my job as a lawyer in this town. I'm helping people, as opposed to some corporate conglomerate that feels the need to enter into one more merger. I even have a few male friends." He laughed. "I never had any friends in New York. I had business associates and I had Hannah. In looking back, I realized my world was very small."

Sam turned away from the ocean and looked at him, appreciating his sincerity. "You certainly seem happy now. But I could never do what you did. I wouldn't have the courage to get up and leave my job, my home. I love New York. I feel comfortable there. My goal is there."

"You want to work sixty hours a week for the rest of your life? Most women want a relationship. A family."

This conversation was getting too heavy. Why was he talking about a family? Is that what he wanted?

She sipped her wine. "I heard what you said earlier. On the boat. I'm not ignoring it. I just need time to digest it. Figure out my priorities. With regard to kids, who knows? I don't picture myself never having any, but I don't picture myself with them in the near future." Especially not now that she was getting divorced.

She swirled her wine and watched it spin in her glass. Earlier today, she had anticipated a hot, stimulating affair with Michael. Unfortunately, they had gotten too deeply personal with each other. Even so, she was still wrestling with the idea, trying to convince herself to overlook all barriers and go for it. Get them both back to more carnal thoughts, which were always there, under the surface. At her dining room table. In her kitchen. On his sailboat. She shouldn't bury them now that she was in his house, ready for him to inflame her.

Walking over to the grill as he turned the steaks, she stood close, too close. "Do you need help?"

A smile curled the corners of his lips, acknowledging her come-on. "I'm sure you can help me later. But right now, there's nothing left to do."

As soon as the steaks were done, they entered the house, and Sam purposefully touched his hand fleetingly while moving with grace in and out of his space. She smiled coyly as she helped carry the salad and wine from the kitchen to the dining room. A bit nervous over her decision at first, she now worked toward her goal with confidence. He would soon be kissing her, and this time she would surrender. There would be no words escaping her mouth, asking for him to stop. And there would be no question in Michael's mind about whether she was ready.

"Why the sly smile?" he asked, breaking into her designing thoughts as they began eating the feast he had prepared.

"Was I smiling?" she flirted shamelessly.

Candles flickered as dusk turned to dark. The pounding background music of the ocean intensified the rush of adrenaline through her body. Her smile disappeared, and she looked into his eyes, trying to communicate her will to be taken.

His jaw tightened as he held onto her gaze, not allowing her to look away. She could hardly breathe as she moved her hand across the table toward him, a not-so-subtle invitation. Desire flamed within.

The blackness of his T-shirt tinted his eyes a darker shade of blue. An imperceptible movement in his jaw gave his chiseled features even more depth. His warm hand covered hers briefly, before he got up and moved behind her chair. In the seconds it took for him to touch her, her body tensed, then melted as strolling fingers brushed over sensitive shoulders, followed by his warm breath. Hungry kisses had every nerve ending in her body screaming for more, and her breasts pushed against the silky material of her top, aching for release.

He fastened strong hands around her upper arms, searing already flaming skin before pulling her up and turning her toward him. His mouth imprisoned hers, sending Sam spinning into a centrifuge of pure physical desire. She reached up and pulled him closer. His velvet tongue roved over susceptible flesh, and she arched her neck, silently begging him to send more delicious sensations to her very core. She moaned with pleasure.

Then he stopped.

She lifted her head to look in his eyes. "Don't stop."

He searched for further confirmation, as if mere words weren't good enough. "If you don't want this, you have to tell me now." His voice was husky, sensual.

"I want this. I want you."

She took his hand and brought it to her cheek, turning her face into it to kiss his palm. She closed her eyes and moved his hand down her neck, down the exposed skin of her clavicle, and over to cup her breast. He fondled her through the material of her top, filling his hand before sliding it underneath the silk to embrace her fullness. Sighing, she moved to find his mouth with hers, seeking his warmth, his wetness.

"Make love to me," she whispered, trailing her tongue along the responsive lobe of his ear.

He groaned as he pressed himself against her, his

arousal apparent. Arousing her more. He then led her up the stairs, never saying a word. His bedroom was dimly lit, so all she could see was the vast blackness of the ocean outside, with no moon illuminating its surface. The only evidence of its presence was the distant rolling thunder of the waves, scarcely audible over the roar within her body.

Michael pulled her to him again, tenderly kissing her eyes, her cheeks, her lips. His hands expertly untied the material at the nape of her neck, and a shock of cool air washed over her as the material fell away. He watched her intently as his hands cupped her breasts, rubbing her nipples with his thumbs, coaxing them to attention. She felt like a goddess being admired by a god.

Unable to keep her hands from moving, she inched his T-shirt up slowly, seductively, then pulled it over his head. She splayed her fingers against his broad, hard chest and moved them upward until they gripped his shoulders, pulling herself against him, skin to skin, engulfed in the hunger he generated. Strong hands grasped her hips before deftly unzipping her skirt, causing its sheer silkiness to fall around her feet.

Unbuckling his belt, Sam pulled it slowly out of each loop, coaxing the leather to ease and curve around his hips until it became free. She then folded it like a whip and trailed it over her torso before letting it fall to the floor, noting his Adam's apple spasm. Her fingers moved to the button of his jeans, and as they brushed his abdomen, the muscles of his stomach tightened reflexively. She looked up into his face, blue eyes smoldering. He bit his lower lip as he watched her slowly ease down the zipper. Then he let his breath escape.

"You're torturing me," he whispered.

"That was my intent."

She kissed his mouth, then pushed his jeans and boxers from around his hips. Her hand stroked his erection, and need throbbed between her own legs as he groaned in pleasure. Within seconds he lifted her and placed her on the bed, pulling off her panties before grabbing a condom from his nightstand. Then he hovered over her, nudging her legs apart. Her mouth sought his as did the rest of her body, straining to get closer, to become one.

He rubbed his shaft against her clitoris, teasing until she was wet with need.

She opened to him, and he inched in slowly until they were one, moving together in unison, desire building within and rolling through her blood, until she could feel nothing but the pleasure and ecstasy of an explosion, white hot and cleansing as she held onto Michael with all her might. His spasms followed seconds after her own.

And then the world was calm.

****

He held Sam in his arms for a long time, touching her, caressing her. He hoped she wouldn't regret being with him—like this. He had wanted to give her room, time for her emotions to stabilize before bombarding her with new ones. But he couldn't wait.

She had seduced him with her eyes, her touch, her scent. And then with her body. Slowly and erotically. Like a magnet, drawing him in. Yet it was much more complex than a simple electrical force.

It was what he wanted. What he fantasized.

But was it what she needed?

As the gravity of the situation set in, would she gather her clothes from the floor, get dressed, and hightail it out of here?

His heart sank at the thought.

Sometime during the last week, she had crawled into his soul. He thought about her constantly—at work, on the volleyball court, out with friends. He'd tortured himself this past weekend, counting the hours until this morning, hoping he might run into her at Melanie's and ask her to go sailing. As he waited for her to show up at the marina, he'd paced the deck of his boat like a teenager, glancing up every other second, waiting to catch a glimpse of her striding down the walkway. Now here she was, lying in his bed after the most incredible sex he had ever experienced.

She stirred in his arms, and he pulled her closer, not wanting her to get up, to leave. She felt so right. He willed her to stay. To see where things went. Not only tonight but in the future. He castigated himself. What a fool. She was going back to New York in a month or so, and that would be the end of it.

She stretched, then looked into his eyes. "I'm hungry."

He laughed in spite of his thoughts. "We didn't quite make it through dinner. I got distracted."

He gave her a tender kiss, but the mere taste of her mouth sent blood pounding through his veins. He aggressively searched for more, turning his kiss into a demand, hard and crushing, gathering her into him. He was hungry too. Hungry for her touch, her kiss, her body, once more. She responded to his demands, rolling on top of him and straddling his hips. Back to where he longed to be. Back inside of her.

Her urgent craving enveloped him, and this time when they climaxed, he knew he was doomed. Not only had she crept into his soul, but she had somehow found her way into his heart.

Chapter Fifteen

Padding downstairs at three in the morning, Michael surveyed the dining room table with Sam in tow.

"What a shame." She pulled the belt tighter around her borrowed robe. "You went to all that trouble to make dinner for me, and it's ruined. I'm so sorry."

He hugged her to him and kissed her temple. "I'm not."

Picking up the plates with the half-eaten steak, he tossed the food into the trash while she poured the wine from their glasses down the sink and placed the salad in the refrigerator.

"How about some eggs?" He pulled the carton from its shelf.

"Mmmmm. Sounds good."

He cracked the eggs, whipped them together with some milk, then tossed a loaf of bread to Sam and directed her to the toaster. Within minutes, Michael had the eggs scrambled with cheese, mushrooms, and tomatoes, and a delicious aroma filled the kitchen.

She tasted the concoction from the fork he held for her. Her eyes glowed in appreciation. "You are some cook. Too bad I can't keep you."

A knot tightened in his stomach at the thought of her leaving. "You can if you play your cards right."

"Oh, sure. What night of the week do I get?

Monday?" Her laugh was lilting and intoxicating.

He had to convince her she was wrong. He didn't have a different woman every night. He didn't have any woman. He dated if the opportunity presented itself. But he was careful to keep things cool and unattached, since the right woman for him had not yet made an appearance.

Sam obviously had a different picture of him, and he hadn't managed to dispel that picture.

"What nights would you like?" He arched his eyebrow, playing her game.

It would do him no good to protest her mistaken belief. She hadn't believed him in the past when he had responded to her queries about other women. It would take time to gain her trust. And time he didn't have.

They sat and ate eggs, laughing and acting silly, interspersed with kisses and nuzzling. After they cleaned up together, Michael glanced at the clock on the kitchen wall. It was nearing four. He should be exhausted, but he was just ecstatically happy.

"I'd better be going." She avoided his eyes as she said it.

"You don't have to leave. You can sleep here."

"Who are you kidding?" That wonderful, musical laugh escaped her throat again. "You know as well as I do we'd get no sleep. And you have to work in a few hours. I'll get my clothes and go home. Maybe you can rest a little before you head in to the office."

She fled up the steps and out of sight. She was right, of course, but he didn't want practicality. He stood by the sliding glass door, hand in his jeans pocket, looking out over the ocean that he couldn't see. What was going on with him? She came up behind him and eased her arms around his waist, then laid her head against his back. He placed his hands over hers and held her to him, willing her to stay. Not just tonight.

"Thanks for a wonderful day…and night." She allowed him to hold her there.

"My pleasure."

"You've made me feel special, Michael, and I thank you for that. This is what I needed. But I guess you knew that. You were in the same position a year ago."

Her words stabbed and sliced at his heart. An impersonal "this" as if she could have been with anybody. Was she really thanking him for their incredible night, as if planned to help her get through a difficult time? He turned to search her eyes.

She leaned into him and kissed his lips. "Good night."

He murmured something incoherent, dazed at what she'd acknowledged. He stood rooted to the floor, as she opened the front door.

And then she slipped away, just as he knew she would.

****

Sam inhaled deeply as she closed the front door, bounded down the steps, and entered the sanctuary of her car. Only then did she let out her breath. She shouldn't have made it sound like he had done her a favor.

Stupid, stupid, stupid.

In attempting to protect herself, she'd aimed to sound blithe, afraid to let him know how she truly felt. Afraid to acknowledge it to herself. She didn't want him to think she was reading too much into it. But her words were cavalier, flippant. She wanted to cry at the same time butterflies skipped and danced in the pit of her stomach. She could still feel the intensity of his passion, his aura. This night had been incredible.

So why did she debase it? Because Michael was a player. She'd seen him on the volleyball court flirting with "the models." A hug here, a wink there. Dinner and drinks after the games, all under the ruse of friendship. She wasn't about to be blindsided again.

Despite her misgivings, the excitement of the night pulled at her every nerve, and the sweet memory of the person who had been so considerate tugged at her heart. Michael was so damn nice. He had given the appearance of caring about her, of wanting only what she wanted. He hadn't rushed her into anything. He'd given her the chance to back out. And after they'd made love, he'd kept her close, stroking and cuddling her, making her feel safe. Not like it was just sex. She marveled at the fireworks he ignited in her. Yet how could she have expected anything less? He had turned her into a hot, writhing, boneless mass in her kitchen the other night, and into molten liquid on his boat earlier today.

Slowly she drove home, basking in the glow of Michael. Her hand drifted softly over her arm, reliving the incredible sensations his touch had awakened, wanting to be back in his bed, feeling his warmth, his hardness. Bristles ran through her blood, and she shuddered at the internal thrill.

Crawling into bed fifteen minutes later, she hoped to get a few hours' sleep. But her body still hummed, and her skin burned every time she thought about their decadent night of lovemaking. How would she ever fall asleep thinking of that? But exhaustion soon overpowered even her most carnal of thoughts, and before she knew it, it was nine thirty.

She practically skipped to the coffee shop, trusting Michael would be there. Swinging through the door with a bright smile clinging to her lips, Sam studied the occupants of the stools and stopped. No Michael. Her smile faltered. It was too late. Of course, he had to be at work sooner than nine thirty. Why did she even think he might be here?

Sam moved through the day, her routine firmly in place but different. Whenever stray thoughts interfered, they were of Michael. His eyes, his smile, his hands all over her body. Chills coursed through her even though the scorching heat of the sun burned her skin.

She had to see him again.

At six that evening, Sam walked to the beach, the ever-present butterflies flitting through her stomach as each step brought her closer to the volleyball court. A group of men pounded the ball over the net, jumping, crouching, yelling, laughing.

Not one of them Michael.

Some looked familiar, perhaps the friends he had made. She stopped to watch from a distance, considering that maybe Michael would show up late.

He didn't.

The rest of the week proved dismally the same. She didn't run into him at his usual haunts, and he didn't call. Well, hadn't she expected that? She was one of many. Another summer fling. And realistically, she wanted it to be that way.

A serious relationship with him was out of the question. A mind-blowing sexual affair was not.

Something that he could clearly relate to. They'd had a great time together, and the sexual combustion proved impossible to ignore. Hot flashes of desire sparked through her at the mere thought.

She should be happy she'd found the right person to help her feel close to whole again. A master of romance.

But negativity invaded her thoughts. While she could talk a good game, it wasn't the way she felt deep inside. She wanted more. But did he? Michael probably used the same date on all his women. A sailboat ride, stolen kisses, and a little groping on deck before an invitation to his house for dinner. She sighed.

Why was he ignoring her? He knew she would only be here for a few more weeks. He had her where he wanted her. Ready, willing, and able.

So what was his problem?

Chapter Sixteen

"I'll let Nicki know you're here." The young receptionist at Snow Leopard Music practically chirped as she directed Sam to a seat in the ultra-modern reception area.

The office of a music producer was a far cry from the staid and conservative law office where Sam worked. Men and women crisscrossed the open space, talking animatedly to each other. The elevator doors pinged open every ten seconds, spewing more people onto the fourteenth floor, and the ringing telephones didn't stop even though the receptionist worked with efficient speed as she pressed buttons and talked through a headset. Nicki's world buzzed and hummed and kicked.

Sam fidgeted on the leather chair, crossing her legs, then uncrossing them, unable to get comfortable. But it wasn't the chair. She checked her watch. A minute after eleven. A sigh escaped.

She had called Nicki's secretary yesterday to check on her friend's schedule, telling her she planned to surprise Nicki. Unfortunately, what she had to report was going to be more like a shock.

God help her.

"Sam?"

She jumped at her name, turning in the direction of the familiar voice.

Nicki frowned as she strode across the reception area, a designer suit clinging to her perfect body. "Hi." She hugged her friend. "Is everything okay?"

Sam stood there awkwardly, the weight of her mission pulling on every last bone. She found her smile, praying Nicki wouldn't notice anything amiss. At least not yet.

"I decided to come into Philadelphia today. I'm going crazy at the beach. I hoped you wouldn't be caught up in some important meeting."

"Any other day this week and I would have. This is perfect." Nicki's frown disappeared, and a genuine smile took its place.

Of course Sam knew that. Which was why she'd chosen today.

"Show me your office." Sam was dying to get out of the reception area and into a quiet space where the two of them could talk. If she didn't get this off her chest soon, she'd explode.

"Sure. This way."

Sam followed Nicki through a series of hallways with open-doored offices on the perimeter and workstations with computers and phones along the inner walls. Every office and cubicle were populated, and the vitality of movement and conversation flew through the air. It must be exhausting to work in a place with such energy.

They finally reached Nicki's office. Sam closed the door before taking a seat. Nicki looked at her questioningly. Apparently no one closed doors around here.

"Is something wrong? Did you hear from Tom? You seem edgy."

Edgy was a good description. Crawling out of her skin would be better. Although she had practiced her speech over and over, now that she was here, sitting in front of Nicki, her stomach bunched into a knot as her anxiety threatened to surround and suffocate her.

"You know Denise's son, Bobby, has leukemia, right?"

"Yes, I know. It's so awful. That poor kid. Losing his parents and now this." Nicki sat forward, worry etched on her face. "Have you heard something new? Has he taken a turn for the worse?"

"No. No. He's the same." Sam kept her voice calm and even. A supreme effort given her mission. "But they've decided on a course of treatment after speaking to the specialists. Chemo, then a bone marrow transplant. I represent Denise and Ben. And Bobby. I filed an application. To obtain his original birth certificate." Her mouth dried up as if a vacuum had sucked out all the moisture, and she licked her lips. Her short sentences and halting delivery were sure to give away her angst. "I got it yesterday."

Nicki smiled. "That's great, right?"

There was no inkling of understanding.

Sam squeezed the fingers of her left hand with her right. "Nicki, you're Bobby's mother."

The words hung between them as Sam waited for them to be deciphered and understood. When they finally sank in, Nicki's eyes grew wide, and her body stiffened. Her lips moved as if to comment, but no words came out. The strain evident in Nicki transferred itself to Sam, and every muscle in her body tensed.

Nicki covered her face with trembling hands, and a scream punctured the air. Sam dashed out of her chair and flew around the desk, embracing her friend. Sinking to her knees, she hugged and patted and murmured, praying that any one, or all three would find their way into Nicki's heart and soothe her.

Nicki cried into Sam's shoulder, her body wracked with sobs, as she let out her emotions in a torrent of tears and incoherent words. After a time, Nicki's sobs abated, and she lifted her head in search of a tissue.

Minutes must have passed, and Sam's ears hurt from the deafening quiet.

Finally, Nicki spoke. "You probably need to know who the father is." Her eyes avoided Sam's.

"No father is named on the birth certificate. You said you were drugged at a party and didn't know who he was."

"I wasn't drugged. I made it up. I was with a classmate, and I didn't want anyone to know. The father is Michael McCain."

A chill ran through Sam's body. Surely she hadn't heard correctly. It couldn't be. But the panic in Nicki's eyes confirmed her words.

Sam sat back on her heels, giving Nicki a little more space—giving herself more space. The shock buzzed through her, and she felt light-headed. It couldn't be true. Yet bleeding into her brain was the undeniable fact that only Nicki knew who the father truly was. *Stay focused, be supportive.* But accusatory words escaped.

"But…you mean you lied to everyone?" Sam's head swirled, and she clung to Nicki's hands to avoid melting to the ground. "Why didn't you tell us you were involved with Michael in high school? We shared everything."

Nicki didn't respond immediately, clearly dealing with her own shock.

Sam continued holding Nicki's hands, refusing to break the contact, wanting Nicki to know she was there to support her. But her mind froze, and her eyes fogged as she attempted in vain to digest the news Nicki had slammed her with. She inhaled and blinked rapidly to fend off a dead faint.

Nicki slid her eyes away from Sam, then shook her head. She was finally ready to tell the story, but Sam wasn't at all sure she could listen to it, comprehend it. She bit her lip hard, expecting the sharp pain to bring her around. Nicki's own anguish overshadowed Sam's astonishment, and she continued.

"We weren't involved. We were friends. He felt sorry for me because I was so upset about my mother's depression after my father died. I felt sorry for him because his father was abusive. I wanted to be there for him, listen to him. He was so angry his mom left with his sister and not him. We talked about that a lot—with me trying to come up with excuses for her desertion so he wouldn't hate her." She looked out the window. "The more time I spent with him, the more time I wanted to spend. I wanted to be there for him, to help him. I wasn't in love with him, but he needed me, and it made me feel good."

Nicki dabbed at her face with a tissue.

"One night, I was with him after his father had beaten him up for some minor infraction. I remember that night so clearly. I touched his bruises, trying to erase them. Before I knew it, we were kissing. Then it went further. I felt so incredibly close to him. Like we were the same person. We were both in so much pain."

A sob escaped from her throat. "He probably didn't feel anything but lust. His real emotions were wrapped up in his dysfunctional family. And I had lost my father, spiraling my mother into another world." She glanced at Sam, a flush of embarrassment heating her face. "He was sweet to me. He cared about me. As a friend."

What Nicki didn't know was that Michael was now a friend of hers. More than a friend. Although this news had the potential to derail those feelings. Sam swallowed hard as her heart cracked into a million pieces.

Nicki had gone through so much, and Sam had never even known. She'd kept it to herself all these years. And such a huge secret. It took every bit of strength and effort to keep from blurting out that Nicki's Michael had become her Michael. Even if temporarily. But she'd have to deal with that later. Right now, she needed to focus on Nicki. And Bobby.

"Did you tell Michael you were pregnant?" It came out in an almost whisper, along with the hope Nicki would whisper her response. Perhaps it would dissipate into thin air so she wouldn't hear it.

"Yes. The night of Alyssa's party. The night he disappeared."

So Michael had known her friend—his friend—was pregnant, and he ran. Unacceptable on so many levels.

Then it struck Sam as if it were a physical blow. "Did he tell you he was leaving?" Did she know all along that Michael was fine and hiding out in New York City?

"No!" Nicki shook her head as if to underscore her statement. "I was as shocked and upset as everyone else. I thought something bad had happened to him."

Sam tried to disguise her skepticism but failed.

"I know you must feel betrayed," continued Nicki. "We told each other everything. I'm sorry, but this was too personal. Too much a part of the bad side of me. I didn't want to share it. I couldn't."

Nicki's pain resurfaced, as if fifteen years had fallen away, stripping her of the dignity she'd tried so hard to salvage. Sam's gut wrenched at the thought that Nicki had kept her secret from them for so long. Did she fear her friends would judge her harshly? Sam reached out and touched Nicki's shoulder, squeezing it in an attempt to reassure her that, no matter what, she'd always love her. "Nicki, you don't have a bad side. You were young and afraid. Your mother wasn't there for you. But we would have been by your side no matter what."

Nicki nodded, perhaps acknowledging her words as true.

"How did Michael react to your news that night?" Sam held her breath.

"It was not a good night for him. He had a new black eye, courtesy of his father, and had just been arguing with that ass, Carl. But I couldn't keep it to myself a second longer. I needed to tell him, to share my fears."

Sam's ears rang, and her head throbbed. But she had to focus on Nicki and not the hurt that weighed heavily on her chest at the thought that Michael had abandoned Nicki in her time of need.

"I think my confession pushed him over the edge," Nicki continued. "He said all the right things—after he suggested an abortion. When I balked, he told me not to worry, he'd stand by me, marry me if I wanted to keep the baby. That was not my plan either. I wanted to talk more, but he was so distracted. I begged him to forget about Carl, but he wouldn't hear of it. He wasn't going to be called a coward for failing to show up for the fight. I was scared for him, scared for me, scared about my future. He must have been too." She paused as if rewinding the video. "I was angry that this thing with Carl seemed more important than what I had just told him. I blurted out I would do what he suggested and get an abortion. That he didn't have to worry about it; I'd take care of it. Then I left." She looked at Sam and whispered, "I couldn't believe he disappeared."

Did Nicki still hold a torch for Michael? Is that why she refused to commit to a relationship today?

Sam stood and leaned against Nicki's desk, recalling the heartache over believing their classmate had met a disastrous end, their commingled theories running rampant in the aftermath of Michael's disappearance. But at the time, they were also dealing with the news of Nicki's pregnancy. Never knowing there was, or could have been, a connection between the two.

The knowledge that Bobby's father was Michael, the person she couldn't stop thinking about, wreaked havoc in Sam's mind. How could he have deserted Nicki like that? Her head was ready to explode, and her stomach ached. He'd bailed out on her friend at the time she desperately needed his support. Even if Nicki said she was going to have an abortion, he should have been there for her.

"Did Michael ever try to reach you?" Sam held her breath, wishing for the best possible answer, although she couldn't fathom what that could be.

"No. I never heard from him. At first, I convinced myself he'd be back. Or at least call me. He wasn't the kind of person who'd leave me to deal with the problem on my own. But when he didn't resurface, I assumed what everyone else did. He'd met up with his fate." The detachment in her voice struck Sam. Was this her protective wall coming up because Michael had hurt her?

Nicki continued. "I went to speak to the officer in charge of the investigation, convinced they'd overlooked something, someone. But they hadn't. In their eyes, he was a missing person who wanted to disappear. And after the officer explained their findings, I began to believe that too." A hint of anger lay below Nicki's words.

Sam couldn't blame her. Because of circumstances, Nicki's future was tied to Michael's, and he'd let her down in a big way, leaving her to deal with the baby on her own. How could he have done that? His faulty character then didn't jive with the man she knew today. Then again, he was eighteen, a kid really, who'd been abandoned by his mother and abused by his father. He obviously didn't think he could shoulder the responsibility.

Nicki stood and started pacing in front of the window. "Don't tell Michael he's Bobby's father."

"I have to, Nicki. I have a legal obligation to Denise and Ben. And Bobby."

Fresh tears watered Nicki's eyes. "Oh, my God. I know who my child is. I saw Bobby at a party at Denise's. When Ben's brother and his wife were still alive." Her voice broke, and her pain reached down to

195

Sam's toes.

It wasn't surprising that this conversation had so many tendrils, given the complexity of the many lives it touched and the emotions evoked by focusing on any one, but Sam had to try to center on one issue at a time. Her headache grew exponentially with each passing second.

"I'll be the donor. He can have my bone marrow." Nicki continued to resist, as if throwing out whatever possible solution came to mind.

"What if yours doesn't match? What if there are other problems? From what I understand, it's not easy to find a perfect match, and Bobby deserves all the help he can get."

"You don't care what your best friend wants?"

Nicki was clearly grasping at straws, and the trauma of everything Sam had laid on her was coloring all reason. But for her to use their friendship as a weapon to win her plea cut deep. Especially since Nicki hadn't trusted her best friend with the truth in the first place.

Nicki must have realized the error of her statement, and before Sam could formulate a response, she said in a barely audible voice, "I'm sorry, Sam. But I don't want to face him. I lied on the adoption papers about not knowing who the father was. And I've tried to bury that awful chapter of my life. It's helped me survive giving up my child, our child, for adoption. I don't ever want to see him again."

"I understand your anxiety over bringing Michael into this. And of course, he'll be shocked. But he's the boy's father, and Bobby needs as many chances as possible to help him get well. You don't have to see

Michael. You don't have to talk to him. All tests can be taken independently of each other."

Nicki deflated. "Of course we both need to be tested." She turned her back on Sam.

Sam reached out and hugged Nicki to her. "Don't worry. I'll help you get through this. I promise."

But how in the world would Sam?

Chapter Seventeen

Michael could feel her presence before he actually saw her. Glancing at the small crowd gathered on the beach to watch the game, he zeroed in on her.

Sam. Her name reverberated in his head, sending an instant buzz of attraction through his veins. Christ. She looked gorgeous, dressed in white shorts and top, highlighting a summer tan on long limbs. His eyes moved to her full lips. Which he yearned to kiss. Desperately.

"Hey, Michael," his teammate yelled as the volleyball whizzed past his head. "Where are you, buddy? That was your ball."

Caught in the act. His face burned as the other guys joined in the taunts. He'd have to try a little harder to reign in his thoughts.

He'd hoped not to see her tonight. Since Monday, he'd successfully avoided her, keeping busy by working late, going so far as to make evening appointments with clients. He'd blown off the volleyball games—until tonight—so he wouldn't run into her on the beach. Then why was he here now? Had he subconsciously anticipated she'd show up?

He should have stuck to his plan. Staying away from her guaranteed his heart's protection. She planned to use him to get over her husband. And he was captivated enough to follow her blindly to his destruction. He had to keep his defenses up.

Yet she'd touched him in places other women hadn't. Figuratively and literally. She'd opened herself up to him, and he'd done the same with her. He never told anyone about Hannah. But he'd poured his heart out to Sam. And she'd listened.

He smacked the volleyball over the net, then glanced unobtrusively toward Sam, trying like hell to play it cool. But it was no use.

He ached to look into the depths of those glistening, violet eyes. To taste those beautiful, full lips, to touch her soft satiny skin.

She looked so good. Like an angel in white while inspiring very unangelic thoughts. For she was no angel. He imagined her pressing her body into his, wrapping her long, willowy arms around his neck, molding herself closer so he could feel the curves of her body through the thin material of her clothing. She drove him crazy.

He wanted her.

Still.

But he didn't want a summer affair. For him it would mean something more. Something too personal. Something like love. Not what she was looking for. Sam wanted someone to get her over the trauma of her divorce. Someone to balance her so she could leave here in a few weeks feeling whole again.

He couldn't afford to be that person. To have his heart broken—again.

He couldn't fall in love with Samantha Winslow.

Despite all rational reason, he ached to be with her again. Maybe he could compartmentalize. If he knew exactly what he was getting into, why not enjoy these last few weeks with Sam instead of being a martyr and trying to ignore her? He'd never be able to anyway. He could do this. He just needed to be strong. Uncaring.

With great effort, he pushed aside the battle in his head and focused on the game.

At least this was a game he could win.

The last set was barely over when Sam came up to him, a strained expression on her face.

"I didn't think I'd see you here." He strove for casual, matter-of-fact, but his heart raced.

She reached for his arm and pulled him away from the crowd. "I have to talk to you about something private."

The edge in her voice sent flickers of worry to his core. "Sure. Are you okay?"

Her face paled, and her eyes avoided his as she steered him toward the ocean. Something was wrong.

She stopped at the lifeguard stand and faced him, her gem-like eyes finding his and pinning him to the spot. "I have something to tell you. It's going to seem a little disjointed and rushed, but please let me get it out before you ask any questions."

Her anxiety-provoking words kicked at his gut. Did he want to hear this? "Go ahead."

She inhaled. "You know Denise and her husband, Ben. They adopted their nephew, Bobby…"

****

The muscle in his jaw tightened, and his fists balled before the curses came flying out. Sam stood there motionless as Michael paced the short distance between the ocean and the life guard stand, head bowed, unintelligible words forming on his lips meant only for his ears.

Passing the wooden stand, he punched it hard, and the structure shook for a second or two before shuddering to a stop. She followed him with her eyes, instinctively knowing the time had come for her silence. At least until the questions started.

"How long have you known this?" he lashed out during one of his passes.

"I received a copy of the birth certificate on Wednesday. I told Nicki yesterday. I went to Philadelphia." She trapped him with her eyes. "She admitted you're Bobby's father."

"My name wasn't on the birth certificate?"

"No."

He swore again. "She told me she was going to have an abortion. But she gave the baby to Ben's brother and sister-in-law?"

"No!" She couldn't allow any misconception to take hold and fester. "Nicki gave the baby to an adoption agency as soon as he was born. She never knew who adopted him. She didn't want to know. She put 'unknown' on the birth certificate under father. She never told us the truth. She made up some story about a phantom guy drugging her at a party."

"This all came out because you had requested that the records be released for Denise?"

She nodded.

He stopped and stared back. A well of hurt and pain shone deep within the depths of his eyes. "Why didn't she name me as the father?"

"I don't know. She didn't say."

His eyes penetrated hers, as if to gauge the sincerity of her statement.

"Why would I lie about that? Why would I lie

about any of this?" She stood her ground, although his piercing gaze sent a quiver through her system. Who was he to question her about this?

Unfortunately, just those words came flying out of her mouth. With more. "Nicki told you she was pregnant, and instead of sticking around to support her through those awful months, you upped and disappeared." Ire pricked through her words and hit its mark as Michael physically backed away with the blow. Rationally, she knew this wasn't her fight. But Nicki wasn't here to defend herself. And an innocent young boy's life was at stake.

He shook his head. "You don't understand what I was living with. What I had become." The bluster seemed to leave him in a whoosh. "I couldn't put a child's life at risk." He sat down on the sand facing the ocean, away from her, away from everything. He bowed his head.

Hearing the anguish in his voice stabbed at her heart.

She took a tentative step and placed her hand on his shoulder, waiting for it to be shrugged away. But instead he put his hand on top of hers and squeezed it. That small gesture melted her soul, and a lump formed in her throat. She knelt down and slid her arms around his shoulders, hugging him.

"I'm sorry," she whispered against his ear so her words wouldn't be carried off by the ocean breeze. "Do you want to talk about it?"

She needed to offer comfort, not accusation. When he nodded, she moved next to him and sat down, her leg touching his—a connection of sorts. The waves crashed along the shore, filling her ears with a dull roar while she waited for him to begin.

"As we grow older, we blame our parents for the issues that haunt us. Isn't that what the shrinks are all trying to get at?" Pain laced through his voice, and she reached over and touched his hand. "Well, I know I blame my parents. You know about my father. Unemployed most of the time, drunk most of the time, and abusive all the time." He stared out at the horizon as if in a trance. "When I started our final year in high school, my mother had had enough. She moved back to her home town with my younger sister. She left me behind because it was my senior year. She assumed I wouldn't want to leave my friends or my position as the starting pitcher for the baseball team. She was so convincing that I believed I didn't want to go. Deep down, she must have known that if I stayed, it would make it easier for her and my sister to leave. My father wouldn't fight as hard if he still had one of us. I thought I could deal with it. Be the man. Help them escape."

He picked up a shell and tossed it into the ocean, watching it skip and plunk into the deep. "Once my father's scapegoat was gone, he turned his attention to me. I tried to stay out of his way, going to friends' houses to study after practice and not going home until he was passed out on the couch. That worked for a few weeks. Until he decided I should work after school to make money to support us. When I argued with him, explaining I'd get thrown off the baseball team, he used his fists to show me who was in charge."

Sam cringed at the picture Michael evoked. His father was a big man. Strong. And back then, Michael had not exactly been built. He must have been terrified when his father let loose.

"After that first beating, I did what he told me, balancing it with baseball. I got a part-time job after school at the deli. But the coach couldn't turn his head the other way. Other guys were pressuring him to give them a chance to pitch, and they constantly pointed out the number of practices I missed."

"Did the coach know how your father was treating you? Did the school administrators?"

He shook his head. "I didn't tell anybody. I was embarrassed. Afraid."

Her stomach twisted.

"The coach made me the relief pitcher because I had to work, but my father still wasn't happy. I knew by then that nothing I ever did would make him happy. Everything seemed to be an excuse to beat up on me."

"Is that when you and Nicki became good friends?"

He stole a glance at Sam, sorrow and pain evident in his eyes. "She listened to me. Tried to talk me into calling my mother. Leaving. But it was so close to graduation. I had gotten a scholarship to Fordham, so I'd be going away to school in September. I just needed to hang in there for a few more months." His eyes refocused on the horizon, refusing to look at her. "Nicki was great. She kept me sane. I didn't look at her as a girlfriend. She was a friend. But one night after my father had beaten me up again, she was there to help me through. We started kissing. And we ended up making love." He laughed without mirth. "If that's what you'd call it. We were both inexperienced, and it was her first time."

Sam thought back to Nicki's take on their relationship. She'd been right about Michael's platonic feelings toward her.

He continued. "After we made that mistake, we agreed it was better for us to be just friends. I was dealing with so much, and she was only looking to help me out, not to get involved in a relationship. She had big plans. Going to the University of Pennsylvania, to their business school. We'd be in two different cities. Two different states. But she assured me she'd always be there for me."

"And then she found out she was pregnant." Sam felt the oppressive weight of her statement, even though it had been fifteen years ago.

"When she told me that night at Alyssa's party, I was alarmed. Not that we'd been smart about birth control. But I knew I couldn't deal with one more problem. And I sure as hell couldn't bear the responsibility for anyone else. I didn't handle it well, but I did offer to marry her if she intended to have the baby."

A painful jolt sparked through her. What if they'd gotten married? Their lives would be so different now. And she wouldn't be sitting here on the beach with Michael, telling him he was the birth father of a teenager named Bobby. It was amazing how one turn of events could change the lives of so many. "What did Nicki say?"

"She said in no uncertain terms that she was having an abortion and promised she wouldn't tell a soul about her pregnancy. So I could relax about it. She was angry that I was going to fight Carl that night. She said she'd never want to marry someone who dealt with problems by using their fists. That she didn't want to end up like my mother, running away to protect herself." He closed his eyes and exhaled. "That really hurt, but her words struck a chord." The strain of the conversation from so many years ago ravaged his drawn face. "She left, and I met up with Carl. I clobbered him and thought I should feel good about it. But everything was coming down on me. Nicki's words scared me more than my father's beatings. Was I becoming like him? They say that abused kids become abusers. I had to get away from him. That night."

Michael glanced at Sam. The weight of his confession pressed heavy on her heart, and all she could do was nod.

"I snuck into the house through my bedroom window, threw some clothes in a duffle bag, grabbed the cash I had kept from my father, and headed for the bus station and New York City, hoping no one would find me. Too many people."

"Did you know anyone there?" She couldn't fathom eighteen-year-old Michael picking up and moving to a huge city to hide. But in reality, kids did it every day.

"I didn't know a soul."

"You were supposed to go to Fordham in the fall. Did you?"

He shook his head. "I was afraid if I went, I'd be found. I never wanted to see my father again. I'd gotten myself out of the hands of that lunatic and saved myself. Even though I had nothing, I felt free."

"Why didn't you go live with your mother?"

"She couldn't protect me. She hadn't before, so she didn't deserve the chance then."

Sam attempted to disgorge the lump in her throat. He had left his family and friends behind, even though he'd still been a child, and started a new life. He'd seen the problem clearly enough to know he had to get away from it or risk becoming a person he'd hate. He'd taken responsibility for himself and become a better person. A strong, successful adult with a law degree and enough self-confidence to throw away his career at a New York City firm. He had friends, a job he loved, a house on the beach, and a sailboat—all indicative of success. And when Sam wasn't bringing him down to unimaginable depths with her unimaginable news, he seemed pretty happy.

"Didn't you ever think of calling any of your friends to let them know you were okay?"

"It never occurred to me that anyone thought I was dead. I didn't know the police were looking for me. But I did know I couldn't let my father find me, so I stayed under the radar. Hidden among millions." He stood and brushed the sand from his butt, his eyes downcast, his mind obviously spinning.

A depressing sadness settled around her. He had only been eighteen, and he'd been alone in the world. Her eyes burned with unshed tears for the teenager who'd been a part of their lives.

"I wish I'd known you better. I wish you felt that someone cared enough about you so you would have reached out."

He held out his hand to pull her up. "Thanks, Sam. I appreciate it." He walked toward the ocean and let the surf spin around his feet. She went to stand next to him, and he turned his gaze on her. "I'll do anything to help Bobby. If he needs bone marrow, it's his. If he needs anything else, I'm there."

"I'm sure Denise and Ben…and Bobby will be

grateful for your support. You have to have a blood test to see if you're a match first."

"Whatever it takes, as quickly as it can be done, I'll do it." His voice was tight with emotion, but his determination showed through. "How awful for that little guy."

She smiled for the first time since she'd pulled him away from his volleyball game. "He's a great kid. So smart. So strong." Like Michael.

"Does he know about me?" He turned toward her, a mixture of hope and fear in his eyes.

"Not yet. I haven't even told Denise and Ben who the birth parents are. When I got the birth certificate, I immediately went to Nicki. Once Nicki told me you were the father, you were next. If either of you weren't willing to help, I wasn't going to name you. Denise and Ben have their hands full with Bobby's treatment and their other two kids. They knew my plan was to initiate contact with the birth parents and we'd go from there."

"Maybe I should stay in the background. I don't want to complicate things any more than they already are."

"Are you saying you don't want to meet Bobby?"

A shadow crossed his face. "I don't know. You're telling me he's my son. But I'm not his father. I've never been there for him. There's no point in getting close—only to break it off after the transplant. If I'm even a match." Sadness drew at the corners of his eyes.

"But you wouldn't have to stop seeing him then. Why not see him whenever you can? Become part of his life."

"He has a family, Sam. He doesn't need me."

So that was it. He was afraid to get too close, for

fear Bobby would cut him off when he no longer needed his bone marrow. What a jaded view he had of relationships. No wonder, given his history.

"How's Nicki dealing with all this?" Michael swallowed, his Adam's apple rising and falling in his throat. "I was such an ass." He shook his head. "Nicki had been a good friend to me, listening to all the crap I had to deal with in my family. It should never have happened. But we got carried away. She must hate me for disappearing the way I did."

Sam recalled her friend's panicked reaction over her obligation to tell Michael. Regardless, she didn't want to tell him about Nicki's refusal to see him. That news was better left for another day. Instead she sidestepped his comment. "Nicki was shaken to learn that Denise and Ben ended up being the parents to her child. Your child. It will take some time for her to process it all. But she wants to help in any way she can. Maybe once everyone gets through this next hurdle of blood tests and hopefully finding a match for Bobby, the other issues can be dealt with."

Not the least of which was her growing attraction for Michael.

Chapter Eighteen

"I'm so glad you have off this weekend." Sam sat across from Alyssa as she skimmed the menu at Rosa's, a cute little Italian trattoria in Crescent Beach owned by a young, talented chef whom Sam had met the last time she'd been here.

After dealing with the emotions and discussions brought to the forefront by Bobby's birth certificate, Sam had lain low this past week, needing some space. But now that the weekend was here, she craved company.

"I haven't seen you in a while and wanted to check in." Alyssa looked over the wine list. "What will it be, red or white?"

Once they decided on the wine and their choice of entrée, Sam studied Alyssa's face. She seemed to glow. "What's going on with you in the romance department? Anyone new?"

"Sort of."

"What does that mean?"

A sly smile inched over Alyssa's lips. "He's an ER doctor at the hospital."

Sam raised an eyebrow. She'd heard murmurings from Nicki that Alyssa was having an affair with a married doctor. But Alyssa hadn't confirmed it. Perhaps this was someone different. "Who is this mystery man?"

A sigh escaped. "His name is Cole. But he's married."

"Oh, Alyssa. Please don't tell me you've moved to the dark side." So she hadn't stopped the affair. *Ugh.* Sam waited for their wine to be uncorked and poured. "Why are you involved with a married man?"

Her eyes sparkled despite Sam's admonishment. "He makes me so happy I can't believe it. He's amazing and exciting and everything I could ever wish for in a guy." Her entire face beamed that happiness.

"Except that he's married." Sam zeroed in on Alyssa's eyes.

"In the beginning, I was good with that." She toyed with her silverware. "I wasn't looking for anything but a distraction after David and I had broken up. Cole took my mind off the *whys* and *what ifs* from that disaster. He made me feel special. Sexy." Her smile held a hint of sadness. "He still does. We've gotten closer over the last month. Meeting outside of the hospital when he can get away. Sharing pieces of ourselves."

Sam's stomach clenched. "Do you think he's going to leave his wife for you?"

"I don't know. Maybe."

Sam exhaled. "Has he said he would?"

"No. He has two little kids." Alyssa's lips turned down.

Of course. And probably a beautiful wife who adored him. And a lovely home in the suburbs where their lovely friends came for dinner parties. But Sam didn't share any of this. "How long has it been since you started seeing him?" Was that the correct term?

"Since January."

Sam's head snapped up. "You've been keeping this

from me for over six months?" The secrets being held by her best friends and soon-to-be ex were staggering.

A flush crept over Alyssa's cheeks as she nodded. "Sorry."

Sam took a gulp of wine. "I hope you don't get hurt in the end." Her half-hearted wish was colored by the scourge she wished on the other woman in Tom's life.

"I know what I'm doing. What I've gotten myself into." Her bravado faltered. "I don't want to talk about this anymore." She played with the salt and pepper shakers while presumably searching for a better topic. "I talked to Denise earlier today."

An acceptable transition. "How is she? I haven't spoken to her in a few days. I know they're waiting for the results of the blood tests that Nicki and Michael took."

"They found out yesterday. Nicki's not a good match. But Michael is."

Sam's heart jumped to her throat. Just the mention of his name did crazy things to her insides. But she hadn't spoken to him since she'd delivered the news that he was Bobby's father. Eight long days ago.

Giving him time and space to process everything seemed prudent, but she missed him.

Alyssa continued. "Denise sounded so relieved. I feel bad for Nicki, though. She was apparently heartbroken to learn her blood type wasn't close enough. I think deep down, she felt she could make it up to Bobby for giving him away at birth."

"I can't imagine the guilt Nicki must be feeling. I'm sure she thought once she made the decision to place him for adoption, she'd be able to forget about it.

To have it all come back like this is incredible. The whole story is incredible. Michael. Nicki. Bobby." Sam sighed. "Life really sucks sometimes." In more ways than one.

"Well, the good news is that Michael has agreed to the bone marrow transplant. Bobby is going through chemotherapy until the middle of August. Then they're going to schedule the procedure. Everyone's holding their breath that it works."

A rush of warmth seeped through Sam's veins. Michael was stepping up to the plate. Big time.

"Do you think Nicki and Michael will get involved in Bobby's life now that they know he's Denise's and Ben's son?" asked Alyssa.

"I'm guessing Nicki will since she's such good friends with Denise. I don't know about Michael. When I delivered the news to him, he seemed to want to hold back."

"It must be so weird for Nicki. Seeing this boy who's her son, yet not knowing him at all. That's probably why Michael's not ready to meet him."

Although Sam knew it was more than that. His father's abuse, his mother's desertion, his fistfight with Carl, all events he locked away with the past were now front and center with this revelation. So many times, she'd picked up the phone to call him. To see how he was doing. To see if he wanted to talk. In reality, she'd been dying to get back to the place where they'd been the night after they'd gone sailing. But too much had gone down since then.

Before this whole mess—a lifetime ago—he'd made her blood simmer and her heart pound. Just the sight of him playing volleyball on the beach would send her stomach catapulting. But if he felt the same way, the news about Bobby had dumped a bucket of cold water over him—over them. Apparently, he didn't want to see her anymore.

Sam's glance fell on a couple sitting across the restaurant by the window.

"Oh, no." Her cheeks burned, and she grabbed a water glass to douse the fire spreading within.

"What?" Alyssa obliviously sipped her wine.

"Nothing, I…I just thought of something I need to do for work." A knot cramped her stomach. Michael was with another woman. She pushed her salad plate away and fought the urge to get up and leave.

At that moment, Rosa came out of the kitchen and headed over to their table.

"Sam!" Her voice was loud enough for the whole restaurant to hear. "It's so nice of you to come back."

On any other day, Sam would have been impressed and flattered that Rosa remembered her name after meeting her only once. But her fear that Michael would hear her name and turn came true within seconds, as he waved at her across the restaurant. Sam pasted a smile on her face, gave a pitiful wave back, and concentrated on the question Rosa had asked.

"What did I order? Oh…uh…"

"Didn't you order penne with vodka sauce?" Alyssa broke in.

"Yes." It was all she could squeak out.

"I ordered the lobster ravioli," Alyssa volunteered, filling the void in the conversation. "I've heard so much about your restaurant from Sam that I couldn't wait to come here tonight. If the pasta is anywhere near as good as the salad and homemade bread, I'll be in heaven."

Rosa laughed and thanked her for the compliment before heading to the next table.

"I have to go to the ladies' room." Sam got up abruptly and headed down the hallway past the kitchen.

Safely behind the closed door, she turned on the cold water and splashed some on her cheeks, hoping to diffuse the colorful red patches that had sprung up. She took out her brush, dragged it through her hair, and swiped at her lips with her lipstick. Taking a deep breath, she counted to ten and then felt light-headed. She breathed in and out more slowly, glanced at herself in the mirror, and shook her head. *You are not a schoolgirl with some silly crush on a boy you just met. Get over it and get out there.* She pushed herself away from the sink and walked out into the hall.

Right into Michael.

"Sam, I want to talk to you." He looked uncomfortable, and his usual megawatt smile didn't appear.

"Outside the ladies' room isn't a very good place to have a conversation." She sounded angry and hated herself for it.

"I know. I would have called you, but I've been busy."

She knew about the blood tests. And of course, he had a job. But she couldn't keep the sarcastic words from rolling out of her mouth. "Not busy enough to prevent you from making a date for tonight, I see." She mentally flogged herself for sounding like a jealous girlfriend. Which was ridiculous. She was the one who'd made their night together sound like it was nothing. She didn't want to have feelings for Michael.

But she did. It would be better to leave things where they stood. Clearly, that was Michael's intent.

"That's my cousin, Eve. She's visiting for the day. I'll introduce you."

The weight on her shoulders lifted as his words sank in. Could she be any more of an ass?

She shifted uncomfortably under his stare as blue-green eyes glided slowly down her body from the top of her white halter dress to her polished toes.

"You look fabulous." His smile, along with his words, dripped with sex and thawed the ice that had formed around her heart.

But she didn't want it to.

"I'm sorry I didn't call you. Maybe you heard that I'm a match for Bobby."

She nodded. His hand caressed her arm, and the heat from trailing fingers burned a path as he skimmed her too-sensitive skin. His smile faded, and he gazed at her with unmistakable hunger. Intense eyes turned from light to dark blue in seconds, and with the change of hue came a serious set to his jaw. He moved into her space, and before she could slide out of the way, his mouth descended, hot and powerful, covering her lips and coaxing her to let him in. Possessive hands slid up and down her bare arms, sending shivers to places she didn't want to awaken. Not here. Not now. Not while Alyssa waited for her. Not while his cousin sat across the room. Despite her reservations, she didn't want him to stop. He felt so good, so warm, so exciting.

She snaked her arms around his neck, then pressed closer, deepening the kiss, losing herself in this glorious feeling. She spun out of control, shedding all sense of what was right and wrong, reveling in the blissful sensations streaming through her inner core. Her fingers curled into soft hair at the nape of his neck as his hands claimed her back, curving around her bottom, pulling her into him, pressing her into his hardness. She yearned to wrap her legs around his hips, but thankfully her dress was too tight. The fact that they were in a public hallway didn't seem a filter to her wantonness.

Dragging her lips away from his, she turned her head so he couldn't mesmerize with those eyes. She breathed in and lowered her lids. "I have to get back to Alyssa."

"Alyssa's here?" His voice was husky, sexy. He cleared his throat. "I didn't notice who you were with. I haven't seen her since high school."

"I'll reintroduce you."

Before she could pull away, he whispered, "Come over later." Those three little words sparked tiny explosions through her veins.

Tamping down raw disappointment, she said, "I can't. Alyssa is staying the night."

He touched her cheek with sensual fingers just as a patron came down the hallway looking for the ladies' room. "It's in there," he said helpfully as he pulled Sam away from the wall and farther down the hall. He shook his head as if to negate what had just happened. "You drive me crazy, Sam. I didn't think we should see each other again since you're leaving in a few weeks. But now that I have, I can't keep my hands off you."

Conflicting arguments zigzagged her brain. He was Bobby's father, Nicki's former lover. Sam still hadn't gotten over the shock, even with his acceptable explanation. She shouldn't blame him today for mistakes made in his teens. He was a different person now. Kind, caring, willing to help Bobby. And the mere mention of his name tripled her heart beat. His presence melted her soul.

Her goal in coming to Crescent Beach had been to heal, to become the strong person she used to be. Her sabbatical had been somewhat successful. She shouldn't ruin it. But the attraction to him was so strong, so addictive, she didn't want to think about how she would feel when she left. She needed him now. His powerful presence, his electric shock to her system, made her forget about the reasons she was here in the first place. She could only hope that her feelings for him would wane as soon as she left town.

"When is Alyssa leaving?" he asked.

"Tomorrow afternoon."

"How about tomorrow night?"

She closed her eyes but nodded. "Okay." Why wasn't she listening to herself? She slid past him and looked back over her shoulder. "Come on."

"What took you so long?" Alyssa dug into her plate of ravioli. "I couldn't wait another second to eat. Sorry."

"That's okay. I want to reintroduce you to Michael."

Alyssa wiped her mouth with her napkin and looked from Sam to Michael with her mouth open. "We were just talking about you. That you're a match for Bobby and it's so wonderful that you're going to do the bone marrow transplant."

He smiled sadly. "It's the least I can do." He touched Sam's arm, searing her flesh.

The heat swarmed through her. "With your help, I'm convinced they'll all get through this."

He nodded. "I have to get back to my cousin. I'll call you tomorrow, Sam."

Alyssa squinted at her as Sam took her seat. "What's going on between you two?"

"What do you mean?" She pushed her penne around the plate with her fork.

"Don't do that. You know what I mean. When the two of you looked at each other, that gaze could have set this restaurant on fire. And I saw him stroke your arm."

"It wasn't a stroke. He touched it."

"With a promise to touch a whole lot more."

Sam chuckled. "You did not see all that just now."

"So you don't deny it. My, my. When did this happen?"

Sam exhaled, her game up. "We ran into each other in the beginning of the summer. Michael lives in Crescent Beach now."

"And you've been seeing him since then?"

"Sort of. A little. Then I had the adoption records unsealed and got Bobby's birth certificate. It's been hard. I haven't seen him since I told him he was Bobby's father. I didn't know he was a match until you told me tonight."

"Is it serious?"

"Of course not." Sam's voice escalated with her denial. "I'm going back to New York soon. Besides, he has trust issues, so he doesn't get close to anyone. From what I could tell, he dates around, but there's no one he's serious about." A streak of gloom shot through her, but she held it in check. "I'm not looking for a relationship. Hell, I'm not out of the one I'm tangled up with right now. Michael's the perfect solution. The person who could help me forget about my broken marriage."

"You're having a summer affair?"

Sam didn't want to get into any of this with Alyssa. She didn't know herself what she was doing. "It's not an affair if neither of us is married." She quickly amended, "Or if I'm separated. All I know is that he makes me feel desirable, sexy. I need that right now."

Alyssa sipped her wine. "Be careful. You don't want to accidently fall in love with someone like that."

This coming from the affair-ee. "What's that supposed to mean?" Sam's question came out a little too sharp, but Alyssa didn't seem to notice.

Sam took a bite of her pasta, moodiness overshadowing the happiness Michael had instilled just moments before.

"You insinuated that Michael's a bit of a player. Men like that break hearts, probably without even meaning to. You're vulnerable now, Sam. I think you should be careful."

"Shouldn't I be giving you that advice? You're the one having an affair with a married man with two kids."

"Touché." Alyssa lowered her lids. "But I'm being careful. I know it's unlikely Cole will leave his wife for me. My eyes are wide open."

Though annoyed with Alyssa for making it sound like she couldn't take care of herself, Sam felt a tug of jealousy every time she glanced over at Michael talking and laughing with his cousin. She wanted it to be her. She wouldn't let herself get hurt. She knew what she was getting into.

It was Sam's turn to make the rules. And it was her turn to be in control.

Chapter Nineteen

Michael picked up the phone and skimmed his contacts for Sam's number with the same mixture of dread and desire that had permeated his thoughts the night before. *What's stopping me? I've had short-term flings before.* If he called Sam to cancel tonight, he'd kick himself the entire day for not feeding into his carnal craving for her. But it would assure that his heart would remain intact. On the other hand, if he invited her over, he wouldn't be able to control himself, and they would end up in bed. Not that there was anything wrong in experiencing mind-blowing, sexual pleasure. And if it ended with that, so be it. Yet Michael feared he would lose a piece of himself in the bargain, and that's where the dread came in.

He hit her number and paced the living room.

"Hello?" She sounded bubbly and much more awake than he.

"Hi, Sam. It's Michael." He gazed out over the ocean, hoping the right words would spring from its depth and enter his mouth.

"Michael. I'm so glad you called. What would you like to do tonight?"

Here was his chance to come up with an excuse. "I thought I would cook on the grill again. At my house. How's six?" *Great excuse.*

As soon as the invitation flew out of his mouth, he

struggled to convince himself he could have her over for dinner and they could just eat. No touching, no soulful looks, and definitely no hot, passionate kisses. That was his downfall. They dragged him into a whirlpool that he found impossible to spin out of. And while there, he didn't want to escape. Since he knew what he had to avoid, he could do it. He was an adult.

"Sure. What should I bring?"

"Just yourself." *Dressed in something sexy.*

She lowered her voice. He guessed Alyssa was right there. "Maybe I should eat before I get there. We didn't quite make it through dinner last time."

"Sorry about that. I promise I'll feed you." He laughed in spite of the anxiety gnawing at his insides. She wasn't going to make this easy with her teasing comments and sexual innuendo.

After he hung up, his angst escalated. But he couldn't be sure if it stemmed from anticipation of the night to come or fear of jeopardizing his heart.

He moved onto the deck. The waves crashed into the surf, giving rise to squeals of delight from toddlers and teens alike. Lifeguard whistles blew and arms waved, cautioning those who swam out too far to come closer. He scanned the beach and reached for his sunglasses lying on the glass table next to the unopened *New York Times*. By now he should have been halfway through the sports section, but his mind refused to allow him to concentrate.

Finally, he went inside for his running clothes. And to assure he'd be too tired to fall prey to Sam's feminine charms, he walked down to the beach, inhaled the ocean air, and started running.

He refused to stop until he had clocked ten miles.

****

Sam slid into her favorite well-worn jeans, which sat on her hips and hugged her bottom. An egg-shell halter top bared her bronzed shoulders and back. She pulled her hair into a ponytail and slid on a pair of sandals. The digital clock in her room added another minute. It was five forty-seven, and she didn't want to be late.

She had gotten back to the house an hour ago, after spending the day with Alyssa. The distraction had been a godsend, for if she had time to dwell on the evening to come, she may have chickened out. Her goal, to have a summer fling with Michael, started out all well and good, except she wasn't cut out to have a fling.

Or maybe the problem was Michael. He enthralled her, tantalized her. And took her breath away. At the same time, he tugged at her heartstrings. She should stay away. Her ploy to replace Tom did not include falling in love with the replacee. He was supposed to be temporary. Fun. A diversion to get her through. Falling for him was not part of the plan.

Standing on the stoop in front of his house, she contemplated ringing the doorbell or turning and running away. As her finger hovered near the button, anxious fear skipped and danced in the pit of her stomach. A déjà vu. Why was she playing this game with herself? Why was she playing this game with Michael? Making out outside the ladies' room of a restaurant while Alyssa and his cousin waited at their tables was practically immoral.

She rationalized her behavior as his fault. He'd told her she drove him crazy. She felt desired, wanted, coveted. If she was searching for validation of her appeal to men, Michael gave it to her. *So ring the damn doorbell.*

Unfortunately, she longed for more. Wasn't that always the case? Just when she thought she found what she was looking for, she herself changed the rules and made it more difficult. Women were impossible!

Exasperated with herself, Sam pushed the button. *If he breaks your heart, it serves you right. You can't change the rules of the game midstream. You confuse everyone.*

Michael opened the door, a cordial smile crossing his face. "Come in." His invitation could be considered cool, casual.

She needed more than civility to rid her growing anxiety. "Hi. I brought some wine." She handed him a brown paper bag. "I didn't know what you were making, so there's both red and white."

"Thanks. I'm making burgers. I hope that's okay with you."

"Fine."

She followed him through the living room and into the kitchen. His reception held none of the torridness of last night's encounter. Something was off.

"Which would you like?" He pulled the bottles from their sack.

"White, please." Sam's tone mimicked his cool cordiality.

He uncorked the bottle and poured the wine. "Let's go out on the deck. It's nice out there this time of evening."

She followed him outside and took a seat. If this had been their first date, she would have understood his distant politeness. But they had been to bed together!

Shouldn't some familiarity, some warmth, penetrate his words? She glanced over at him in profile. No trace of a smile surfaced. He looked pensive, serious. His aquamarine eyes peered out at the ocean. A slight movement in his jaw signified tension.

"Is everything okay? Was tonight a bad night for you to have company?"

"No. Everything's fine." He sipped his wine without turning to look at her.

Maybe it had something to do with Bobby. "Did you talk to Denise today?" She held her breath, praying the question wouldn't shut him down even more.

"No."

He didn't sound angry. Maybe talking about it would be a good thing. "It's wonderful you're a match for him. I know Denise feels this bone marrow transplant will work. Don't you think it would be nice if you met Bobby now that you're doing this for him?"

He didn't answer, so she continued. "Maybe you'll find a connection with him, something you haven't had with your family."

His Adam's apple rose and fell in his throat, telling her she was treading on thin ice. "I don't need a family. I'm fine without one."

That might be true, but she couldn't stop from pushing. "What about Bobby? Maybe he'd like to meet his biological father. He's been through so much. His parents' death. Now this. It might be good for him."

She should shut up. Her words—meant to suggest a possibility—were instead bordering on coerciveness and manipulation.

She glanced over at him, and his face seemed set in stone.

Following his gaze, she watched the ocean in silence for a few minutes, but the calming effect she needed eluded her, and instead had her stomach rising and falling with the swell of each wave.

"Listen." She stood, not knowing whether anger, embarrassment, or hurt drove her. "I think we may have made a mistake getting together tonight. I'm going to leave. Call me later in the week if you want." Her face burned, and she moved to the sliding glass door as quickly as her legs could carry her, before he could see the disappointment so evident on her face.

"Wait, Sam." Michael jumped up and grabbed her arm, pulling her back. "I'm sorry. I want you to stay." He held her within inches of his body, and she could feel his penetrating stare, but she refused to raise her lids for fear of what he'd see.

He put his index finger under her chin and raised it, forcing her to look at him. His magnetic gaze held hers, and she felt herself slipping under his spell. The intensity of his eyes, the serious set of his jaw, the sensuousness of his mouth, sent shivers through her bloodstream, cautioning her to flee before it was too late. Within seconds, his mouth covered hers, coaxing her lips to kiss him back, warming and thrilling her with his tongue as he ran it back and forth, dizzying her with each stroke. It shouldn't have been so easy for him to do this to her. She had almost been out the door. Yet one look, one kiss, turned her upside down.

She slid her arms around his neck, bringing him closer and at the same time preventing her knees from buckling. She willingly parted her lips and let him in, deepening the sensations that sent her spinning. His hands rubbed her back, each time moving lower.

A voice inside told her to stop, to not permit the overpowering thrill of his kisses to rule her body. But she was losing this battle.

She silenced the conversation in her head and simply felt. She felt his soft chestnut hair, his strong, broad chest pressed against hers. His arms encircled her as his hands stoked flames wherever they touched. His tongue plunged and swirled in her mouth, causing a hunger within that could only be satisfied if they were naked and connected. A moan escaped her mouth. She wanted him. All of him.

But when her fingers tugged at his shirt, he dragged his lips away from hers. She waited for them to brush across her neck, her cheek, anywhere.

"I invited you over for dinner." He held her wandering hands, then moved away. "I'm not going to be as rude as I was last time and not allow you to eat." He took in a breath and exhaled slowly. "Besides, I think we might need the strength to get through the night."

His slow smile sent fireworks exploding through her heart. She ignored the voice of reason in order to bask in what was sure to be a night of ecstasy. The anticipation would make it all the more arousing.

For the next hour, everything flowed smoothly: the meal, the wine, the conversation. Sam prudently stayed away from the issue of Bobby, and none of his prior chilliness resurfaced.

"How was your day?" he asked.

"Good. It was fun to spend time with Alyssa. She's high energy."

He nodded. "She was a cheerleader in high school, right? Four sisters?"

"You have a good memory. She still lives in Lawrenceville, so she's only an hour away. We played tennis at the high school, then went to the boardwalk in Point Pleasant where we ended up in junk-food heaven. Ate caramel apples, saltwater taffy, and soft pretzels. It was wonderfully decadent."

His warm laugh melted her insides. "It's a good thing you played tennis first."

"I'll say." She hesitated, questioning whether she should divulge the part of their conversation that still had her off balance.

"You look puzzled."

She dove in. "Alyssa's been having an affair with one of the ER docs at the hospital where she's a nurse. He's married with two kids."

"That can't be good. Is she single?"

"Yes. She and her fiancé broke up last year after eight years together. As a result, she's disheartened with relationships. Thus the affair. At first she looked at it as an exciting distraction. Now, I'm not so sure. She's developing a relationship with him. If you could call it that."

"Someone's going to get hurt in the end. Alyssa. The wife. The kids."

"I get the impression she's not even considering the consequences. She's too caught up in her blissfulness. And after what she went through with David, she deserves to be happy. But this is a disaster waiting to happen."

"Maybe it will fizzle out before tragedy strikes."

She considered his words. "Maybe. She should just stop the affair."

"Did you give her that advice?"

"I did. Alyssa didn't want to hear it. She's so content with things the way they are. Excited to go to work. Thrilled to see him when she can. Although Alyssa's my friend, all I could think about is Cole's wife and compare her situation to mine. The longer it goes on, the worse it's going to be. Either Cole's marriage will blow up, which will assuredly affect the kids, or Alyssa will get dumped before his wife finds out."

He took her hand and massaged her palm. "You can't force someone to listen to the voice of reason. But I'm sure you'll be there for her if she needs you. It's nice you've stayed so close to your high school friends."

She nodded and smiled ruefully. "We were always there for each other, and we still are. They've been wonderful in helping me get through this tough time. I love them dearly."

"You're lucky to have that. I haven't had any good friends in a long time. Although I guess I'm getting pretty tight with the guys I play volleyball with. Back in high school and college, I had teammates from soccer and baseball. But I can't say there was anyone who I would talk to about personal things. When I lived in New York, I had coworkers, but again no real friends. We'd go out to lunch or for a drink after work. No one I ever missed."

"Nicki was your friend." It came out quietly, reverently. And although she knew she shouldn't be raising Nicki's name here and now, it happened. And it was too late to take it back.

"She was," he acknowledged easily, looking into Sam's eyes. What did he see?

She lowered her lids. "I guess I'm feeling a little guilty for being here because of what's come out about you and Nicki. I haven't told her that we've...gotten together." Was that the right phrase? She certainly didn't know what else to call it.

He took her hand in his and brought it to his lips. That tiny gesture sent her into a dizzying spiral.

"She's okay with it."

"What?" Had she heard him right?

"I went to visit her. We needed to talk. To clear the air. Get on the same page for Bobby's sake."

Sam's blood pumped in her heart. "And did you?"

"Yes. I also told her about us. Or at least what little there is to tell. She acted like a true friend would and threatened me if I didn't treat you right."

She tried to read something further from his eyes, but the corners crinkled as he smiled.

"What?" he asked, looking confused by her inspection.

"Nothing." But she couldn't contain her grin.

And her heart swelled with the knowledge he'd cared enough about her, as well as her and Nicki's friendship, to talk to Nicki about "what little there was to tell" about them.

She reached over and covered his hand with hers. A hint of emotion flashed across Michael's eyes before he stood and started clearing the table. The chill of his absence underscored her feelings for him.

Not good on any level.

****

Michael walked into the kitchen, needing some space away from Sam. She was creeping into his heart without even trying, and he couldn't afford to let that

230

happen. Yet her easy conversation and insightful comments made him want to be around her. Her empathy for her friends superseded her own feelings, and he knew that trait was so much more important than her intelligence, drive, and beauty. She was probably right about Bobby. He should reach out to him. It was just so damn hard to get his mind around it. What if Bobby rejected him? What if Bobby died? He couldn't think about that now.

His gaze followed Sam as she moved gracefully into the kitchen, carrying the glasses. What an amazing woman. In a few short weeks, she had him all turned around. It sure didn't hurt that she looked great in shorts or jeans, her long legs tantalizing whether bare or covered. She generally wore little or no makeup, and her glossy hair, when pulled back into a ponytail, had him fantasizing about flicking kisses along her very sexy neck. Her huge, violet eyes were impossible to ignore when filled with compassion, but even more irresistible when filled with desire.

And that desire became so evident when he kissed her. Her carnal craving ignited each time he moved his mouth over hers. Just thinking about it aroused him. He shouldn't have invited her over. He didn't need this. He didn't fit into her plan. He didn't want to.

She had made it clear his role was temporary. Was he willing to pay the price for a few thrilling weeks? So that by the time she left to go back to New York, he would have his heart thrown back at him as if it didn't mean anything?

The black thoughts swirled through his mind, the same as when she'd first arrived. As if they weren't bad enough, she'd made him feel guilty about avoiding

Bobby. His sullenness had almost made her leave. And he should have let her. Instead, he had gazed into her eyes and seen the pain he'd caused by his silence and icy facade. And in that second, he had wanted her more than he'd wanted to protect himself.

Sam stood before the screen leading out onto the deck, watching the last rays of light fade to dusk.

"What are you thinking about?" He moved behind her, staring out over the ocean.

"That it's so beautiful. I can see why you'd rather live here than in New York City."

"What about you? Do you think you'd ever change your mind about going back?"

He held his breath. Hating himself for asking the question. Not wanting to hear the response. Did he sound as pathetic as he thought?

"I can't imagine not going back. It's all I have right now. I own a co-op there, and I have a job."

He let out his breath. She didn't exactly say no. Perhaps she was softening. Getting used to the idea of living here. "There are lawyers everywhere." He was careful not to specifically mention Crescent Beach. "Coming from a big New York firm, you'd be able to write your own ticket."

"I'm definitely calmer here, more laid back. But I'm on a leave of absence, so whatever feelings I have about this place, or a place like it, are somewhat of a fantasy. It's so perfect here. But this isn't the real world."

Maybe not hers, but it was his. "You'd have a better quality of life if you left the rat race of the city."

She looked at him skeptically. "Wouldn't I just be changing locations? If I were at a law firm in the area,

I'd still be working six days a week. This career we've chosen is so demanding. Besides, I don't think I'd change my work ethic just because I moved from the city."

This conversation had the potential of taking on a life of its own, and Michael's mood couldn't tolerate a serious discussion about the practice of law—in any locality.

His ringing phone interrupted their discussion, and he sent up a *thank you* for the break in conversation.

He meant to press the button to decline the call, but in his haste, he accepted it and the speaker was on. A woman's flirty voice filled the air.

Chapter Twenty

"One of your cheerleaders?" Sam inquired, an amused smile playing on her lips after Michael quickly disconnected the call.

He hung his head and sighed as he mentally ran through his responses to that same heavenly Being he had mistakenly thanked. *Why now? Very bad timing. How could you do this to me?*

He said aloud, "She's a friend. Nothing more." He moved closer to Sam from behind and encircled her with his arms. "You, on the other hand, are much more." He inhaled her jasmine scent, willing the intrusion to fade into oblivion.

She followed his lead. "How much more?" Her raspy voice begged for him to show her.

He lifted his hand to touch the smooth silkiness of her shoulder, dragging it down simmering flesh. An unmistakable intake of breath and whispered sigh spurred him to kiss that delicate skin between neck and shoulder. Her passion lay barely below her surface, and he felt erotically powerful awakening that passion with such a simple touch.

She leaned her head to the left, silently begging him to press kisses along the length of her neck, her eyes closed, her lips smiling. She reached down for his hands and covered them with hers, drawing them up to trace her breasts over the silky material of her top. His jeans grew uncomfortably tight, and he pulled her back against him, encouraging the roundness of her bottom to press and tease. Roving fingers slipped under her shirt, working their way to her hardened peaks. She moaned before turning her head to find his lips.

"Let's go upstairs," he whispered, his voice husky with desire.

She nodded, her eyes heavy, her lips smiling. He reluctantly withdrew his hands from the warm mounds of her breasts before guiding her up the steps.

Darkness had fallen, and a small desk lamp cast a rich sapphire glow over the room. He stood before her, needing to drink in another hot, erotic kiss. With his mouth firmly over hers, he drove his tongue through her parted lips, entwining it with hers. Moving his hand down her torso, he fingered the button on her jeans and unfastened it, dragging the zipper down while brushing his fingers over her abdomen.

Muscles tightened as he played with the smooth skin of her stomach, aching to feel all of her, but keeping the pace slow to maximize erotic pleasure. She grabbed the hem of his shirt and moved it up his chest, breaking their kiss to remove the impediment. Flirty fingers trailed back down their path, stroking his torso. Her teeth nibbled at him playfully between licks and kisses, driving him to the point between pleasure and pain. He had to get her clothes off.

Tugging at the material around her neck, he quickly unfastened the loop, letting her top fall around her waist. Magnificent breasts, full and round and silky, called to him. He cupped them before teasing her nipple with his tongue, then sucking it until it was hard and erect. He turned his attention to the other one as a moan vibrated through her chest. Absolute heaven.

He broke away to slide her jeans over long, shapely legs, taking in Sam's lean, tan stomach. Very sexy. Dipping his tongue into her belly button produced another moan of pleasure, encouraging him to drag her satin panties down the same path as her jeans. She was finally naked, and he ached with desire as he gazed at her.

Much faster at disposing of his remaining clothing, he pulled her into his embrace, needing to feel her warm skin next to his, her silk against his roughness. He gently pulled the band holding her hair, sliding it down the thick mass until luscious tresses spilled out and down her back. He threaded his fingers into its strands and worked them through until they reached the end.

Then he led her to bed.

****

By Monday afternoon, Sam's feelings for Michael penetrated every synapse. For the past six hours, since she'd left his house, she had toyed with the idea of calling him, then dismissed the thought as imprudent. She'd just be one of how many? Instead, she sent mental messages convincing him to dial her number, all for naught. The tug of war in her mind went on endlessly. The rules of dating, as she knew them, didn't apply in this case, making it impossible for her to know what to do.

The stab of pain that pierced her chest every time she thought of him proved Michael had invaded her heart, without warning, without her wanting him to.

She knew he felt something more for her too. His tenderness and passion surfaced within minutes of their being together. And not only last night. He couldn't react this way with every woman he dated. Besides, hadn't he tried to persuade her to move to New Jersey?

But convincing herself she was somehow special to him only made the fact he didn't call or text worse. And preventing her from calling him was the fear he would be too busy to see her, translated to mean he was seeing someone else.

Sam needed a diversion.

Flipping through the local newspaper, she searched for an idea that would jump off the page. Nothing. She stopped at the *Help Wanted* ads. Maybe she could get a part-time job waitressing for a few weeks. The idea tickled her, but who was she kidding? She had never waitressed in her life. And she wasn't about to start now. Her eyes moved down the page and touched on the word *Volunteers* in bold lettering.

Cherubs' Wing at Crescent General Hospital needs loving, warm adults to care for children displaced from their homes. Only a few hours per week can make a difference. Apply at hospital.

Caring for children whose parents had neglected them? That should be distracting enough. And what better way to spend her time?

Sam grabbed her purse, jumped in the car, and headed for the hospital.

****

"What does lemonade taste like?" Penny, a precocious four-year-old with curly black hair, raised her huge brown eyes to Sam.

Penny hadn't seen her parents for weeks and probably wouldn't for a very long time. They were both in jail, busted for selling drugs out of their apartment.

Sam cuddled her in her lap as she read her a story about a mouse picnic. Momma mouse had just poured lemonade.

"It tastes sour and sweet at the same time. Like lemons with sugar."

Penny's brow furrowed. "What's a lemon?" Her adorable face scrunched up in wonder.

"A lemon is an oval fruit that can fit in the palm of your hand. Like the size of this ball." Sam demonstrated as she pulled a small ball from the toy chest. "It's yellow. Have you ever eaten an orange?"

"Yes." Penny nodded, her eyes wide. "I love oranges."

"Well, it looks like an orange inside, except it's a different color. It doesn't taste like an orange though. In order to make lemonade, you squeeze the juice from the lemons and add water and sugar. I'll bring you some the next time I come. How does that sound?"

Penny's head bobbed up and down, her curls bouncing against small shoulders.

Danny heard the last part of the conversation and came over to Sam, his dirty hands gripping her shirt as he pulled himself up into her lap. "Bring me something too, okay?"

"Do you know what I'm bringing Penny?"

"No. But I want a toy. A train. A toy train. Red. No, blue. And it needs a whistle."

Sam's heart cracked. What Danny requested was against the rules. The volunteers were not to bring individual children toys. Donations made to the wing were fine, as long as the items could be used by all the children. And a special treat, like food, was acceptable. But the social workers didn't want these children to get used to presents or treats on a daily basis. It would make it that much harder for them to go back to their families, or into foster care. And no one wanted that.

"Danny, I can't bring you a train. But I am bringing in lemonade. Would you like some too?" She hugged the boy in her lap, and he permitted it for a few seconds before wiggling free.

"Okay. But I'd rather have a train."

Sam smiled at Danny's back as he went to play with two other little boys. She finished reading the book to Penny and stood up to stretch. She had been here since noon today and had initially planned to leave at four. But one of the volunteers for the evening shift couldn't make it, and the director asked Sam to stay through dinner.

"Penny, I'm going downstairs to the coffee shop for fifteen minutes. Beth's here if you need anything. I won't be long."

"Can I come?" Penny's huge eyes pleaded as her tiny arms latched onto Sam's leg.

For the past two days that Sam spent on Cherub's Wing, Penny had followed her around like a little duckling. Yesterday, she had begged to go home with her. It broke Sam's heart to tell her no.

"I'm sorry, honey, but you need to stay here. You see that clock on the wall? When the big hand is on the six, I'll be back. Why don't you play with Barbara? She looks like she could use a friend."

Penny looked over at Barbara sitting on the floor playing with a doll, then back to Sam as if weighing her options. "Okay. I'll wait for you."

Sam grabbed her purse and slid out of the room quickly, before another plea came her way. These children clung to each of the volunteers, never wanting them to leave, hoping they wouldn't disappear like their parents did. How would Sam ever be able to quit without a backward glance when the time came for her to return to her real life? In just two days, she had become attached to these children. The director told her she shouldn't come every day, although that had been her plan. The children would start depending on her. So she intended to skip Thursday and come back on Friday. To ensure she wouldn't change her mind and show up, she invited Denise and her two little ones to the beach tomorrow, since Ben was taking Bobby for his treatment.

The hospital coffee shop buzzed with activity. Doctors, nurses, technicians, and administrators grabbed sandwiches that purported to be dinner, while visitors took a rest from seeing sick relatives. Sam found a table in the corner and sipped a lukewarm cup of coffee. Her mind wandered from the kids upstairs, to the legal brief she'd worked on this morning, to the status of her divorce case, to the need to get to the grocery store before Denise showed up tomorrow.

"Sam! I thought that was you. What are you doing here?"

Standing before her in a beautifully tailored suit was Michael. His perfect white smile and gorgeous eyes lit up his tan face. He held a shopping bag.

"I'm volunteering on Cherubs' Wing." She kept her voice even but feared her racing heart would betray her. She hadn't seen or heard from him in fifty-seven hours, which fed into her assumption that other women filled his free time, despite his protests to the contrary. It was all for the best. Her powerful attraction to him could only hurt her in the long run. "What brings you here?"

"I came by to see a neighbor. And I thought I'd stop in to say hello to the kids on Cherubs' Wing."

"You know about the organization?"

"I help out once a week. Usually the five-to-ten shift on Fridays. They have a hard time finding volunteers for that slot. It's not much, but…" He shrugged.

She couldn't picture Michael sitting there reading a book to Penny or playing dolls with Barbara or even trains with Danny. But then again, maybe he didn't have to. The kids were surely sleeping by eight or nine. "What do you do during that shift?" Curiosity got the best of her.

"I usually play basketball with them on nice days, then help them get ready for bed. Some of the kids can't sleep. They miss their moms or dads. They cry. They get out of bed. So I sit up with them. We talk, play, read. Whatever it takes to get their minds off their troubles."

Sam's throat clogged. How could Michael have such a warm heart for displaced kids? It couldn't have anything to do with the guilt over his own son, since he'd just learned about him.

"Would you like to sit down?" she croaked, wishing he had to go, while wanting him to stay.

Up until now, she thought his social and business lives were full. Yet here he was, admitting that at least one night a week, and a Friday night no less, he comforted children.

"Sure, for a few minutes. I have to be in municipal court at six."

She nodded, not trusting herself to speak. Her heart fluttered like a schoolgirl's, and she hoped it wasn't evidenced by a blush on her cheeks.

"When did you get involved with the kids here?" His easy conversation would have one believe everything was fine between them. Like he hadn't ignored her for almost three days. Like she hadn't evaded him.

"Monday. I decided I had too much time on my hands. I needed to do something more than sit on the beach and read. So I looked through the newspaper and noticed an ad for volunteers. I've been here the last two days."

"I thought you were trying to take a well-needed break from the rat race. But you're still working, and now you've added this."

"I'm taking a break from my life in New York City. Since I put my brain back together, I figured I should do something constructive." She paused. "Of course, I still love going to the beach and relaxing. But I don't need to do it every day. This is perfect, and I feel like I'm making a difference."

"I'm sure you are." His clear eyes found hers and held them in his gaze, mesmerizing, hypnotizing, pulling her into his spell.

She had to disconnect before she entered the danger zone. "I better be going," she rasped. "I promised Penny I'd be back by four thirty, and I'm sure she'll hold me to it."

"I'll walk up with you. I need to drop this off anyway." He motioned to the shopping bag, which Sam could now see was filled with books.

His voice caressed her, sending heat to places she

didn't want to acknowledge right now. Warm fingers grazed her back as he escorted her out, and the heat turned to a sizzle.

They took the elevator in silence, with Sam slipping out of his grasp in order to give herself some space. She supposed his casual style regarding relationships allowed him to act warm and friendly whenever he ran into…into whom? His lover? His friend with benefits? *Ugh!*

Perhaps she could look at this time in Crescent Beach as a learning experience. There were all kinds of men in this world. Some who needed one woman at a time, but not necessarily a long time—like her cheating husband—and some who treated their dating relationships so casually it assured them of remaining blissfully uncommitted. Now that she knew at least two types to avoid, she could start her search in earnest for the type that would satisfy her.

"You're awfully quiet today," broke in Michael. "Is everything okay?"

"Everything's fine." She pasted a smile on her face and aimed for cheeriness in her voice.

"I haven't seen you in Melanie's or taking a walk on the beach in the evening."

"I've been busy." In reality, she had purposefully stayed away from the beach at six and made her own coffee in the morning. "Between work, coming here, and going out, I guess I've changed my routine." Of course, she hadn't gone out on the town as she'd made it sound, but she wasn't about to let him think she had nothing to do at night but wait around for him to call.

"Oh."

He sounded disappointed. *Good.*

They walked through the doors together into the children's wing. A collective scream of "Michael" went up as the kids swarmed him, hugging his legs with their sticky little hands and faces, and grasping at his fingers as more than one endeavored to climb into his arms. It was an incredible sight. Michael, in a sea of children, calling each one by name, laughing, smiling, hugging, oblivious to the smudges they wiped onto his suit and white shirt.

"I have to go now, kids. But I'll be here Friday night. How's that?"

They vocalized their approval, and he extricated himself from the mass, giving them high fives and pats on their backs. He looked over at Sam.

"How'd you like to get together tomorrow night? I can pick you up around seven, and we can grab something to eat at Rick's."

The push and pull played war on her heart. She had successfully avoided their shared spaces for a few days so as not to make it easy for them to casually get together, while at the same time longing for his attention. And now an invitation.

"I can't." Both relief and regret collided. "Denise is coming to visit with her two younger ones tomorrow." She felt strange mentioning Denise, given the circumstances. Their lives were crisscrossing, but instead of feeling closer to him, a wedge seemed to be driving them apart. She swallowed her discomfort. "I don't know what time they're leaving." She added quickly, "They may even stay overnight." Of course, they weren't, but Sam killed the possibility of leaving the door open to a later invitation.

"That's too bad. I've missed you."

The sincerity in his voice pulled at her heart and almost eclipsed her frustration over his lack of communication. She broke their contact and looked down. Her frail excuse for not getting together would not be tossed aside with a look. Besides, his candidness was suspect.

If he had really missed her, why hadn't he texted or called?

****

That's just what he needed.

Michael headed out of the hospital muttering to himself, without having stopped to see his neighbor, the main purpose of his visit. Although he had casually looked for Sam the past two and a half days at her usual haunts, he knew avoidance would be the safer route. His fingers had itched to pick up the phone and call her, but he'd resisted the impulse and replaced it with jogging, working, volleyball, and dinner with friends. Staying busy was key, and he had intended to keep it going.

He'd succeeded in getting through the past few days, and then, of all places, he ran into her at the hospital coffee shop. Her white pants and yellow striped shirt sported smudges and wrinkles. And wisps of hair escaped her ponytail, framing her beautiful face. Her dishevelment made her even more beautiful because of its cause. She had been playing with the kids on Cherubs' Wing.

A grunt escaped as he removed his suit jacket and tossed it into the back seat of his car. At first, he'd thought she was upset with him for not calling. But it had become clear that wasn't the case. She was too busy going out!

He slammed the door shut, his jaw tense.

Thoughts of her invaded every waking moment, interfering with work, play, sleep. He'd hoped time away from her would dull his feelings and free his mind. It hadn't. And the second he saw her again, it all came back with a vengeance. He told himself to act casual, be friendly—and don't ask her out. So what did he do the second his brain wasn't focusing on his demands? He invited her to dinner.

And she'd refused.

Could this get any worse?

Chapter Twenty-One

"Would you help us build a sandcastle?" Jennifer, Denise's four-year-old daughter and obvious spokesperson for her and her younger brother, stood before Sam with her pudgy little hands on sweet toddler hips.

"Of course." Sam pulled herself up from her sand chair on the beach. She looked pointedly at Denise.

"I didn't put them up to that, I swear." Denise giggled before removing a magazine from the diaper bag. "Since they only want your attention, I think I'll page through *Vogue* and see what I should be wearing this summer."

It had taken them nearly a half hour to unpack Denise's car—a port-a-crib, umbrella, beach blanket, net full of buckets, shovels, and watering cans, diaper bag, cooler, beach chair, stroller—and walk to the beach with most of it in tow. Sam marveled at Denise's efficiency and stamina in dealing with two tots every day. In addition to a fourteen-year-old with leukemia. Could Sam ever do this?

She picked out two brightly colored watering cans with daisy spouts from the array of sand toys. "Who wants to walk down to the ocean to get some water in these buckets?"

"I do. I do." The kids jumped up and down as if this were the best invitation they had received in months.

"Okay. Each of you hold a bucket in one hand and hold my hand with the other."

They dutifully complied and accompanied Sam to the surf. But once down there, Sam couldn't convince them to fill their buckets and head back. They jumped over the shallow waves, splashing and laughing, letting go of Sam's hand for a second before grabbing for it again. Johnny sat in a small hole dug out by some other child, letting the water run over him, puffing up his diaper and adding wet sand to the mix. He squealed and giggled as each new wave spun around him, clapping as it receded, then calling for the next one to fill his pool.

Jennifer picked up shells and carefully placed each one in her bucket, caring not whether they were broken or whole. Adorable curly blonde hair blew in the wind, framing her porcelain face and drawing attention to blue eyes wide with glee. Her image mirrored Ben's, so different than Denise's darker, Mediterranean features.

"Sam, could you help me catch a crab to take home for my daddy?" Her plea involved her whole body.

"I don't think the crabs want to leave their home. They want to be with their families under the sand. But maybe we can catch one for a few seconds, look at it, then let it go. What do you say?"

"Okay." She plopped down on the wet sand and waited for Sam to do the work.

Sam inwardly smiled, then got down on her hands and knees and explained, "After the wave rolls back, you'll see tiny holes form in the sand. You have to dig real fast before the crabs go too far under. Here are some holes. Use your hands like this." Sam dug with Jennifer, as Johnny watched from his pool, but each time they uncovered a crab, it burrowed deeper into the sand before they could catch it. Not that Sam tried too hard. "I guess we're not fast enough."

"I came down to see what happened to you guys." Denise shaded her eyes with her hand. "I thought you were just getting some water."

"We got distracted." Sam rubbed her hands together to remove some sand. "You should be relishing this time alone. Why aren't you reading your magazine?" The invitation to the beach was partly meant to give Denise a little break.

"I don't know how to relax anymore. Instead of enjoying the peacefulness, I kept looking down here to see what you were doing."

"Don't you trust me?" A grin escaped as Sam placed her hands on her hips, trying for an incensed pose, before brushing sand from her legs.

Instead of answering the question, Denise squinted at her. "I keep wondering who you are and what you did with the real Sam." She chuckled, shaking her head.

"What do you mean by that?"

"You've never shown any interest in kids before, that's all." Denise shrugged, then smiled. "It's nice to see this change in you."

"Thanks." Sam dismissed the faint annoyance that initially bubbled up.

After all, if this had been a few weeks earlier, Sam wouldn't have even offered to play with Denise's kids. She hadn't been a kid kind of person, never knowing what to say to them. At least she didn't find them as annoying as Nicki did. Maybe her time spent on Cherubs' Wing had changed her. Maybe it had something to do with Bobby. Or maybe she was hitting her stride in that department.

"Mommy," broke in Jennifer, "Sam was helping me look for a sand crab."

"Ick." Denise wrinkled her nose. "I guess you don't need me, then."

Johnny's shriek of joy confirmed that conclusion as she momentarily watched him clap and laugh as another small wave swirled around him.

"We're fine." Sam smiled, shooing her away. "Go and relax. We'll be back up to the blanket when we're finished."

Sam sat on her heels and watched Jennifer dig furiously with both hands, spewing sand in every direction. The furrow of her brow and intent look on her face showed purpose in her quest. Johnny sat in his puddle happy as a clam, spraying water on himself as well as Sam each time he slapped his palms down. They were adorable, sweet, happy children who so easily invited Sam into their lives. Like the kids on Cherubs' Wing. So trusting, so open.

Her heart swelled with emotion, filling a void she hadn't even known existed. *So this is what it's all about.* A smile curved her lips, and she knew it would remain there the rest of the day.

The morning sped by, and before Sam knew it, it was noon. The children were starving from their hard work at the beach, so they gathered the diaper bag, cooler, and stroller and headed back to Sam's house for lunch. All four of them washed as much of the sand off as possible in the outside shower, then entered the kitchen where Sam made sandwiches for the kids and a salad for her and Denise.

Halfway through lunch, Jennifer turned to Sam.

"Would you take me to the potty?"

Denise chuckled and kept eating. "You've made a very good friend, Sam. She doesn't ask just anybody to do that."

Ignoring Denise's teasing remarks, Sam stood. "Sure, Jen. This way."

"You may need to help get her bathing suit off. There's a hook in the back," Denise called after them.

Sam brought Jennifer to the bathroom and helped her, answering a stream of questions about why the tile was pink, why the sink was so small, why Sam had on shorts over her bathing suit, why she wore her hair in a ponytail. The "whys" were endless, but given that she hadn't seen Jennifer since Christmas, she was glad the little girl felt comfortable enough to talk to her at all today.

After lunch, Johnny took a nap so he wouldn't be a bear for the rest of the afternoon, and Jennifer ensconced herself in front of the television for a dose of *Sesame Street*. Looking forward to some down time, Sam invited Denise out to the porch where she poured iced tea from a pitcher into two tall glasses and set them on the table before them. Denise flopped into the padded wicker chair and propped her feet up on the edge of the sofa, catty-corner to her.

"How are things going?" Denise sipped her drink.

"Fine…" Sam could feel Denise's eyes inspecting her face but couldn't bring herself to look at her.

"Now there's an answer full of secrets." Denise peered at her friend above the rim of her sunglasses.

"Why would you say that?"

"Because of the way you said it. Because you're blushing. Because you refuse to look at me. Take your pick."

Sam laughed despite being caught. "You know me too well, kiddo."

"Does your secret have something to do with Michael?"

Sam's heartbeat skipped at his name, preventing her from responding.

"Spill it, Sam, before I have to torture you by tickling." Denise shrugged when Sam looked at her questioningly. "That works with the kids."

"I better come clean, then. I hate being tickled." Sam paused, considering her words. "As you know, I've been sort of seeing Michael."

Denise leaned forward in her chair. "And?"

Sam failed at containing her smile. "When we're together, he sends me to the moon, and I never want to come back." Her smile faded. "But then I don't see him for a few days, and I feel like some lovesick teenager waiting on pins and needles for the phone to ring, or to bump into him around town. I hate it. I don't want to feel that way about him. I'm not looking for a relationship. And neither is he."

"Oh, Sam. This is trouble." The corners of Denise's mouth turned down.

"At first I thought we could have a casual affair. Nothing serious." She idly spun the glass in her hand. "He makes me feel special when I'm with him. I figured he would help me get over this rough patch in my life. Then I'd be ready to face the big, bad dating scene in New York when I return. But now...I don't know."

"He's a pretty special guy. He's been wonderful in dealing with Bobby's medical issues. And to think this whole thing was recently dropped on him. Never knowing he even had a child." Denise shook her head. "When he first started calling, he walked on egg shells, not wanting to step on our toes as Bobby's parents yet wanting to help."

"He calls you?" Why was he continuously surprising her?

"Almost every day. He's even offered to take Bobby to chemo, to help us out. Or to take care of Jennifer and Johnny if we're busy with Bobby."

"Has he met Bobby?"

"No. But he asked us if it would be okay."

Sam's breath hitched in her chest. "You're kidding."

"No. Why do you look so surprised?"

"Because of a conversation I had with him not too long ago. I'd gotten the impression he was afraid to meet Bobby. At first I thought his fear came from thinking Bobby would be angry with him for giving him up. But then I realized he didn't want to commit to someone who might reject him after he was no longer needed."

Denise nodded. "I could tell he had reservations. He didn't say why, and I didn't want to pry. When he's ready, we'll make it work."

Sam sighed. A good sigh. Except that Denise's revelation was making her fall in love with him more. "He is a wonderful person. And so easy to talk to. We have a lot in common too. But he moved out of the city, and I'm going back."

"What made him leave New York?"

"He found his fiancée in bed with another guy."

"Ouch." Denise pursed her lips and looked over at

Sam as if trying to glean something more. "Are you thinking of moving out of the city too?"

"No! Of course not. Where would I go? What would I do?"

"You could move here. You seem so relaxed. Even happy."

"That's because I'm on sabbatical. Who wouldn't be relaxed with ten weeks off after working sixty-hour weeks for the past eight years?"

"Are you looking forward to going back?"

Sam had never asked herself that question. There was no reason to. Her life revolved around living and working in the city. She had always loved it before. But now, forced to answer the question, she surprised herself. "No, I'm not looking forward to it. As a matter of fact, I dread it. I don't know if it's because I'm going back to an empty apartment or because I finally realized there's more to life than working my butt off to become a partner."

"What are Tom's plans? Is he returning to New York soon?" Denise set her empty glass on the table and her eyes on Sam.

"I have no idea. I told you about his call a few weeks ago. I haven't heard from him since, not that I expected to. Not that I want to."

"Is your mind made up about him?"

"Yes. After working my way through the hurt and anger, I realized we didn't have a whole hell of a lot in common."

"That didn't bother you before," Denise pointed out ever so rationally.

"I know. I thought we would find shared interests along the way. But instead of growing closer, we became mutually exclusive. I did my thing. He did his. In retrospect, that sounded the death knell. Tom didn't want to go to the opera or museums by himself. He wanted his wife to share those interests with him. And if I had been smart, I wouldn't have spent every waking minute practicing law or reading about it."

"When did you have this epiphany?" Coming from anyone else, the question would have sounded sarcastic, but not from Denise.

"Over the past few weeks. It started when I went sailing on a Monday with Michael. He decided, just like that, to take the day off and enjoy himself. Being the beneficiary of that little pleasure, I began to see how much richer this type of life could be. Don't get me wrong. Michael works and he works hard. It's just not his life."

"You've been so driven since high school, Sam. What would you do with yourself if you had free time?" In her subtle way, Denise asked the questions that made Sam really think about her decisions.

"I started volunteering at the hospital on a ward called Cherubs' Wing. For displaced children. And I feel so good about helping them. It's much more important than representing someone who's fighting over a piece of art work. These kids crave love and warmth, and when they get it, it's like you gave them the stars. When I worked in New York, I never even thought of volunteering to help kids."

Denise smiled. "Do you realize you talked about working in New York in the past tense?"

"That's not what I meant," protested Sam. "I just meant when I was working. Don't go reading anything more into that statement, Ms. Freud."

"There's nothing wrong with changing your life, Sam. You're still young. You can have a career in New Jersey as easily as in New York." Denise paused. "I know you're a very career-oriented woman, but you must think about having a family someday."

Sam blushed. She had given Denise such a hard time about giving up her banking career to stay home with her kids. "I have," she finally admitted. "Of course I would still work."

"Of course." Denise nodded, her lips twitching as if to keep a grin from curling the corners of her mouth. "Is it Michael who has you so turned around?"

The mention of his name sent her heart thudding and adrenaline rushing. She got up and paced the grass in front of the porch. "I don't know. I never felt close to being ready to have a child when I was with Tom. Maybe I'm mellowing. Or maybe it's the air around here. It's possible I'm too relaxed and don't know what to do with myself, so I'm conjuring up ways to fill my life. Once I'm back to work, I'm sure that idea will fly right out of my head."

"That's too bad." Denise swirled the ice in her glass with her finger. "Children can add such a wonderful dimension to your life. But you've already learned that."

Before she could stop it from falling out of her mouth, Sam said, "Michael must love children." She stopped pacing and glanced at Denise to see if her non sequitur had stunned her, but Denise just looked at her as if to say *go on*. "He volunteers at Cherubs' Wing too, although I only found out yesterday."

"That's admirable."

Sam examined Denise's expression to see if she

hid any well-deserved criticism under the surface, but she couldn't detect any. "What do you think?" Sam craved her opinion, even though it might come with unwanted condemnation.

"What do I think of what?" Denise blinked, looking very innocent.

Sam sighed and threw her hands up in the air, continuing her pacing. "About the fact that I'm having an affair with someone while I'm still married? About the fact that I really, really like Michael, but it can never work out? About the fact that I now volunteer helping children? About the fact that I would even consider having kids? Doesn't any of this shock you?" She stopped and turned to Denise.

"No. Why should it? From what I can see, your marriage is over. Tom left you for another woman, and you filed for divorce. Even if he came back, it doesn't appear as if you'd consider a reconciliation. So the fact that you're seeing someone else is great. Whether Michael's the man for you remains to be seen. But you have all the time in the world to figure that one out. You'll go back to New York, back to your apartment, back to your job. There's nothing to preclude you from seeing each other. The city's not on the other side of the continent. It's only sixty-five miles from here. Maybe you'll even decide to move out of Manhattan. Who knows? As for your newfound love of children, that was just a matter of time." Denise gave her a wink. "I'm thrilled you're helping kids who need it, and that you eventually want a family of your own. It will change your life for the better."

Denise's positive attitude rained over Sam and calmed her soul. There was no censure, no criticism.

Given her steady, rational words, Sam ventured out on a limb.

"Would you think I'm absolutely insane if I tell you I've been daydreaming about moving here? About having some fantasy life with Michael?" She held up her hand to preclude Denise from responding. "Please explain what's wrong with me."

Denise's smile was genuine, not mocking as she had feared. "You're not insane, Sam. You've finally discovered there's more to life than a career."

Sam exhaled, allowing the kind words of a great friend, who only wanted the best for her, to penetrate. "Thanks, Denise. I needed to hear that."

"Mommy," called Jennifer through the screen door. "Johnny's awake. He's crying."

Denise stood up and headed for the door. "So much for adult conversation. Back to kid duty. How'd you like to come with us to the boardwalk in Point Pleasant later? I promised them a ride on the merry-go-round."

"When I said I've become much better with children, I didn't mean I would go on the rides with them." Sam laughed, following Denise into the house.

Denise winked over her shoulder. "It's all part of the plan."

Chapter Twenty-Two

By Friday, Sam had decided on her own plan. No longer willing to let fate dictate when or where she saw Michael, she jogged on the boardwalk in the early morning before the sun blasted the area with its blistering heat, singing along to the Rolling Stones as they claimed sympathy for the devil.

After showering, she spent some time reviewing documents and telephoning the office, although her focus wasn't as sharp as usual. Instead, she rushed through her work in order to enjoy the other parts of her day before heading off to see her kids on Cherubs' Wing—and Michael.

She felt a little sneaky about seeing him this way, but she rationalized she had planned on working at the hospital today before she even knew he would be there. It would be easier to run into him and see how things went, rather than calling him to set up a date. This way, either one of them could disappear without making further plans and without any guilt. She just hoped she'd be the one to make the decision to walk, if that was the decision made.

Thrilled to see her after a day away, the little girls cuddled and showed Sam their dollhouse, and the boys jumped on her and threw paper airplanes in her direction to get her attention. A warm feeling of purpose invaded her body, and she wondered if this undertaking was changing her life forever.

Sam didn't forget her promise made a few days earlier. She brought lemonade and poured it into paper cups for each of the children, getting mixed reviews on the taste, evidenced by comical faces. Halfway through the tasting, she heard a familiar voice, and fireworks cascaded through her body.

"How are the little angels?" Michael bent down, getting pummeled with hugs and shoves and screeches. All ten children encircled him, trying to get a piece at the same time. "Whoa." He stood and held out his hands so he could ruffle hair. "It's good to see you guys. Is it time for dinner? I'm starving."

The brilliance of his smile lit up his face and reached those aquamarine eyes, transmitting warmth straight to the pit of Sam's stomach. The scene was so endearing a lump of sentimentality clogged her throat. As if she were watching a heartwarming film.

Michael's movie star looks only enhanced the fantasy, despite faded jeans, navy T-shirt, and scuffed sneakers. His hair had been tousled by the children's hugs, making him look even sexier. A surprised gaze met Sam's, and his smile widened. "Hi, Sam. I didn't know you'd be here today."

"I'm here until eight. I promised to help get the kids ready for bed tonight."

"Good luck with that." He chuckled, sending a playful wink her way. "After dinner, I'm taking them outside to play basketball. That always gets them wound up."

"Then I assume you'll be here to help get them wound down too." She grinned, picking up the pieces to Candy Land and putting them back in the box.

"Of course. I tried to sneak out in the past before bedtime, but that didn't work. Right, kids?" he asked as they still hovered around his legs.

"Yeah," they yelled in unison.

Sam and Michael helped the children with dinner, buttering rolls, cutting their meat, pouring drinks. It was a noisy affair with everyone talking at once, silverware clanging and chairs scraping against the floor. Although excited about playing basketball after dinner, they were told they had to clean their plates before everyone could leave. And they did.

"Sam, how's your game?"

"I haven't played since high school, so probably not so good."

"Oh, no! I forgot you were on the team. And here I thought I could whoop your butt."

Looking at the bunched muscles of Michael's biceps and the powerful thighs under his jeans, Sam would be no match for him, but she wasn't about to slink away. "We'll see," she said slyly, arching her brow before walking away. Playing head games was all part of the battle, and she could do that with the best of them.

"I'll take the girls, you take the boys." Sam moved onto the court with her posse.

"That may not work out too well for you, Ms. Winslow." He smirked, obviously thinking he had the better team.

"I'll take my chances," she said coyly. "We'll practice for a few minutes on this half of the court. Feel free to practice on that half—unless you think you don't need it." She couldn't contain her grin.

"I don't know how to play," cried Penny as Sam

gathered her girls for a quick pep talk.

"That's okay, honey. Look for me or one of your other teammates. If you get the ball, throw it to one of us. We're here to have fun. Don't worry about the rules."

"That's your problem," commented Michael under his breath as he passed her.

"What are you talking about?"

"Forget it." He dribbled the ball around her and passed it to Danny as he rallied his troops.

When the game began in earnest, the children ran around the court, throwing, passing, dribbling, yelling, and of course, laughing. They learned as they went, and more often than not, passed the ball to the wrong team. Sam took great satisfaction in stealing the ball from Michael when the occasion presented itself, and she got her game back after the first five minutes of playing, managing to keep Michael at bay and never failing to use her hips to maneuver him out of her way.

"That was a foul," he yelled at her, after she stole the ball from him again.

"I didn't hear the referee's whistle." She ran past him, heading for her team's basket.

"There is no referee," he shouted as she made the basket.

"Score." Sam and her teammates cheered, ignoring his comment.

Michael bounded underneath the basket and grabbed the ball, passing it to Eddie. "Now you're in for it." The gleam in his eye suggested the gloves were off.

"In for what?" Sam asked innocently, hands on hips. "I thought we were just having a friendly game of basketball." The corners of her mouth slid up in a smile, and she ducked back to bring up the rear, encouraging three of her teammates to move in and surround Michael.

Just as Billy was about to pass the ball, the little girls ran in front of Michael, with one pulling on his shirt, one gripping his hand, and the third jumping up and down enthusiastically and coming down on his foot.

Sam dashed in and intercepted the pass, dribbling around Michael for effect. "Is this what you meant when you said 'I'm in for it'?" She raced past him and up the court.

He murmured an incoherent oath and carefully disengaged himself from her cohorts. "Come on, guys. We have to stop her." He motioned to Danny and Charlie who were sitting underneath their basket, apparently taking a break.

Michael clutched Sam around the waist and lifted her easily off the ground as the ball bounced away from her, out of her control.

"Put me down." Her shriek turned to laughter as she struggled to extricate herself.

The girls leapt to her rescue and started pulling and tugging on Michael, while the boys dashed in to help their hero, all adding several decibel levels to the racket. Within seconds, they all ended up in a heap on the ground, tickling, giggling, and laughing until they were out of breath.

"Okay," Sam shouted over the din. "Game over."

"Awww." The kids complained, even though they were dead tired.

"It's seven thirty. Time to get ready for bed."

She and Michael corralled them back into the building and up to the bathrooms, one for the boys, one for the girls. Sam turned on the shower for the two older girls and started a bath for the three younger ones. They talked about how much fun they'd had playing basketball, sang a few songs that everyone knew, and washed the dirt of the day away. Sam could use a bath herself, but that would have to wait. The sweat had trickled down her back during the heat of the game, and she feared she smelled like a little kid herself, one who just came off the playground.

After brushing teeth and hair, the girls moved quietly into the room where their beds were set up. Michael already had the boys in there, sitting around him on the floor, ready to read a story.

"Hey, slowpokes," he called to them good-naturedly. "We've been waiting for you for hours."

Barbara looked up at Sam. "Were we that long?"

"No. Michael's teasing." She patted the top of her head and stroked her hair. "Go on over and listen to the story, honey."

The girls filled in the spaces and listened to one of the *Berenstain Bears* tales. Sam sat nearby and watched, as the children hung on to every word Michael spoke. They laughed, asked questions, and commented, dragging out the story as much as possible.

Sam's head spun as she captured this picture for posterity. These innocent little children, so trusting. They adored the strangers who came to play with them and feed them and help them. Life wasn't fair, but they still laughed and giggled and had fun. They slept in a room with ten beds and hadn't known each other until they'd been thrown together in the sterile environment of an institution, becoming fast friends and playmates. Then they were torn apart again when a foster family took one or two of them away. A lump formed in Sam's throat as she watched them fight to stay awake, begging to hear one more story, to be with Michael, a man they clearly adored.

"Okay kids. It's time to get into bed." Michael pulled them up and pointed them in the right direction. "Sam will help me tuck you guys in. You played a great game of basketball tonight. We'll do that again real soon." He covered Charlie with a sheet and bent over to kiss his forehead before moving to the next bed.

"Sam, will you play again too?" asked Penny.

"I sure will." Sam smiled as she too pulled up sheets and tucked the children in.

When they finished, Michael took hold of Sam's hand and pulled her to the other side of the room. "I think we tired them out enough so they'll sleep tonight."

"I know I will." She massaged the tops of her thighs, where the muscles started tightening.

Within seconds, soft breathing came from each of their beds.

"They do look like little angels, don't they?" whispered Michael, nodding in their direction. Then he turned to her. "The social worker on duty tonight can take over from here. How'd you like to grab something to eat?"

The hairs on her arms stood at attention, and her heart flipped in her chest. This was what she had hoped for. "As long as it's someplace casual," she heard herself saying. "I feel a bit grubby."

"Me too." He laughed, then added, "And tired."

She assumed his latter statement was meant to clue her in that this date would only include dinner. At least now she wouldn't have to worry about ending up in his bed.

And that was fine with her. *Right?*

****

His assumption that avoidance would keep him safe slapped him in the face. Instead of thrilling, this roller-coaster ride had him so confused he felt ill. He wanted Sam so badly it hurt, but he knew it would hurt more when she left. So he'd tortured himself by trying to ignore her. But each time he saw her, his good intentions of steering clear did a hundred-eighty-degree turn and drew him to her like a magnet. Each time, the force became stronger and the effort to keep away harder.

Tonight proved no different.

If he wasn't careful, he might become a masochist. Yet he gained no pleasure from punishing himself like this. Why didn't he give up his plan to avoid Sam and enjoy her while she was here? His mouth seemed to ignore the instructions from his brain anyway. All he needed was to be within two feet of her, and an invitation fell out of it.

Like now. After dinner. "Would you like to come back to the house?" The offer held no mystery, his intent ever so clear.

A pretty blush crept into Sam's cheeks. "How about a walk on the beach?"

Was that a yes, no, or later? He might never understand women.

The beach stretched out before them under the muted light of a million stars, the moon conspicuously missing. Dimly seen in the vastness before them, whitecaps rolled over each other as they made their way to the surf. The crashing water filled the air around them, forcing them to talk louder than either may have wanted.

"I don't know what's going on with us." Sam looked as confused as he felt.

"We're too attracted to each other for our own good." He grabbed her hand and kissed it.

"Is that why I don't hear from you? Because you're attracted to me?"

It sounded so ridiculous, but the truth couldn't be hidden. "Yes."

"I thought this is what you did during the summer months. Dated women who came to the beach for the season."

"I do. Sometimes. But I…" Did he want to acknowledge this out loud? To her? "I feel differently about you."

She stopped and turned to him. "How differently?"

His pupils had adjusted to the dark, and Sam stood very close. He could see her huge eyes look to him for the answer she needed, pulling it from his soul. "I'm falling in love with you."

She opened her mouth as if to speak, but nothing came out. The strain in her face disappeared. In its place a softness, the hint of a smile, a glow in her eyes, all surfaced as she brought her hand up to stroke his cheek. "I feel the same way," she whispered.

The wall crumbled between them, and euphoria surged through Michael as he leaned in to cover her lips with his. She tasted so sweet and warm, like melted molasses, and she opened her mouth to let him in, allowing his tongue to explore leisurely at first, before his hunger grew. His mouth became insistent and demanding, as she ran hot palms up his chest and around his neck, sending sparks, then fire wherever she touched. Graceful fingertips fondled the ends of his hair and his neck, transmitting shock waves to his extremities. Her lithe body molded into his, making him feel like molten liquid in some places and cast iron in others. She made him weak with passion, and he pulled her down to the sand with him, never breaking the hot, erotic kiss that sapped his strength.

He slipped his hand under her shirt, and the moan from swollen lips drove him wild. Sliding her shirt up and the lace of her bra down, he moved his mouth to her breast and teased until it was taut and peaked. Sam's back arched as she ran her fingers through his hair and over his shoulders, sending shivers of desire down his spine.

He looked into her hooded eyes, yearning apparent in their depths.

"Will you come back to my house now?" His voice was raw with sexual tension. "At our age, it's not necessary to do it on the beach. Besides, with your record, we'll probably get arrested for lewd behavior."

Sam didn't even laugh. "You have me so damn aroused I don't know if I'll make it back to your house." Her violet eyes bored into his, serious, solemn, almost begging him to take her right there, right then.

The temptation was so great and his lust so close to the surface that Michael momentarily considered her plea. But practicality took over. He slid her shirt down and took her hand, pulling her up with him. "Come on. My house is less than a half mile away."

****

They started running, as if in a race, laughing like giddy lovers, the wind now in their faces, making the trip harder than Sam would have preferred. Despite the anxiety of getting hurt again, she had come to the decision she wanted to be with Michael, no matter what. She would throw caution into the ocean and enjoy the moments he might be willing to give. Not in her wildest dreams had she imagined the reason he'd been scarce had to do with his feelings for her and his fear of letting those feelings surface. Her heart jumped and skipped at the thought of his words. *I'm falling in love with you.*

She knew she had fallen in love with him. Every time she ran into him, her blood pounded through her veins, and her face flushed with need. But seeing him with the kids had sealed her fate. And knowing he would form a bond with Bobby made her heart soar. He'd become a real person, a caring person, not just a sexy, drop-dead gorgeous guy she'd had a crush on in her former life and met again years later. How would she be able to let him go?

They climbed the stairs from the beach to his deck, and Michael slid the glass door open, stepping aside to let Sam through. Peace enveloped her as she moved into the house, away from the wind and crash of the ocean, almost too quiet. Her insides squirmed, and the exertion from their run heated her skin. She inhaled to calm the internal turbulence, but to no avail. She scratched at her skin, which now itched from the salt and sand and warmth.

"I feel so…sticky," she admitted.

"Would you like to take a shower?" Michael's

eyebrow arched, indicating something more than a mundane ritual.

"I'd love to." She smiled at his duplicitous suggestion. The thought of clear, cool water sluicing over their bodies as they washed away the film of sand covering them sounded like pure heaven. Especially since the pleasure wouldn't stop there.

He led her upstairs to the master bathroom, bigger than the kitchen of her borrowed shore house. A huge double-stall shower stood to the left, a picture window opposite, overlooking the ocean.

He turned on the shower and lowered the shade. "I'll be right back with some towels."

Sam quickly shed her clothes and stepped under the firm spray, the tepid water running over her body, ridding it of the grit and grime of the day. She stood under the deluge, as she slid the soap across her skin, sexual tension continuing to build within her.

The steam around her drifted and settled in every pore as she lifted her face to the shower head, luxuriating in each drop of water striking her shoulders and sliding down her back. Very sensuous.

Outside of her haze, the shower door slid open, tingling her body with a whoosh of cool air and the knowledge that Michael had come to join her.

"You started without me." His low, sexy voice enveloped her as he moved into her space, his chest to her back.

She purred in response as he kissed her ear, tickling it with his tongue until the sensation became deeper, more erotic, sending shivers from her neck to her toes. He moved his arms around her and took the soap, palming it in his hand before sliding it over her ribs and breasts, his other hand massaging the smooth, satiny skin left in its wake. He continued to assault her neck with his tongue, harder, slithering. She leaned back against him and moaned with the pleasure he gave, eyes closed, head against his shoulder, willing him to hold her up for fear she would dissolve and slide right down the drain.

She angled her head to find his lips, drinking him in, turning in his arms to face him. Taking the soap from his hand, she lathered his chest, his arms, his hands, before moving lower. His jaw clenched, and he closed his eyes as she stroked his hardness, leisurely, lightly, teasingly. Without giving her time to explore farther, he took the soap out of her hand, put it down, and gave the water barely a second to rinse them before turning the faucets off.

"What are you doing?" Sam asked, stunned by his abruptness.

He pushed open the door, grabbed a towel, and wrapped it around her before taking his own. "You're making me crazy." His voice was husky. Raw.

"That was the idea." She smiled lazily, moving in slow motion.

"I know. I need to move it to the bedroom."

"Anxious, aren't you?" she teased, wiping her face with the towel.

"I've been anxious since five o'clock this afternoon. The anxiety is killing me."

She felt the same way and reveled in the anticipation that hummed through her body, setting her senses at high alert. He guided her to the bedroom, then faced her, sliding her towel from around her shoulders and letting it fall to the floor—next to his. He then drew her to his bed.

The covers had been pulled down, and she lay on cool sheets, the luxury of fine cotton against her back and legs. Michael settled next to her, leaving no distance between the two of them, lowering his head to find her mouth. He covered her lips with his—hot, firm, and searching—sending every nerve in her body a jolt of electricity. She glided her hands around his shoulders and caressed the back of his neck, pulling him closer, feeling his ardor.

Arching toward him, she silently begged him to take more, to take all of her. Her breath caught in her throat as his hand trailed down her abdomen and between her legs. She was so ready for him.

Sam couldn't distinguish between the sound of the ocean crashing against the beach, and the hum in her head creating white noise and fog as she opened herself up to Michael. Every touch, every kiss, every stroke brought her closer to the edge until she could hold back no longer. Waves of orgasmic pleasure washed through her, ebbing and flowing, taking her further into the fog, bringing him with her as he climaxed seconds later.

Chapter Twenty-Three

"I think it's time I left." Sam sipped a glass of wine on the deck, watching the sea gulls swarm and swoop near two children who threw bread into the air.

"It's still early." Michael took her hand and kissed it as he watched the same scene.

For the first time in months, she felt like a whole person. She'd spent the last few days in a blend of utter contentment and pleasure. She and Michael cooked on the grill, walked on the beach, and sailed on his boat. They even went grocery shopping. And in between each activity, they made love. By Sunday night, her muscles ached, and she was dead tired, but the lightness and happiness that came with Michael permeated her soul.

Despite her euphoria, she stuck to her resolve. "I know, but you need to work tomorrow, and I need to check in too." Deep down, she didn't want to be so practical. She could have stayed here, wrapped in Michael's cocoon forever, feeling his warmth and love surround her, never again venturing out into the real world. She smiled at the thought. "Besides, I don't want you to get tired of me. I've been here since Friday."

He looked over at her and smiled. "I can never tire of you." Beneath that smile was a smoldering look that would have her in bed within minutes if she didn't leave now. She would never tire of him either.

She stood and brushed a kiss on his forehead, afraid that anything too close to his lips would crush her determination to give him some room. And hopefully some time to miss her. "Thanks for the wonderful weekend, Michael." Her voice caressed him instead of her arms.

He rose and cupped her cheek. "I don't know how I'll sleep without you tonight."

She laughed playfully and moved through the glass door into the living room. "Considering we don't get much sleep when we're together, I think you'll do fine." She noticed his jaw tighten at her attempt at a joke. "I'm sorry. I didn't mean to be flippant."

She picked up her bag and headed for the door.

A sharp pain stabbed at her heart, catching her off guard. She couldn't bear to even think about what would happen to them after the next thirteen days. She would miss him terribly. She missed him already. And she wasn't even out the door. Wanting to ask when they might see each other again, she opted against it. She didn't want to push. And considering her silent vow to keep things light between them, despite their blissful weekend, she said goodbye.

He followed her out. "There's a volleyball game against our biggest rival tomorrow night at six. If you're not doing anything, come by and we'll grab something to eat afterward."

She exhaled. Thank God for small favors. "Sure. I'd love to."

They gave each other a chaste kiss, and she left. How odd that formality had replaced passion. She had disconnected from Michael, and the absence of intimacy sprayed her with melancholy.

As a little girl, she had hated Sunday nights. The end of a pleasurable weekend brought apprehension and even dread of the week to come. Sleep would elude her until the wee hours of the morning, and Monday would start out with her tired and grumpy. Back then, all she needed was an hour or so to get back into the swing of things, and the new week ahead would transform itself into new possibilities instead of dread.

But this was different. Her ecstasy and happiness when with Michael were turning to anxiety and longing without him. And that was while she was still here in Crescent Beach. What would happen when she returned to New York? Would she ever see him again? Or would their obsession fade into the inconvenience of the commute?

She should never have wandered into this quagmire. Yet she had convinced herself she could handle it.

She should have known better.

****

The volleyball game began at six, and Michael was pumped. The men's voices filled the beach with shouts, laughter, and grunts as the ball spiked and plummeted into the sand. Quite an audience had assembled for the games, cheering and clapping for their favorite team. Michael's team consisted of men his age; the opposing team, younger. But what Michael's team lacked in youth, they made up for with experience, and the youngsters were getting their heads handed to them, much to the chagrin of the college girls ogling on the sideline. With no lack of team spirit on either side, gibes and taunts flew across the net with the ball, yet none of the remarks were given or taken with ill will.

Even team pride dissipated a few minutes after the game was over, when both teams and their guests agreed to meet at Harry's for burgers and beers.

Michael wended his way through the spectators toward Sam. She wore denim shorts, a white T-shirt, and a smile that made him want to drag her back to his house and skip dinner. But it was Hal's birthday, and he had promised his teammates they would join them.

Pulling a black T-shirt over his head, he gave her a quick kiss. "I know I invited you out to dinner tonight, but I forgot about Hal's birthday. Would you mind having that burger with a few of my closest friends?"

A small crowd headed off the beach in the direction of Harry's.

"I'd love to meet your friends. By the way, great game. It looks like you guys have so much fun out there."

"We do. It's a good bonding experience," he teased.

Sam gave him a sideways glance. "I'm sure it is. You said yourself you didn't have any friends in the city."

They brought up the rear of the gang, lagging behind by at least a block.

"I'm working on it. I see how great it is for you and your friends. You're so connected. So helpful to each other. I never had that." He glanced at her. "But these guys are a good group. I think they'd do anything for me if I needed it. It's a nice feeling."

He wished he'd had that kind of support system in high school. But there was no sense making the comparison or feeling any anger or regret over the past. He'd come through it as a stronger and better human being. He hoped. And now he was breaking down barriers. All because of Sam. She'd convinced him to reach out to Bobby. And she'd taught him the value of having friends.

Sam brought him back to the conversation. "Do your friends all live in Crescent Beach?"

"Either here or in one of the surrounding towns. None of them lives more than ten miles away." Michael grabbed her hand, and an immediate surge heightened every nerve in his body. They walked in sync, their connection reinforced after twenty-four hours apart.

"What do they do for a living?"

"Rob and Pat are accountants, although they work for different companies. Tony owns a restaurant in Spring Lake, Joe manages a bank, and Hal is a lawyer too."

"Where does Hal practice?"

"In Red Bank. For a branch of a New York firm. He's one of us. A former city workaholic who found peace in the suburbs."

"You can't include me in that 'us.' I'm a temporary transplant."

Although her words didn't surprise him, they twisted his heart. Did she have to sound so chipper about it? He had hoped she was interested in finding out about his friends' jobs to see if there could be anything here for her. He should have known the thought hadn't even crossed her mind. A die-hard city girl would be impossible to break, and apparently she still lived, breathed, and loved Manhattan. Even though it was only sixty-five miles away, their worlds would assuredly defy bridging.

"Hasn't Crescent Beach gotten to you just a little?"

He brought her hand to his lips and kissed it, hoping a little more than Crescent Beach was getting under her skin.

"Of course. And so has the local prosecutor." She smiled coyly. But her words, which meant to flatter, only served to punch him in the gut. What difference did it make if she liked him? Even loved him. She was still going back.

The long weekend they had spent was magical, joyful. Two and a half days of laughing, kissing, and making love. He hadn't wanted it to end. He'd almost begged her to stay last night, but she was right. He had to work today, and a good night's sleep had delightfully eluded them throughout the weekend. And although he'd slept, his waking hours had proved unproductive, when thoughts, no dreams, of Sam—in his arms, in his bed, in his shower, in his kitchen—had flashed through his mind like euphoric hallucinations from a psychedelic drug. He should never have tried that drug. Addiction could prove fatal.

"What's the matter?" she asked, breaking into his thoughts. "You're awfully quiet."

"Nothing." He couldn't tell her she was killing him slowly. "A little tired from the game, I guess."

"Getting old, huh?" She playfully poked him in the ribs with her elbow, and he caught her arm and pulled her into him.

Iridescent violet eyes shone with laughter, and her wide, sensuous mouth smiled as she made a half-hearted attempt to pull away from his hold.

"If I'm not mistaken, you're the same age as me, Ms. Winslow. And we all know that women age less gracefully than men."

"Oh! Now you're in trouble." She fisted her hands and gave him tiny punches on the arm, dodging and running around him, until he grabbed her wrists and held them over her head.

Breathing hard with the exertion of their little fight, her chest heaved, pushing her breasts out toward him. He managed to take his eyes off her chest to study her face. All vestiges of playfulness were gone, and pure desire pooled in the pit of his stomach and lower. He leaned over and kissed her, hard, demanding, proprietary.

"Let's skip Harry's," he said, coming up for air and immediately returning to her mouth.

She pulled away, her lips swollen from his assault. "We can't. You promised your friends."

He sighed. "You're right. We'll order the second we walk through the door, have one beer, eat fast, and get out of there."

She laughed, a low sexy laugh, and grabbed his hand, pulling him toward the restaurant. "You're on."

****

Her last Saturday in Crescent Beach loomed over her like a wave, building and growing in power and strength. When it came crashing down, Michael would be washed ashore in Crescent Beach and she would land in New York City, wondering what had happened to destroy the rapture they'd experienced over the past two weeks.

And what a blissful two weeks it had been. Blurred into a snapshot of pure delight and exhilaration, Sam had spent some part of every day with Michael, and they were bonded like glue at night. July at the Jersey shore put businesses in the black for the year. Every house was rented or occupied by its owners, every restaurant and bar packed to the gills, and every square yard of space on the beach covered with chairs, umbrellas, and blankets.

But Sam and Michael only had to contend with the crowds when they chose. When able to take off from work in the middle of any given day, Michael would hunt Sam down at her favorite haunts—Melanie's Coffee Shop, her house, the beach, or Cherubs' Wing—and cart her away. They'd spent their time lazing on his deck or in his bed, with his friends at local bars after volleyball games, at Sam's house where she'd experimented with dinner, or on his sailboat. The two of them had been inseparable, lost in the haze of new love.

While the days were lazy and sun-kissed, the nights were wild and passionate. Sam couldn't get enough of Michael, and by his actions, she assumed he felt the same way about her. Although he wouldn't admit it. Except for that one night on the beach, no further declarations of love were uttered. She ached to hear those lovely words again, but she understood the vulnerability that came with such words, and couldn't fault him for avoiding that trap. For she avoided it too.

And then her last day arrived.

Sam's eyes hurt from lack of sleep, and she rubbed them as she walked out onto the porch, coffee mug in hand. Michael slept, sprawled in her bed, and although she couldn't bear to leave him, she had to get moving. Most of her clothes were packed. All she needed to do was finish cleaning up the kitchen and bathroom before noon, the time her friend, Bruce, and his family were taking their house back.

The screen door squeaked as it opened, and she looked up to see a groggy Michael stumbling out to the porch to join her.

"Morning." He set his coffee cup down on the table before sliding onto the sofa next to her. He kissed the side of her head.

"Morning." All hope and lightness slowly exited her body.

"How'd you sleep?"

"I didn't. I couldn't."

He held her hand and massaged her palm with his thumb. "This sucks. How dare your friend kick you out of his house today!"

Sam smiled at his attempt to joke. "I can't believe I'm going back to work on Monday. I hope the last ten weeks hasn't warped my mind."

"You didn't let it. You continued to work through your sabbatical. But even if you do feel a little rusty, before your first day is over, you'll wonder what happened to the calm and serenity you channeled here. You'll be juggling client meetings, settlement conferences, and preparing for oral arguments on motions. It'll feel like you never left."

"Sounds like you have experience in returning from the black hole." She gave him a sideways glance.

"I do." He lifted her hand and kissed her fingers. "Although I didn't return to New York City like you are, I found my way back to practicing law. The first day was tough. But after that, the routine set in. With me, it was exciting. I started out in a new place with a new outlook on life." He paused. "You'll find your center again. You're a strong woman and a wonderful person." His words, meant to encourage, sounded hollow, sad.

Tears welled up in her eyes, and she couldn't look at him for fear they would spill over her lashes and down her face. She couldn't cry now. But when he put his arm around her shoulders and drew her into him, the floodgates opened.

"It'll be okay, Sam." He rubbed her arm and let her cry, making soothing sounds to ease her sorrow.

"I'm sorry," she hiccupped. "It's just that I ended up having such a great summer…with you. I can't stand the thought of leaving. Of going back to my co-op. Of picking up the pieces to lead me back to the partnership track." She knew the real strain was integrally connected to the reality of losing him.

"Sam. You'll do fine. You were able to clear your head here. You told me yourself that talking to your friends was the best therapy. And you made a life-changing decision to file for divorce. It may seem overwhelming to go back, but once you're there, you'll see that all this angst was unnecessary."

He held her for a long time, reassuring her, comforting her, saying all the things she needed to hear, yet she was dying inside. She wanted him to convince her she shouldn't go back. That she should give up her co-op and her job in New York and move here.

But she knew he had to let her go. She wouldn't toss aside her responsibilities. She couldn't just quit. So there was no use in making it harder on either of them by pretending otherwise. She needed to return, even if only to find out she no longer desired that life. Icy fingers of dread strangled her insides at the thought of leaving Crescent Beach.

Of leaving Michael.

Her throat constricted, and she swallowed to push down the lump. She was in love with him, and it hurt.

She pulled away and sat up. "I better finish cleaning. I don't want the Taylors showing up to a dirty house." She stood and headed into the kitchen.

"What time are they coming?" he asked through the screen door.

"Noon."

She looked at the kitchen clock. It was nine. He followed her inside.

"I told the kids on Cherubs' Wing I would stop in to say good-bye." She washed out the coffee mugs and began tidying up the rest of the kitchen. "Penny cried when I told her I was leaving. I promised I would write to her."

Sam continued making small talk, avoiding any words that would cause more pain. But even these words pulled at her heart. How could she leave those kids? She loved playing basketball with them, reading to them, kissing them good night. With Michael right beside her, sharing a piece of himself.

"Don't worry. I'll take good care of them."

Of course he would. Like he was helping Bobby. "I talked to Denise the other day. She said the bone marrow transplant is scheduled for mid-August. You didn't tell me."

He shrugged. "I've been selfish. I didn't want to spoil our last few days together by talking about Bobby's leukemia." He looked at the floor as his jaw tensed.

She walked over to him and placed her hands on his shoulders. "You're a good man, Michael. You're doing more than anyone else could to help him. He'll be fine once the two of you get through this procedure."

The hint of a smile crept across his lips. "I need to keep hearing those positive words from you. It's sure to bring us luck."

"You'll hear them from me every day if that's what it takes." She held his eyes for a fleeting moment.

"Well, I guess I'd better be going." He moved away from her abruptly. "Let you get done what you need to."

She looked up, startled. He should stay until the end despite the melancholy look, the sad eyes. The useless words.

"Don't forget the Labor Day party." He took her hand fleetingly. "I'll call you. Or you call me."

It sounded so trite. So unemotional. Her eyes found his, and she pleaded for something more—something that would make the pain go away. But the pain inundated his eyes too.

He gave her a quick kiss, then turned to go. Sam ached to cry out "Wait." But the plea died on her lips as the door closed softly behind him.

There was nothing more to say.

Chapter Twenty-Four

The keys to her apartment slid easily into the three locks that protected their possessions. She pushed the door open with her foot and set one suitcase in the foyer, carrying the second one in. The air hung still and stuffy, and the heat from the summer's day closed in around her as she moved into the living room. Everything stood as she had left it: the silk pillows just so on the linen couch, the shades pulled down to the sills, the coffee table books angled to the left, the ottomans under the sofa table. Very modern, very sleek. Very sterile.

She walked down the hallway toward the bedroom, her sandaled feet crushing the nap of the oyster-colored carpet, leaving dark footprints. Eerie silence followed her, and uneasiness settled in the pit of her stomach. This was her home. Why didn't she feel comfortable, even cozy? She looked around the bedroom. Nothing graced the top of the bureau but emptiness, coldness. No clothes were strewn on the chaise. The closet door remained closed instead of slightly ajar, as it had always been. The nightstands held no books or pens perched on their surfaces. No one lived here.

She threw her suitcase on the bed and moved into the bathroom. Stark and empty. No towels on the bar, no toothbrushes in the holders, no soap in the dish. She toyed with the idea of calling a realtor right then and there. This place was in perfect condition for sale. Why not list it immediately? Why wait for Tom to come back? Or not. This was no longer their home.

But where would she go? She needed to look for a new place. A smaller place. Something for herself. The thought intrigued her. She would begin her search Monday at lunch time, and every day after that. And when she found something, she would put the co-op on the market unless Tom preferred to buy her out.

After setting the air conditioner temperature to a reasonable seventy-two degrees, she unpacked her suitcases and began the task of making the place look like someone lived there. It would never approximate the coziness of her Crescent Beach home, but at least it no longer looked like a museum.

Grocery shopping was next, a dreaded, necessary chore that would never move up on her list, but she pushed the cart up and down every aisle, filling it with a mix of comfort food, healthy choices, and staples. Unfortunately, she had overdone it and struggled off the elevator with her purse, keys, and three bags full of provisions.

But she didn't need the keys. The door stood open, and standing there, filling the frame, was Tom.

"Hi, Sam." He said it as if he had just seen her that morning. He took two bags from her arms and headed toward the kitchen.

She stopped in her tracks, her mouth open, her feet cemented to the marble floor in the foyer.

He retraced his steps and looked at her rooted in her spot. "Aren't you coming in?"

She finally found her voice. "When did you get here?"

"About fifteen minutes ago. I figured you would arrive either today or tomorrow, since you're going back to work on Monday."

"How do you know?" Her annoyance was barely hidden, but she didn't care.

"I called your office. Carol told me."

"Humph" was all she could come up with. "I thought you were staying in California through the summer…or longer."

"I cut it short. We need to talk." His words were clipped, and no warmth surrounded them. As if she were the culprit.

"It's too late for that."

"Now, Sam. Let's not be unreasonable." A condescending tone invaded his voice.

"Unreasonable?" She kept her cool even though her face burned in anger over his gall. Placing the bag down on the counter, she strode over to him. Then the absurdity of the situation tickled her, and she started to laugh.

"Are you okay, Sam?" Tom looked at her with something resembling fear in his eyes.

She shook her head and pulled out a stool from under the counter, before plopping down on it. "Don't worry. I haven't gone off the deep end. I'm actually fine. I'm just surprised, maybe a little shocked. I didn't expect to see you today. I certainly didn't expect to see you here."

"I needed to get back before this crazy divorce thing got any further."

He had to be kidding. Did he really think he could waltz back into her life now and change her mind? She raised an eyebrow, intrigued. "Go on."

"I know you didn't want to dismiss the Complaint when I called you a few weeks ago, but now that you've had a chance to relax a little, I thought maybe we could go to counseling. Figure out what went wrong with us. Fix it."

He looked at her pleadingly. He was so handsome, his straight blond hair cut to perfection, light-green eyes like crystal jade, and a smile to die for. The Ivy League preppy type.

So different from Michael's sensual, surfer look.

She sighed and gazed out toward the window. "Tom, I don't know how you and Sherry got together. I would like to say I don't even know why it happened. But I do. You felt I spent too much time at work, and you resented it. You told me as much that night at Winston's. But whether you had a good reason to have an affair or not, I'll never be able to forget that you betrayed me. Not only did you cheat on me, but you cheated on me with someone I considered a friend. Obviously I was wrong. She was clearly just a friend of yours."

"That's not…"

Sam held up her hand. "Please let me finish. I had a lot of time to think while I was away. And I had a lot of help from my girlfriends analyzing our marriage, my feelings, and the consequences of getting divorced. I don't trust you anymore. You never came to me and told me you were unhappy. You never gave me the opportunity to know my sins, at least in your eyes. Instead, you confronted me with it the same day you moved out. How could the person I married throw me away like that? With no regard for my feelings. No discussion. You basically told me I wasn't worth it."

Anger crept into her voice, and she inhaled to disperse it. "I don't know whether divorce is the right thing for you, but it's the right thing for me."

She rose from the stool and stood against the counter. "It took some time to get over my anger and face the reason that you left. I was a workaholic. I spent all my time either working at the office or here. I admit I wasn't available for you. But never once did you call me on it. Never once did you tell me how unhappy you were. Instead, you replaced me."

His shoulders slumped, and defeat took up residence in his eyes.

She felt sorry for him. "If I had to do it all over again, knowing what I know now, I would find the time to take a break, to relax, to have fun. It took me this summer to realize that my career is not my whole life. It's a means to allow me to enjoy life."

She thought about Michael and how happy he would have been to hear these last few statements from her. Apparently so was Tom.

He perked up. "That's great, Sam. Then why can't we try it again? Why can't we do things together? Try to rise above what happened to us?"

"I take it you and Sherry split up. Otherwise, you wouldn't be standing here begging me to give our marriage a chance. What happened?" She had become so calm she amazed herself. Here she was, asking her husband what had happened between him and his girlfriend. As if she could help ease his pain.

"I don't know." He hung his head, avoiding her eyes. "I guess the thrill of our affair didn't translate well into the humdrum of everyday life. We started fighting. She accused me of still loving you." He looked up at Sam, his eyes serious, his jaw set. "I still do, you know."

"You may think you do. I think you're just sad it's over. I am too. I'm sorry I spent so much time on my career. I'm sorry you didn't have the courage or the desire to talk to me about it before you walked out. We may have been able to work it out then. But we can't now. It's over."

Sam dipped into the grocery bag and started putting the food away. Tom sat there, his eyes downcast, twisting his wedding ring around his finger.

After a few minutes he said, "Are you sure?"

She turned and looked straight into his eyes so there could be no mistaking it. "I'm sure."

****

"Hey, Eric, do you have a minute?" Michael stood in Eric's doorway at the end of a long day of office appointments and business meetings.

"Sure. Come on in." Eric put his pen down and loosened his tie. "What's up?"

Michael eased into the chair in front of Eric's desk. "I've been thinking about your offer. To become a partner here. Have you ever thought of opening a New York office?" Although it was half said in jest, he couldn't help thinking it could possibly work.

Eric chuckled. "No. But if you'll commit to being my partner, we can talk about it."

"Then I'll do it." Michael leaned over the desk to shake his hand.

"It took you long enough." Eric grinned. "You've been here for a year. But I'm glad you finally made the right decision." He sat back in his chair with his hands behind his head. "What made you finally decide?"

Michael sighed, the weight of his decision pulling at him from both sides. "I've been skirting around the issue because I wasn't sure I should tie myself down. But I realized over the summer that commitment can be a good thing. It's been great spending time with Bobby and his parents. Even though the circumstances have been tough." And even though every time he thought about Bobby, he agonized over losing Sam. "This whole thing has grounded me. It's even changed the way I deal with the kids at Cherubs' Wing." He smiled as he replayed his basketball games with Sam and the children. How he'd learned more about each one of them when Sam was around. How it made him care more.

Eric's gaze seemed to question his statement. "So you're committing to me, and you've committed to Bobby and the kids at Cherubs' Wing." He paused. "Why haven't you committed to Sam?"

"What?" Where did that come from?

Eric attempted to hide a smile, but it didn't work. "You've changed this summer. For the better. Don't you see it's because of Sam? She's the one who convinced you to spend time with Bobby. She's the one who got you more involved with the kids at Cherubs' Wing. Now you're ready to be a real partner here. The only person you're not committing to is her."

Although it came at him shrouded in a white glove, Michael felt the blow as if it were physical. "In case you haven't noticed, she moved back to New York." How could Eric be blaming that on him? "She always intended to leave. Her career is in New York. Her life is there. She could never live in Crescent Beach." Even as he said it, the painful truth ricocheted through his being.

291

"That's why I asked about a New York office." Michael bowed his head. "I'm not sure I can go on like this."

"Did you ever ask Sam to move here?"

Michael's defenses kicked in. "Not in those specific words. But I encouraged her to think about moving out of the city to a place with a better quality of life."

Eric shook his head in disgust. "You're a great lawyer, Michael. Don't you know that sometimes it's necessary to spell it out? To get right to the point?" Eric's cutting advice caught him completely off guard. But apparently he wasn't finished. "Seems to me you didn't ask her because, even though you say you've changed, you're still afraid of commitment—at least where Sam is concerned."

Michael closed his mouth, but he guessed the shock etched on his face was a little harder to cover up. The accusation had his adrenaline pumping, and he would have loved to pummel Eric with a witty but snide come-back. But all he could manage was his tired excuse. "Sam needs to make up her own mind. I can't ask her to change her whole life, her career path, to move down here, just so we can keep seeing each other."

Eric shook his head, but a chuckle escaped. "For such a smart guy, you're being awfully dense on this subject. There is an alternative path to casual dating."

Then the light dawned, and it splintered into a thousand strands—like fireworks.

"Are you suggesting I ask her to marry me?"

Eric shrugged, obviously playing it close to the vest. For a change. "I'm pointing out a major flaw in your thinking. As your new partner, but mostly as your friend, I think you should consider your options and act on the one that makes the most sense." He looked at his watch, stood up, and grabbed his suit jacket. "Gotta go. I'm meeting my wife for dinner."

Michael couldn't help but notice the satisfied look on Eric's face as he headed out the door.

****

Tom didn't move back in. He left that day and settled temporarily into a hotel. Sam and he talked through their attorneys, negotiating the terms of a property settlement, and once Tom put his mind to it, it was easy. They listed their co-op for sale, and Sam started, in earnest, looking for a place to live.

But her heart wasn't in it. The life and the spirit of New York City, which she'd once loved and couldn't live without, evaded her. She tried hard to make up for lost time, but the electricity that had always defined the city fizzled and died.

She missed Crescent Beach. How a small town had gotten under her skin and into her blood she couldn't fathom. Yet the draw came from its friendliness, its open arms. By becoming one of the locals, Sam could walk into the coffee shop, the office supply store, the pharmacy, the post office, and have a warm conversation with not only the employees but the customers.

During her last two weeks, she'd gotten to know and like Michael's volleyball friends who'd welcomed her into their group like she'd been there all along. She even found she had a little something in common with each one of them. Sam was embarrassed to learn she'd become a New York snob, thinking only Manhattanites were intellectual and cultural and on the cutting edge.

However, Michael's friends could hold up to the best Manhattan had to offer. They were intelligent, professional men who spent more time taking advantage of the city than most city dwellers. Their quality of life allowed it, and their zest for culture demanded it.

One more mental barrier broken down.

She didn't need the city anymore. She didn't even want the city anymore. Not if Michael wasn't there.

She missed him. Ached for him. Her love for Crescent Beach was inextricably intertwined with him. She couldn't imagine one without the other.

Sam had talked to Michael by telephone a few times leading up to the bone marrow transplant. It was the only thing keeping them connected since they'd gone their separate ways. They both seemed to have silently agreed that a long-distance relationship wouldn't work, so they didn't even try. With Sam working six days a week, what was the point?

As she sat in her office dictating a Complaint the Thursday before Labor Day, Phil Bennett, the managing partner, stepped in.

"How's it going, Sam?" He took a seat in one of her client chairs.

"Fine." She swiveled away from her computer and looked at him. "Why? What's up?"

"Have you been able to settle back into your work?"

"Yes. Of course." Why was he asking? Was there a problem?

"You don't seem like your old self. I wanted to make sure you were okay." Concern underscored his words.

"That's very nice of you, Phil. But I'm fine. My upcoming divorce has me a little preoccupied. It's going through next week." True enough, except the real reason for her funk had to do with missing Michael.

Phil nodded as he crossed his leg. "I never had a chance to ask you how your leave of absence went?"

"It was wonderful." She felt her face light up. "I needed to get out of the city for those two months. It was great for my mental health. Of course, you know I worked from Crescent Beach."

"I knew you would." He smiled. "You're too dedicated a lawyer to desert your clients."

"I think it worked out well." She leaned forward, waiting for the real reason for his visit.

"I'm sure it did." He looked at her, his expression serious. "That's not what I came to talk to you about." He paused, and her stomach sank. "As you know, you're up for partnership in September."

She held her breath, not daring to move. This was it. What she'd been working toward.

"You've been such a dedicated, hard-working lawyer over the years, Sam. Your clients have the utmost confidence in your abilities, and you've won over most of the partners here, who not only respect your intelligence, but your drive."

Uh-oh. He said *most* of the partners. What about the others? She didn't dare ask.

He continued. "There's been some talk among my colleagues that your leave of absence came at an inopportune time for you, and the time off should push you back a year."

Sam gripped the arms of her chair as a combination of bitter disappointment and misplaced anger collided.

Of course, some would feel that way. Was she truly surprised? It was extremely difficult to make it to the partnership level at a firm like this. Only two other attorneys, of the sixteen who'd started with her, had survived. Would they choose one of them? Would they postpone her chance until next year?

"But I convinced the skeptics." A smile replaced his intensity.

Her spine tingled. Her skin tingled. Her hair tingled. But no words came out of her open mouth.

"Sam, are you okay?"

"I…I think so. Are you saying that…?" She was terrified to say it out loud.

"Yes. I'm saying you're being offered a partnership." He stood and stuck out his hand to her. "Congratulations."

She rose and shook his hand, feeling light-headed, dizzy. *Yes*! She had made it! Her smile escaped, the only release for her bottled-up emotions.

Phil sat back down. She took her seat as well, unable to wipe the stupid grin off her face.

"Have you talked to Bruce Taylor lately?" he asked.

The quick transition startled her. As well as the question.

"No. Not since I left Crescent Beach at the beginning of the month." When she'd turned over her keys to his summer house. And her heart to Michael. "But I'll probably see him this weekend. Why?"

"Oh? You're going down there for the weekend?" Phil's eyebrow inched up, and Sam almost laughed at his puzzled look.

"Yes. I've been invited to a Labor Day party."

"So you made some friends there, huh?"

"You could say that." She smiled but refused to elaborate.

"I guess you've heard Bruce is leaving the firm to open up his own office near Crescent Beach?"

Her stomach dropped, and her eyes opened wider. "What? Are you serious?"

He chuckled at her reaction. "Bruce has been pushing for us to open a Red Bank office for at least a year now. He'd done the research and felt it was the perfect New Jersey location for a branch office. He wanted to field it since he has a house down there. But we weren't ready to make the move and invest in a satellite office. So he decided to do it on his own." He sighed. "I, for one, will be sorry to lose him."

She tried in vain to tamp down her excitement over Bruce's decision. "How wonderful for Bruce." But the irony didn't escape her. Bruce was leaving the city and moving to Crescent Beach—about to live her dream. Envy spread through her. She couldn't let Phil see it. She was supposed to be ecstatic over her partnership. Yet this news overshadowed hers by a longshot.

Phil steepled his hands and rested his chin on them, clearly musing over the subject. "Do you think the people who live in the Crescent Beach area would go to a New York firm for legal services?"

She trod carefully, not sure where he was going with this. "There are a few small firms in Crescent Beach. As a matter of fact, I'm using one of them for my divorce. It appears that the local firms mostly handle municipal court matters, wills and trusts, and real estate." She sat back in her chair, finally relaxing. "I met a few lawyers there, and one of them works at a

New York spin-off in Red Bank. He does estate planning and tax litigation." Fond memories surfaced at the thought of Michael's friend Hal. Which led to delicious thoughts of Michael. "The area could certainly use a great land use and zoning attorney like Bruce."

Maybe the area could also use a divorce lawyer. Her stomach flip-flopped at the thought. She inwardly laughed at herself. Would Bruce even consider it? Would she? How absurd! She'd just been offered the partnership she'd been working so hard for.

Phil stood. "Maybe we made a mistake by dragging our feet. I hope, for Bruce's sake, he's successful." He turned toward the door and called over his shoulder, "Congratulations, Sam. There will be a formal announcement about your partnership next week."

Sam stared at the empty space Phil had left, wondering if an angel was watching over her.

Chapter Twenty-Five

Sam hit the brake again in the stop-and-go traffic on the New Jersey Parkway. Squeezing the steering wheel in frustration, she let out a curse. Everyone from Maine to New York clearly intended to spend the Labor Day weekend at the Jersey shore. She wanted to be in Crescent Beach now. She wanted to see Michael. Now.

She couldn't wait to tell him about her decision. He probably wouldn't believe it. She couldn't believe it herself. If she weren't so happy, she'd think she'd lost her mind. Risking so much uncertainty. And after she'd been offered partnership.

The pesky questions bombarding her brain sidelined her pure joy. Would she be able to get a family law practice off the ground on her own? Would she be happy being a solo practitioner in a small town? Would she fit in? She sighed, knowing she was avoiding the biggest question of all. Still, it reverberated in her head like an echo.

Was she making this decision for the right reason?

Her resolve to leave New York and relocate to Crescent Beach was about more than being with Michael. She would strive to find balance between having a successful and independent career with a fulfilling personal life—complete with love and companionship. Months from now, if she discovered Michael wasn't right for her, or vice versa, she didn't want to castigate herself for moving out of the city and giving up her job there. She couldn't make this decision for the wrong reason.

Serious thoughts shifted to those more carnal in nature—Michael's welcoming arms caressing her, his insistent lips kissing her. Anticipation fluttered in her stomach. She'd have a whole weekend to bask in what she hoped would be the resurrection of their relationship.

For she'd made the decision whether she questioned herself or not.

All her life, her choices had been based on her need to be independent, in control. After seeing what her mother had gone through, she'd vowed never to rely on a man for money or for anything else. And she would do whatever it took to assure herself she'd be fine. More than fine. Her definition of independence had included success, money, and power. All of which were within reach with her firm's offer of partnership.

But now she didn't want it. At least not to the exclusion of her personal life.

The uncertainty Sam carried around with her throughout her last weeks in Crescent Beach, as well as New York, had been draining. The ecstatic highs followed by death-defying lows took her on a roller-coaster ride that only the strongest of heart could endure. Not knowing how to deal with the issue of Michael tortured and tormented her. Until she realized what she had to do. Insight had finally and miraculously lifted the oppression she felt and freed her to make the right decision—the only decision.

She smiled, despite the crawling traffic surrounding her.

Now all she needed to do was tell Michael. Her heart soared at the thought of seeing him.

When she finally arrived, every space on the street in a four-block radius contained an automobile. She pulled into Michael's driveway as if she belonged and grabbed her overnight bag from the trunk. Taking a deep breath, she headed up the steps and through the front door.

It was noon, and the kitchen and deck were already crowded with people—some of them familiar faces, although Sam wouldn't swear to their names.

"Hey there, Sam!" Hal gave her a bright smile as he made margaritas in the blender on the counter.

"Hi, Hal. Starting early, huh?"

"You bet. It's a gorgeous three-day weekend, and the sun is shining. Here you go." He held out a plastic cup filled with the light-green, frothy mixture.

"Thanks. Do you know where Michael is?" She attempted to keep the anxiousness out of her voice but didn't succeed.

"Missed him, eh?" He gave her a knowing look. "He's out on the deck tapping the keg."

"I'll be right back to help." She put her drink down and moved toward the back door.

"Take your time." His teasing words, punctuated by a wink, made her want to deny the truth. But what was the point?

Instead, she threw her bag into the office off the kitchen and headed outside. Michael stood over the keg, pumping the piston, holding a cup under the spout. Bronzed biceps bulged and relaxed with each pump, and his jaw tightened with the effort. Sam's breath hitched as electric sensations shot through her body and surrounded her heart. Magnificent aqua eyes glanced her way and caught her staring, but she wasn't embarrassed. She was hypnotized as he held her gaze, so intimate, so private, so personal. Then he dropped the cup and smiled broadly as he closed the space between them in several long strides.

****

"Samantha." Michael breathed her name as he took her into his arms and held her tight, crushing her, losing himself in her jasmine scent, her feel. They could have been alone on a desert island, for he blocked out every person, every sight, every sound, except for her. He whispered into her hair, "I've missed you. Terribly."

He found her mouth with his and gave her a long, hungry kiss. Be damned his aversion to such a public display of affection. The beauty in his arms had returned, for whatever brief period, and he truly wished he could ignore his other guests and whisk her away to his bedroom. He tilted his head back to look at her, her violet eyes shining with happiness, her bright smile dazzling in perfection, her mahogany hair gleaming in the midday sun. He brushed his hands over her shoulders and down her arms, feeling the silky smoothness of her skin.

"Where did you put your suitcase?"

The non sequitur caused her brow to furrow. "In your office. Is that okay?"

"Let's get it and take it upstairs."

He grabbed her hand and pulled her through the crowd on the deck and into the house without waiting for her response. Of course there was no need to deliver her suitcase to his bedroom this very minute. Of course the job didn't require two people. But if he didn't get her alone for at least a few minutes, he would burst.

Unfortunately, his guests had other ideas. "Michael, where should I put this macaroni salad?" asked Hal's girlfriend.

"On the counter would be great, Lisa. Thanks."

Every two feet, he was accosted with questions, hellos, kisses, and handshakes. He tried not to appear rude, responding quickly and keeping up his forward momentum with Sam in tow. They finally made it to the seclusion of his room, and he shut the door behind them. He said nothing as she stood before him. He had to drink her in, or he wouldn't be able to function. She still sported a rich tan from her days in Crescent Beach, which time in the city hadn't destroyed. A red halter top plunged low in front, and white shorts made already long legs go on forever. How he longed to have those legs wrapped around him.

Her nails were polished in the same red as her top, something she hadn't bothered with while living at the beach. The sophisticated look of a New York City woman, although tamed, was hard to miss.

"You look wonderful…beautiful." He moved into her space.

She raised her hand to embrace his cheek while her other hand drifted down his arm, sending shock waves through his system.

"So do you." Her low, sexy voice did nothing to calm his pulsing blood.

"How's New York treating you?" Perhaps a change of subject would douse his desire.

"Okay." She didn't sound convincing. That was good.

"I assume apartment hunting is going well."

"No. Not so good. I can't find the right place." A sly smile inched over her mouth.

"That's too bad." Sincerity was lacking since he was unable to keep his true feelings hidden. He held his breath, waiting for her to continue.

"I was thinking—" She paused, boring into his eyes and holding him prisoner with her gaze.

He couldn't help himself. He leaned in for a kiss. "What were you thinking?" he murmured against her lips, tasting their sweetness.

"That I want to leave the city."

Had he heard her right? He searched her face.

"The summer here spoiled my love for New York. Everything I thought I couldn't live without, I did and had a ball doing it. I explained to myself that the circumstances of this summer could never be replicated." She traced the logo on his shirt, her delicate fingers sending ripples of sensation straight to his heart. "It was a once-in-a-lifetime opportunity to kick back and relax. Logically, I know that if I move here, it will be completely different. And the thought of making such a drastic change based on a fantasy isn't very smart." She ventured a look at him, and he tried in vain to subdue his smile. "I lost my connection to New York. This past month, I felt like a bewildered child, moving between my apartment and work. The thrill of being in the city is gone."

He wrapped his arms around her and pulled her closer. "I miss you, Sam. I miss you so much I feel empty inside when you're not here. This summer became a fantasy for me too. A part of me left when you did."

She smiled and took his hand in hers. "So we've

both been miserable without each other."

He kissed her temple and trailed his fingers over her arm. "As a matter of fact, I even talked to Eric about opening an office in Manhattan. But if you're leaving the city…"

Her eyes widened. "You did? What did he say?"

"If I agreed to be his partner, we'd talk about it."

"And did you?"

Michael inhaled. "I had to talk to you first. See what you thought about it." He was hedging instead of taking Eric's advice to be direct. What he really needed to know was if she wanted to continue a relationship with him. No matter what city they were in.

Sam bit her lip. "I was offered a partnership at my firm."

Confusion pummeled his brain. Hadn't she just said she wanted to leave the city? Now she was telling him she'd achieved her lifelong goal. In the city. The two were mutually exclusive. Weren't they? Or was she contemplating adding a ninety-minute commute each way to her already long day? He trod carefully, afraid to say the wrong thing. "I don't understand."

Her musical laugh warded off the uncertainty that came with her announcement. "When our managing partner gave me the news, it was a temporary high. Then I realized I wasn't ecstatic. I didn't feel the way I should have. It was my goal, my dream. I'd made it. I should have been doing flips, but I wasn't. And I knew why." Her eyes softened, and she touched his cheek.

He lifted her chin with his fingertips, forcing her to look at him. "Why?" He shamefacedly had to hear it.

"Because of you. I love you, Michael. And I'm ready to move down here and leave it all behind to be with you."

He could barely contain his happiness. But he shook his head. "I want more." Her lovely brow creased, and he smoothed it with his fingers. "I want you to marry me."

It came out so easily, so effortlessly. Like it was second nature. All the angst he'd worked through since his conversation with Eric fell away. "I love you, Sam. Will you marry me?"

A tear slid down her cheek, but her eyes lit up as she nodded. "Yes. Yes, I'll marry you." The fireworks that had started in his core a week ago over the possibility of committing to Sam now exploded all around him.

He loved her.

And she loved him.

Michael lowered his mouth onto hers, intending to steal a few more kisses, but the power from that first, soulful kiss exploded into fire, and all intentions of letting go quickly burned up with the heat. He hungered for her, and the famine of the past month came to a sweet and ravenous end. He pulled her into him, melding her body against his, stroking her shoulders, her bare back, her exquisite behind. She moaned, and an intense desire fueled him until he was tearing at their clothes, impatient to remove the barriers that kept them apart.

He hated that they had to be quick, but his need for her made it impossible to prolong the ever-so-sweet torture. Thankfully she was as frantic as he and came within seconds of their coupling. Her cries of ecstasy pushed him over the top, and the two of them clung to each other, panting, trying to catch their breath when it was over.

"I can't believe you did this to me." She laughed between gasps.

"I did this to you? Oh, no! You did this to me. And to think I have seventy-five people milling about downstairs, probably wondering where I am. We better put ourselves back together. And no looking guilty when we walk downstairs. That's a dead giveaway."

"I'm sure tongues are wagging as we speak." She chuckled as she untangled discarded clothes.

He pulled her into another hug and kissed her luscious mouth.

"You better stop that," she murmured against his lips, "or we'll never get back to your guests."

"Okay. I'll be good." He smirked.

"I know you're good. That's what I'm afraid of."

****

Sam floated halfway down the steps, then stopped to gaze out over the scene before her, a smile permanently carved on her face, impossible to erase. The day was picture perfect with blue skies in every direction. The sun blazed over the ocean, but a mild breeze and a canopy over the deck saved everyone from its intensity. Those who aimed to worship the sun moved down the stairway to the beach. The others milled between the deck and the house, eating, drinking, and socializing.

She joined the fray five minutes behind Michael, after pulling herself together—mentally and physically. Her life had changed in the space of an hour, and the ebullience surrounding that change was almost too hard to tame. But she did her best, moving easily from one guest to another, initially catching up with Michael's friends from the volleyball team. They chided her for deserting them for the big city, teased her about preferring to bill sixty hours a week instead of enjoying a better quality of life, and scolded her for making Michael miserable without her.

She never let on that she was just as desolate without him. Nor that they'd made a decision to be together for life. They'd make that announcement together.

She spotted Bruce and his wife on the other side of the deck and made a beeline for them. She had to hear the details straight from the source.

"Hi, Bruce. Sandy." She gave them each a hug. "I heard your good news."

Sandy smiled. "I'm going to get a drink. I've heard this story before."

Bruce winked at her, then turned back to Sam. "I finally made the decision. A huge weight has been lifted. For the past year I've been trying to get our firm to open a branch office. But they were moving too slow. I want to be down here. Now." His words could have come out of her mouth. "As a matter of fact, I think I've found the ideal location."

His excitement buzzed through her. "Where?"

"An old Victorian house on Main Street in Red Bank. It's perfect. If you're staying for the weekend, maybe I can show you. You'll love it." He beamed.

She hadn't seen Bruce this happy in years. It was contagious. Not that she needed anything more than Michael to fulfill that role.

"I never thought in a million years you'd leave the firm. You're a partner there. Besides, I thought you were a city man." She sipped her margarita and leaned against the railing.

"I was until we had kids. The city isn't the place to raise them. They need a yard to run around in and a place to live that permits pets. They should be able to go to a school without us having to apply while they're *in utero*. And we shouldn't have to pay a college tuition for preschool. I could go on, but you get my drift."

"I guess children do change things." She thought of Denise.

"You've assimilated well down here. Lots of friends. And I don't want to pry, but you and Michael seem to be quite the item." A hint of a smile crossed his mouth.

Sam blushed and glanced over at Michael, who winked at her as he talked to two couples. She beamed. "I'm crazy about him. As a matter of fact, I've decided to move down here." Shock registered on Bruce's face, and she laughed at his expression. She held up her hand. "I know. I know. It's out of left field."

He watched her intently as he spoke. "Why don't you join me in Red Bank? I'd love to have you as my partner."

Hope shot through her at his suggestion. "Are you serious?"

Her response seemed to ignite his enthusiasm. "It would be great, Sam. I could use another practice area to bring in work. We'd be a formidable team. Of course, we'd have to do some advertising and spend a lot of nights out getting to know the community and touting our services. But once we get our name out there, we can capitalize on our New York City roots. I think it could really work."

She strove to tamp down the excitement building in

her chest, but soon she started pitching ideas and brainstorming with him on what they could do to grow a firm down here. The game of "what if" had them immersed in conversation for at least an hour. But finally Sam had to reign herself in.

"This is crazy," she admitted. "I'm so excited about this. When Phil Bennett told me I made partner, I didn't feel any of this."

"You decided to move down here after you were offered a partnership?"

"Yes. I'm certifiable, right? And until you started talking about working with you, I had no idea what I was going to do when I got here."

"Stranger things have happened." Bruce clinked his beer bottle against her plastic cup. "Taylor and Winslow. Sounds good. Don't you think?"

Sam threw her head back and laughed with pure joy. It sounded great.

****

The last guests left at midnight. Sam staggered over to the sofa and fell into it.

"I'm beat." She yawned, surveying the mess that had to be cleaned up.

Michael came over and sat beside her. "Me too. I'll clean this up tomorrow. Let's go to bed."

"I would, except I don't think I can make it up the stairs. Your friends don't like parties to end, do they?"

He laughed. "It's the last hurrah. The end of the summer. It's sad in a way. Although I love it here more during the fall, when all the vacationers have left and the town becomes ours again."

"It seems as if every season here has its advantages." She snuggled under his arm and closed

310

her eyes, wondering if she would feel the same way when Crescent Beach became her new home.

"The summer's great because of the weather, but the other nine months have their own charm. It's calm and peaceful. A real community of people who care about each other."

She nodded. "I imagine there's not much to do here over the winter." She hoped to hear differently.

"It's a little slow. Yet everyone who lives here prays this place remains their little secret. They want it to continue being the lazy town it is. It's peaceful, sane. You'll see."

A momentary fear skipped through her, and she couldn't tamp it down. "What if I don't like it here?"

"Then we'll move." He kissed her temple.

"You mean you'd go back to the city?" Her heart stopped at his easy implication. She searched his eyes.

The gleam that had been there while talking about Crescent Beach disappeared, but at least he smiled. "I don't want there to be any mistake about this. I love you, Sam." His eyes glowed with their intensity, and his words melted her fears. "I'd do anything to make you happy."

Warmth moved through her like a tidal wave, crashing over her heart and soul and carrying them toward him. She tilted her head to look into his eyes. She needed to see the truth, the sincerity. She needed to feel it. And there it was. So clearly.

She didn't think she could speak over the lump in her throat, but she couldn't leave those blissful words hanging between them without a response. "Thank you. I love you too."

They sat enfolded in each other's arms, and Sam

knew she'd always remember this moment in time, when peace, contentment, and love collided to make her whole.

At least until the next doubt surfaced. "I know you probably think I'm overanalyzing this, but what if I can't take a day off here and there to go sailing? What if I have to work nights to help get the practice off the ground? Are you going to understand my commitment?"

"So now you're afraid I won't understand your workaholic ways?"

She shook her head, exasperated. "I don't know. I definitely learned a lot from this past experience. And I want to put things in perspective and enjoy life more." She stood and walked over to the glass door, looking out over the ocean. "But I'm always going to work hard—maybe just not as hard. I need to know you won't write me off if I make some mistakes. I need to know you'll talk to me if you're not happy about something and not walk away."

He joined her at the door, then took her hand and squeezed it. "I'm not Tom. I don't intend to replace you if you're not paying enough attention to me." He pulled her into him and hugged her. "I'll just have to convince you it's in your best interests to spend more time with me."

His magnificent smile washed over her, spreading warmth and love with just the right amount of reason. If anyone could encourage her to change her ways, it was him. Those eyes, those lips, that soul.

She inched closer and embraced him, laying her cheek against his shoulder, closing her eyes, and inhaling his unique, delicious scent. "Thank you," she breathed. "I never dreamed we'd end up together. I love you so much it hurts."

He held her face between his palms, gazing into what felt like the depths of her being. No longer afraid, she let him read what lay deep within.

"Have you made the right decision?"

"Yes." She smiled, never taking her eyes off his. "It took me this whole summer to find myself. I looked to my best friends and searched their lives, their decisions in trying to figure out what I should do. In the end, I had to find my own way and do what was best for me."

She looked at Michael and continued. "The same is true now. I have to let go of my preconceived ideas of what I need to be happy." And she had to let go of her history. She didn't have to work sixty hours a week to assure she wouldn't have to rely on a man for support. She had become successful. She could support herself. She would never be in the position her mother had been in. She had made sure of that. It was time to let it go. "I can see more clearly now."

"And what do you finally see?"

"You. Me. Love. Happiness. A quality of life living near the ocean, away from the craziness of the city. I can't even believe I'm saying these words." She laughed.

It only took seconds before he lowered his mouth to hers and gave her a sweet, soulful kiss. It only took seconds before that sweet kiss turned demanding, hungry.

It only took seconds for her to take what she wanted and demand more.

The playing field was now level, and both she and

Michael had an advantage; the knowledge of each other's love.

What could be more powerful than that?

Epilogue

On the Friday before Memorial Day, the beach was not yet home to the thousands of vacationers who streamed to the Jersey shore for sand, sun, and fun. But there were some. A small crowd had assembled, wearing jackets and ties and flowery silk dresses instead of bathing suits and shorts.

There were Sam's best friends from high school, Michael's volleyball buddies, and their respective colleagues from work. And then there were the people who made Crescent Beach special. The waitresses from Melanie's Coffee Shop, the clerks at Mort's Office Supply, the bartenders at Rick's, Harry's, and Bill's, the town council who worked with Michael so closely, and the police that kept him in municipal court until all hours of the night. They had all become their family.

Sam stood on the beach facing Michael, dressed in a simple but elegant white silk gown, her short veil puffing softly in the warm breeze. It was six o'clock, and the sun hung low in the sky. A perfect day for a perfect wedding.

Just one year earlier, Sam had walked this path, a cold, bitter woman, isolated in the misery of her lost relationship. Today she glowed in the devotion of a new one. Gazing over the crowd, she dallied in the memories each person brought with them.

There was Nicki, Ms. Independence, who had been

whispering in her ear—*be like a guy, play the field. And don't get involved.* Afraid to love, Nicki sabotaged her relationships, her fear borne from her father's death and her mother's grief. She'd claimed she was never going to experience that pain of loss. Although she'd been ready to ignore her philosophy for Dex. They were supposed to get married last month, before Nicki cancelled the wedding after her miscarriage. She stood alone, sadness in her eyes. Hopefully, Dex would show up. Maybe they'd talk today. Figure out how to get past their issues. Like she and Michael had.

Her eyes found Denise. So happy and in love with her husband and her kids, including Bobby, whose prognosis was excellent after Michael's help. Sam smiled at Bobby and gave a little wave. Despite Michael's initial reluctance to form a bond with him, he'd done just that, adding favored uncle status to the many hats he wore.

Amazingly calm Denise, their rock, gazed at Ben as they talked privately. She'd given up her career for her family and had been happy to do it. Even after Sam's badgering questions and clear indignation over her life choices, Denise, the ever-rational voice of reason, had encouraged, by example, to look at both sides. She seemed to have known Sam would instinctively find her way to happiness. And that happiness would eventually come from a husband and children, even if Sam initially fought it on principle.

Sam turned her focus to Alyssa, who talked animatedly to a few of Michael's friends. It would be so good if she made a connection with one of them so she'd stop her crazy affair with Cole. Nothing good would come of it, although she refused to acknowledge that truth.

Sam turned her gaze back to Michael. The expression on his face left no doubt about his love, and his eyes shone with expectation and promise and intimacy. That look, always the cause of her undoing, made her feel like a queen, special and sexy, like the only person he could see.

Sam blinked back the tears of emotion threatening to well up and spill over. But this was no time for tears. Michael had helped her find peace within herself. With gentle pushing and careful prodding, he had encouraged Sam to see the world beyond career ambitions and solitary goals. Life was more than working six days a week and climbing the ladder of professional success. It included sailing and friendships and laughter. And helping displaced children with a hug and a smile. As well as the occasional game of basketball.

A year ago, Sam would never have guessed how much her life would change. In the space of one short year, she had turned her goals upside down—leaving her marriage, her job, and the city she thought she couldn't live without. It hadn't taken long for her to start up a matrimonial practice in Red Bank. And she and her law partner complemented each other famously. Although Sam worked hard, she'd finally found the balance between work and pleasure that had eluded her in her prior life. Thanks to Michael.

Now, here she was, dressed in white, standing before the man who had shown her the way. Michael pulled her close and kissed her cheek, as sensually as he would have invaded her mouth. His warmth and adoration spread over her like the rolling waves of the ocean. His hands slipped over her hips as he pulled her close.

Then he whispered, "Lady…will you marry me?"

An unchecked tear slid down her cheek, but happiness built from within until it took over her entire being.

"I love when you call me lady."

A word about the author…

Maria Imbalzano is a retired matrimonial lawyer who now writes full time. Instead of drafting motions, legal memoranda, and briefs, although those were fascinating, she spends her days creating memorable characters and taking them on their emotional journeys through her contemporary romance novels.

She is also a motivational speaker on the issue of perseverance.

When not writing, she enjoys spending time with her husband, daughters, and granddaughters at home and at the Jersey shore.

http://mariaimbalzano.com